CAFE PURGATORIO

FREDERICK MARK KRAMER

Sagging
Meniscus

Set in Bembo with LATEX.

ISBN: 978-1-952386-58-9 (paperback)
ISBN: 978-1-952386-59-6 (ebook)
Library of Congress Control Number: 2022950634

Sagging Meniscus Press
Montclair, New Jersey
saggingmeniscus.com

For Irit, David and Julia

The past is never dead. It's not even the past.

—William Faulkner

CAFÈ PURGATORIO

N O ONE WILL SING FOR ME, no muse will supply me with undying fame, I am a mistake born to bring two complimentary beings into wholeness but you can't bring wholeness to the dead-living. But they gave me a name so I was sewed into this world. My parents planned for me in order to forget and bring wholeness into their lives, after that it's only chance. Is this how it starts all by chance? What I took for permanence was only temporary even as it took me a long time to figure this out. What about God's will? Or God works in mysterious ways. Maybe he or she doesn't work at all? Not another monologue on freedom versus fate, better the fate of a character caught up in an historical situation, now that's an old-fashioned idea but nobody believes in that anymore. We moderns don't believe in being anymore let alone God that is until the ghosts came to haunt me—the older you become the more religious you become, not because you fear death, which you do, even if you are curious and want to face it alive, even when you know nothing's out there and still you would like to be able to poetize it, face it alive, curious, as opposed to in your sleep where someone would have to tell you that you're dead. That's what children are for? No the older one gets the less friends you have at your funeral not because they're dead or out of town, but because long ago you decided not to keep up with contacts that bored you; only family is left and they bored you as well but you would not leave and even if in death you will no longer be, it's that moment before that you want to feel. What is all poetry about anyway if but that moment and if the poet doesn't discuss it how can you read him? Schooling had driven all love of poetry out of me yet now I only reread what my uncle had told me to read in the first place. Still in waiting the adventure of living has left me and all I see is decay and as a protest against the modern world memorize poetry as if I can hold it inside me a moment longer; and I now study ancient Greek and German to read the poets in the original. Translation is not good enough especially where there tenses shift from poet to character—to grasp meanings of those who tried to understand freedom versus fate—coward that I am never once questioning always lying—not a hundred percent true as a young man I fought the good fight then years of analysis showed me the fight was a symbol of the knot inside me; the gap not allowing me to sit and write; giving up the good fight I would awake at dawn sit at the windowsill as night became dawn, and how I suffered in modern apartments when windowsills became smaller and I had to write on top of the refrigerator until I actually bought a refrigerator that was the perfect size for both writing and holding magnets on. Even when I have nothing to say I write, to write and have nobody listen or to write what nobody would read hasn't it all been said before only now we try and say it more cleverly? Clichés abound, television, radio, song, even the poem as if enough *mea culpas* can wash away the tears. At first I liked Homer and Virgil—the heroic poets until I was introduced to Plato and Goethe, thinking poets not action poets, by my uncle. Silence, complete silence, I listen for the silences between beats and after dawn the silence slackens, the car horns begin, the sanitation trucks beep, the lawn blowers start, it's only before dawn before the sun rises can you hear the dawn and then only then can you create. By dawn I can look at the pretty women who pass by the window, joggers, workaholics, and bird-watchers—when do they exercise their mind, or play the violin or piano? How can they get through the day by eating, exercising, commuting then coming home to television screens as big as movie screens—when do they exercise their mind? How many times did I give up my day job in order to find the long way, and not worry that I had nothing to think about except what should I eat in the morning, do at work, and come home to a night of bar hopping or television watching. I even became interested in what was going on in the world, had every conceivable point of view, actually thought some of the news commentators made sense, until I found freedom in my solipsistic ways, sitting at my windowsill, when the sill was big enough, or standing by the refrigerator oblivious to the world yet more connected then when I was out with my buddies or playing with myself. The chatter that came after the fall was unbearable and only in solitary thought is language possible, even if sometimes if it isn't possible in words it is in music. Yet in the silence the spirits now come back to haunt me, interestingly I didn't hear them when young now—I killed in 'Nam now the middle of the night their spirits come back and haunt me, can you see how many spirits are haunting me before I stopped and made sure I would never kill again. They come in my dreams, slowly, at first I didn't understand what/who they were—spirits in the modern world? Now doctors have a name for this, and they don't use such an old-fashioned term, instead they medicalize it calling it Post-Traumatic Stress Disorder, weakness not evil, the old shell shock of the First World War, as my uncle called it. He said I had the same far-away look as him and my facial fixtures were like his father's after having killed British, French and later I realized Americans, usually it was British and French, he said, he never really saw the Americans they came so late. Americans know how to fight wars, keep them over there so that their country is not destroyed by the killing, and after the war there were boom times in Germany except for the soldiers they were damaged. He told me how the spirits of the dead haunted him when I told him I enlisted and he told me my grandmother raised him not to be a soldier, that was the refrain then but I joined for adventure. He told me this to help me he didn't want me to be a soldier, but it didn't help me I became a ghost. Escaping home seemed more glamorous than going to college, besides I wasn't too good at my studies—idiotic boy with dreams of glory, medals on my chest and girls on my arm, but instead of an around the world tour I was sent to Vietnam. We shot guns that killed people I never saw, and never would have seen except in Saigon I met a man who started the *Shoeshine Boys Project*, a Catholic conscience, the kind that destroyed the old Roman Empire, who was setting up an orphanage for those boys whose fathers I might have killed, a do-gooder, the kind we laughed at until I bumped into him at a whorehouse, bar, restaurant, and we chatted, a nice man, older than me, but not by much, who had come to this world voluntarily, working a little racket I thought, anything that wasn't military-related I thought was crooked—only the Army was true until I realized he wasn't a phony. Initially I thought he was running a game taking the kids' money for some nefarious activity, but all he did was give them a place to stay and tried to teach them right from wrong in a war zone. Like I said a real do-gooder. He failed most of the time, the orphans were too far gone for him to have much of an effect, but he was a nice drinking partner and we'd sit in a hooch and drink and I'd go back to my day job and shoot "gooks"—I never met the Vietnamese I killed but now I saw them as individuals, fathers, mothers, of the children he helped with lives not only as the enemy who I have to kill before they kill us on my mission which we military only understood. I even actually thought of making the Army

4

my home, good benefits, early retirement, until I started realizing
what I had done. From then on I made sure my gunfire would
always be over the heads of the enemy. Even when I got back into
the world their spirits wouldn't haunt me only now they do. At
first I didn't support anti-war demonstrations I thought they were
giving aid and comfort to the North Vietnamese. But then like in
'Nam I got caught up in the times and where before I thought we
were doing right even if I wasn't killing now I believed we were
doing wrong. I was lucky my tour of duty was early on in Vietnam
before we bombed Hanoi and Haiphong back to the stone age and
my killing was not as great, but as my uncle said war is fought by
idiots and one of the generals said our god is better than your god,
but they are control freaks and didn't say that too often in public
but in private I saw how ruthless they were. And now at night all
alone those killings come back to me, sometimes, I even become
a soldier who's lost before I realize it's me buried in an unmarked
grave or blinded trying to find his way home again, sometimes it
would be my uncle even if the country he fought for is no longer
even on the face of a map—don't tell me there's no such thing
as spirits no matter how much modern psychology tries to deny
it. When did I stop becoming a schmuck? When I first came back
into the world I would not leave my room, what I had so wanted to
get away from was now my jailer, would dream of suicide, wake up
in a cold sweat, sometimes screaming, my mother would say you
need a woman to cure you of your nonsense, and she didn't mean
sex but settling down; never have I seen a boy try to look so ugly
with my crew cut and untrimmed beard—and she was correct, one
day I saw myself in the mirror and I looked grotesque. Why don't
you shave your beard you look like my grandfather from the shtetl.
Once she said that, of course, I couldn't shave it off. My mother
didn't like to be reminded of the old ways, she thought that's what
brought ruin on her and her people. She refused to socialize with

anybody, but specifically Jewish refugees who spoke Yiddish, but I wasn't from the shtetl only the Bronx i.e. the provinces, as if the borough meant anything compared to the sophistication of Manhattan. But you have to learn that. I learned nothing sitting in my darkened room, the door always shut, which didn't matter my mother would never knock, sometimes the radio on and the only light being the neon bulb of the radio as it played FM record after record with no interruption. For months I would not leave except for an occasional walk well past midnight when I was sure not to encounter any of my high school buddies still in the neighborhood. Until one night I ran into Jeff on the street, he seemed to have it all together, finishing college, living with a woman, and we said we would keep in touch. I lied. But he didn't. He would call from time to time and even when I didn't return phone calls he would call back. Finally I tried to find new friends and went out drinking in the pubs that dotted the area. I would call the friends I made there but not Jeff—I had no life, how quickly it came to pass what I escaped from in the first place came back to haunt me after the service. All the time in 'Nam I couldn't wait to be in the world and vowing my new life would be different and how soon the old life returned. It was easy to join the Army difficult to leave behind the Bronx. I should have gone to college away from home like my friend Freddy did, none of my other friends escaped, all were still living with their parents or had married, or like Jeff were living with a woman, but still in the neighborhood. Freddy changed his name to Fred then Frederick and became a novelist. And when Jeff called over thirty years later and left a message on my voice mail— you bastard why didn't you let me die years ago. My good deed was well rewarded! I should have let him die when he wanted to kill himself because Liliana left him and he just got out of prison and couldn't stand this world anymore, I thought maybe he had an incurable illness, or his new wife had left him, but no he was sick of life. That night I had stayed on the phone with him talking him out of suicide and I thought I was doing him a favor and even slept well afterwards: he had a vociferous urge to spill his guts that usually means you want to stay alive and he didn't kill himself and I slept easily with good conscience—his cowardice prevented him from killing himself. Instead he ran away to Vermont, Burlington, Vermont. Now he wants me to know I did him no favors. He hung up. I didn't have caller ID. But this time I wasn't as sure I would call him back. We were best friends, next-door neighbors, who would walk into each other's apartment without knocking, blood brothers, after seeing a cowboy movie together at the local movie theater, we pricked our fingers with his mother's sewing needle and let our blood run together. When I finally did call him back because I could no longer stand being with myself, and said do you want to hang, he said he would have to check with his girl-friend. Are you pussy-whipped? I said. I never liked my friend's wives, usually they were dull women bought off easily, now I see women have trained their daughters to see men as wimps, easily controlled or manipulated and mothers have to say don't marry someone you will have to support. Then all women could do is cook and sew so my buddies married to escape their parents home and their wives became their mothers. Culture changes! One old friend once asked would I let my wife work. Now I say she can drive a cab on weekends besides her regular job. They're divorced, he's hobbling around working as a night watchman drinking after his body shop went belly up, and she's making a fortunate in real estate. And when his doctor said he couldn't go on like this he drank even more. We weren't taught this growing up. I believed the future had promise, after leaving the Army I thought I would never have to follow orders again—imagine when I first left the States I thought we were the greatest country in the world, boy did the schools brainwash me, if not fail me. My uncle had wanted me to go abroad, he suggested I spend a year abroad at his expense, instead of enlisting, but I didn't want to take money from my uncle. I could have met draft dodgers in Stockholm and German women who wanted to be with a wandering Jew, and maybe wouldn't have been a schmuck for so long. But it was only in reading my uncle's books that really got me started on my intellectual path. All my reading is now re-reading and he had no truck with gobbledygook incomprehensible writers he only liked the artists who forced you to think—subjectivity is the ultimate reality not what others tell you to think, he had told me over and over again as I didn't listen over and over again. Of course when professors told me to read textbooks I belched and when I eventually finished college started reading from the books in my uncle's bookcase. Meanwhile the war was still going on—not simply the big one that everyone was against but the little ones that ended up upsetting my stomach while I sat in my darkened bedroom lit only by the neon light of my radio tube, looking out my window, which I never did as a child, as a pigeon landed on my window, I shut the radio lest I scare him away, watch him intently while he looks back at me, I want to take his picture but only have a flash camera and that would scare him away, I stare intently as I can—it's a sign, only what does it mean, omens are ambiguous but I know it means something—at first I think it's injured, can't fly away and I'm worried—the thought of touching it frightens me, but if I must, I must, only how do you fix a broken wing, and we stare at each other intently and I'm waiting for another sign to appear to confirm it's an omen, only nothing comes except each of us staring at each other and me not listening to music: this is important I tell myself when my mother comes into my room, unannounced, sees the bird on the window and says it's a crow they bring bad luck. I thought it was a pigeon, she gives me my camera, he still stays on the sill behind the shade and I keep watching wondering what he wants, I snap the picture and the bird gives a cry which I still have etched in my soul but what I most remember is how dumb I was thinking it was a pigeon. Eventually it flies off to my relief because I don't have to care for it. That was then and that night Jeff calls and I finally agree to meet with him and his girlfriend. He was my only friend who didn't shun me or blame me for being in the war. He tells me about his "freedom summer" where they met helping to register Negroes to vote, practicing non-violence, passive resistance, and generally having a good time except the pizza and Chinese food are terrible outside the city but the music was fine and everywhere they went the Unitarian Churches that put them up were hospitable, and they had a good time and when pork or ham was served for dinner they made sure there were alternatives for him. I was so embarrassed I actually ate the alternatives—they made me Jewish he said, since he loved sweet-and-sour pork—the Chinese kind that we had been eating in Chinese restaurants that dotted the Bronx. And in the small towns in the South one never hollered "police brutality" because you never knew when you would need the police lest the rednecks get restless, and even if the police were fat and fit every stereotype of a cracker, they were generous and made sure nobody got hurt. Yet Liliana said I don't know why we didn't reach for a gun, if I was raised in that situation I know I would be angrier than those who preached non-violence. I get so angry at the police blocking doors and not letting people register or allowing the kidnappings and intimidation to take place. Yet Jeff said the police were decent, I wasn't a congressman's son that had to be protected—and years later when Hollywood made movies about the "freedom summer" with the FBI playing heroic roles in solving the murder I could only snicker that this is what the young think is history. All the FBI did during those years was protect congressmen's children so that the congressmen would be beholden to them and vote appropriately to increase their budget. Useless crackers! And historically they are seen as the good guys and the local police scum. We also helped build a church, Liliana said, we started at dawn worked for a couple of hours and then we could see why rural people eat such hardy breakfasts we were starving after a couple of hours of loading beams, milking cows, digging foundations, all before it got too hot. I never did so much physical labor in my life, Jeff said. The good part was there was always something that had to be done so the days went fast and before I knew it my time was up. He laughed when I told him in the Army when the sergeant asked who's smart, my buddies all agreed since I was Jewish I must be smart and I was picked to be a sniper. I don't know if that's true but they saw me as different—the wandering Jews who kept to themselves and were clannish is how Liliana described her upbringing meeting a few Jews in the Midwest, mostly non-athletic types. It was shocking for us to find out we were considered different when we basically saw ourselves as American—i.e. we have a childhood photo of us in our cowboy hats, toy guns, Jeff in his cowboy boots I was not allowed to own shiny black leather boots in fact that was the only time I saw my mother cry when I wanted to buy them she said it reminded her too much of her past I, of course, had no idea what she was talking about, and cowboy shirts, and we had pricked our skin afterwards to become blood brothers. But I didn't know what I know now don't believe you know the future—we weren't friends for life, we didn't live next door to each other forever, nor have children who would walk into each other's houses; he didn't even go into the Army with me on the buddy system but we did meet for a few years after the Army and before he went to prison and I stole his girlfriend that he had asked me to take care of. She asked me what plays I had seen. Plays? You live in the city, don't you, you must have seen off-Broadway plays? You must take advantage of intellectual life in the city. That's why I came to the city to be near the theater, how many trees can you talk to? I had been to one musical as a class trip. I heard of Broadway Theater but never off-Broadway—except as the joke we're off Broadway when the play was not produced on that street, I didn't know it referred to a genre of theater. If you want to go one time, Jeff isn't that interested in theater unless it's political, we saw *MacBird* (an antiwar play comparing President Johnson to Macbeth) together and he loved it but I found it superficial agitprop. My uncle explained agitprop was twenties theater designed by communists to convince the workers to seize power. However he was glad I started going to theater with Liliana who then felt she couldn't go to the theater without an escort. He told me about Liliana and wondered if she would have enough stamina to make it in the theater—the constant rejection takes its toll on you, she will have to steel her soul against rejection—you can be fooled by the superficial glamour but you don't make money in the theater. And when I reported these thoughts to her as my own she thought I was profound. Take small doses of the theater otherwise you'll gobble it down all at once and you won't have any conversation, was the advice my uncle gave me. We started going to the theater together because Jeff was busy with his anti-war work and afterwards we had coffee or a drink to discuss what we had seen. I never discussed theater before. You see it that's it what is there to discuss. What you see is what you get. But she was taking theater courses and for her there was plenty to discuss, she came to New York for that purpose and went to this private school that I had never heard of, but I only heard of the big football colleges anyway besides City University, not small private liberal arts colleges where all students who went had dog (little) noses, as Jeff said. I sometimes went with her and Jeff to school affairs and had fantasies about women and having affairs with these rich women who actually played tennis and served tea but found most of them disappointing all they wanted to do was lay this Wandering Jew—and to my surprise as well they too had never met Jewish men—and they thought of us as carriers of civilization. Me! Who had never been to a play, except on a class trip, who had never read poetry, and who didn't read novels, who needs fiction it's the real stuff I want. However an intellectual insight did dawn on me when Liliana took me to an art gallery and I saw the English school: Bacon, Freud, and Frank Auerbach. She asked what paintings I liked and really I fell in love with the texture and the thick layering of paint of these guys so unlike the French Impressionists and their view of nature as arcadia. From then on I started looking at painting more seriously not simply as decoration or color scheme and thought of my uncle's place with paintings on his wall. He was the only person I knew who had objects for the sake of beauty not just for their utilitarian value. And even though I couldn't afford it did go to the outdoor art fair in Greenwich Village and actually bought a painting—after looking around forever and debating with myself forever about spending so much money on a painting and that my mother said what's this, where are you going to hang it, you can't put nails in the wall, why are you wasting your money, actually had bought a work of art and hung it over my desk, which was my mother's vanity table that she didn't use anymore. I liked it; I bought it, end of story. But there never is an end of story just a chapter ending, and I continued from that moment to save to buy works of art, sometimes better, usually worse, who says you learn from your mistakes all you do is learn how to disguise them better to fool yourself. Subjectivity is the ultimate reality even if we live in an objective world where we make excuses for all our misdeeds—Jeff reminded me I was able to save money because I didn't smoke, and I was still living with my parents so didn't have to pay rent. Now Jeff is dead, hung himself and he said on the answering machine that hanging is the least painful way of committing suicide he had researched it, and his daughter is going to have a memorial service for him in the Bronx. Did he hesitate before doing it? Did he say one moment here the next oblivion? Did he dream he was a king on a throne but the throne was a potty from which he shat down because he couldn't manage to hold it in? He made the ultimate sacrifice did he want his ashes interred with hers? After all a prayer without sacrifice is just words. At first when I did it (kill), I did it quickly so as not to think, only later when I realized what I was doing (killing) aimed higher at people, in tin-pan boats, temples, bridges, villages—always carrying out my mission of choosing targets, accurately gauging the wind, confirming the hit, until near the end when I wouldn't even do that anymore. They threatened to court-martial me and that scared me but I still made sure I missed targets—not purposefully at first but after two or three failed missions realized I was missing on purpose and could no longer hit targets—the targets became images of people looking up at me with hands of supplication—of course impossible to see we were too far away to see actual human beings, but not impossible to imagine that their large rolling eyes, hands palms up in supplication as bullets whizzed by them, and as the image became sharper the bullets would always go off target—my buddy told me that our warlike nature arose out of early ancestral struggles in nature that could rarely be kept under control, and since his father fought in the second world war and his grandfather in the first, I thought he knew what he was talking about: we were men of a primitive age, but I was able to use a little bit of reason and keep these feelings under control. Only when I got back to the world did I see how easy it is to resurrect them. And I would have been like many if I hadn't run into men who said there was a different way—I saw the children of the parents I had killed—metaphorically, since who knows whom we killed. Like Zeus throwing down thunderbolts, we fired our guns and chance decided who lived who died, I was part of a sniper team, I was a ghost. It took me a long time to realize I was stuck in a situation not of my making and stuck in moments of distorted time: some people challenge all rules so they don't have to obey the Law. Did Jeff feel what he could no longer put into words? I doubt if my words held him back the first time, he just wasn't ready to do it. As far as I know he didn't try again, married a couple of times, had children from each spouse, had a job and was a responsible adult and didn't try to kill himself. Yet Allisson the daughter from his first marriage says she will now help raise the children of the second marriage. Maybe his final act was not to allow his first child, a depressed-sounding woman now, the final act of committing suicide now that she has to help raise her half-sisters. Did he really do it to help his firstborn? She's now in her thirties but her youthful illusions are still there—she still expects a prince charming to come and sweep her off her feet, but no question about it her younger siblings must be helped but can she do it. Will the pain of her father reach her wherever she goes? Is there somewhere to go? How did he face his last moment? Was he thinking about it in control of his consciousness until no more? Did he say I fucked up, the boy genius that had so much potential—he had a great singing voice but never developed it, he could have been an opera singer or maybe a saloon singer, or did he say my bags are packed, enough already, or maybe he didn't want to be alone in an empty house, or walk into a room that was all darkness. Is one aware of it or are you numb already? But even if you are numb there is a moment before you go numb, even if you don't know it's the last moment you have to know it will end—isn't a moment now divided into a yoctosecond (a trillionth of a trillionth of a second). I wonder listening to Allisson on the voice mail that's inviting all his old friends in his address book to the memorial service. She tells me she knows so little about her father, he never talked about his days growing up only leaving New York to start anew in Vermont. She wants me to contact his sister but I have no idea where she is, only later do I think maybe she can leave a message at her methadone clinic telling her to call home. It's not my problem, yet I do like his daughter and she told me he had no truck with his sister since his mother died, they tried to be friends after the funeral they met and she didn't hold it against him that he left her with his mother, but they continued on their separate ways. I didn't even know he had married, had a child, divorced, remarried and had more children. At least he called to say goodbye, he didn't say goodbye to his ex-wives or children. Now that would be a last supper, a man surrounded by all his wives, girlfriends, children, grandchildren and their families, better than in a hospital bed with the family gathered around him: night time and the living isn't easy. I sit up and wonder why I'm thinking about the memorial service, I haven't thought about him for years—and I'm wondering what to wear, as if anybody would be looking at me. Clothes mean nothing by itself but they are a sign of what I've become—not that his children will know what I was, and they'd only know him as this sophisticated adult, I'll have known the real him—the untrammeled and broken boy inside the man—unless success had beaten it out of him. How many three-piece suits did he own? Hardly anyone is alive who knew him in blue jeans and a tie-dye tee shirt, and they will only know me from the clothes I show up in. I'm tempted to wear a three-piece suit but that indicates membership in a clan, and a three-piece suit means stockbroker. I want to wear the uniform of our youth but since dungarees shifted to designer jeans the uniform is kaput and probably nobody would get the symbolism. So I wear black pants, a sport coat and a tie—totally out of it but nobody will pay any attention to me. Allisson comes up and asks that I say a few words about her father. I can't. How can you sum up a person's life in a eulogy—one funny comment, maybe two, then a serious note—not that the people he left behind will never be whole again. Or when he ran away from the city he met this woman, the mother of Allisson, who thought she made a good catch, a wounded young man with a job, that he happened to fall into, and he liked it because he could work all the time and he didn't have to think, which allowed him to give up on living—and at his funeral nobody from his office came. He made life miserable for everyone else because he was so competent but in doing so he didn't have to be home and raise Allisson, yet he did enjoy his children more the second time around, according to his number one daughter. Children sucked him dry, she said, yet the only ones truly mourning him are his children, especially number one whom he knew least. She couldn't recall one time he took her to the teeter-totter or as you New Yorkers call it the seesaw, such a funny name. Yet he never abandoned her even when her mother abandoned him. He always saw her on weekends and when she became a teenager moved in with him through high school, and since she was never without a boyfriend allowing the boyfriend to live there as well. He was proud, she said, that in high school I could go out with a boy who was younger than me. He even came to the funeral, Allisson said, we parted after high school but have stayed in touch and he always liked my dad. She tells me he married some useless thing that transferred things from his mommy's apartment to my apartment and now just sits home on the couch and watches the big screen. I wonder when it got too much for Jeff. Did he have an illness? No he's been living in emotional poverty for so long I'd have thought he was used to it. One day he simply said he was tired of IT. You know his new wife is younger than me. He loved little chickadees. Did he think that before he pushed the stool away? One last adventure before he left. Or did it come to him suddenly. I look around at the mourners all wearing black—no pretty women in the crowd, friends from childhood, and some friends of his children, I can see the crooked grins on their faces, they love acting the part of an adult but the crevices haven't become permanent yet when the

sadness sets in, that's when they become interesting, give them another ten years or so, and none of my high school buddies have a
charm in their look. I sassy up to his sister ask her how she's been,
assuming that she would remember me; she hasn't a clue who I
am. Have I changed that much? Or has she forgotten. We weren't
childhood friends so there is no reason she should remember me,
and when I introduce myself she hugs me, a politician's hug she
hasn't the slightest memory of me. That's a shame. I wanted to ask
her if she's been in touch with his friends from the neighborhood,
but she just flew into New York when Allisson called the clinic
like I suggested. She didn't know him either. I wasn't special after
all just one of the names in his black book that he never threw out
just kept adding additional names; he probably kept the address
book because it held the name of his first love. How else was I
called nobody in his new family knew me? But first I have to ask
his daughter how she reached me my phone number has changed,
I've moved a few times since he left New York, she says everything
is available on the Internet. Sy, Simeon, Simeon Cobbler, she ac-
costed me coming from my left, I didn't even see her come up to
me, but she didn't say you're not going to remember me, because
I would never forget her, and luckily she didn't change her last
name—modern feminism, so she too was available on the Internet.
She thinks she still knows me but I've changed since then, ergo,
she must have changed as well, but Liliana seemed the same except
her chestnut hair turned salt and pepper, and when she put out her
hand to mine, I noticed her ringless finger. She too has memories
of this "golden period" while I stand here in fear and trembling,
yet at the same time laughing at myself for being so self-conscious,
it's been over thirty years. I remember Jeff's letters to me telling me
how he met this new women who seems to be different from all
the girls in the neighborhood; intelligent, articulate, going to some
private college which he never heard of, while most of the girls we

hung with were getting married or planning a wedding. He was impressed that she could talk current events not simply about boys and shopping. I wondered if she had been married, how many times, does she have any children from different men and had she been in contact with Jeff, but she didn't seem to grasp the stony emptiness of his life since they parted. First love never leaves you but who can keep up the intensity, the only way you can is in the dream imagery, being together ruins the image. I want to hug her but she only puts out her hand to me still I do and feel her go tight. But then she loosens and I think poor Jeff made a fool of himself over love. She asks how long we've been apart, I tell her thirty-some-odd years; she says chronological time has nothing to do with inward time. I wonder did Jeff have a premonition of old age, a sliver of an illness or did he want to see Liliana one more time. Is this going to be an ecumenical memorial she asks, Jeff really had no religion, even if his daughter now considers herself Jewish, he had no truck with religion and never set foot inside a temple. Did he try and keep his fears at bay especially as he aged and worried about his children, the eldest being the product of a broken home, like so many children are today, did he think of how he messed his life up—it was easier going through life trying to change the world than changing yourself—communism proved that until some people finally stood up and said no and presto their edifice came tumbling down unfortunately with nothing in its place, so now I love to listen to the young radicals talking Sovietization and when this generation builds communism it will be pure not corrupt like the former Soviets or as my daughter now says dictators practice communism in everything except economics; a bankruptcy of thought like pain doctors who have no idea what works but can measure the caliber of pain and whatever gives less pain they adopt—as if you can heal the soul from an old love: boredom, regrets of life, or whatever else you want to call it, only not the truth. It's better to dull your psyche and pray to oblivion like a junkie who can't live without a high so becomes an alcoholic when he has no veins left rather than face truth. I want a drink, I don't let go of her hand, an old friend from high school seems to be coming in my direction, I see some other people I knew back in high school—friends have a far less powerful hold on me now, then friends knew my inner life now nobody does except maybe new-found friends but they never knew me as a crazy adolescent only know me as this poet—interestingly now my attempts at poetry are recognized whereas when younger the question was always and how do you expect to earn a living writing poetry, are you going to be a school teacher? Liliana says I first heard of you when Jeffrey called you in 'Nam to tell you that he had found the new love of his life after we just got back from demonstrating in front of *Woolworth's* for practicing defacto-segregation in the North. He was the first person I heard from when I got to 'Nam I told her, she was surprised, she said, that he actually knew somebody in the service, everyone she knew was against the war even early on. One of the reasons he joined the movement was to look for pretty girls, the prettiest girls were into civil rights and anti-war he told me once while we were walking the streets at all hours of the morning having nothing to do and not wanting to go home on one of our nocturnal walks. And pretty women brought more men into the movement then all the self-righteous speeches or rock-music (now I can hear Bob Dylan coming from the sound system, a nice touch; he would have preferred Phil Ochs but nobody knows him anymore), a new wave of women became important because it led to the early stages of feminism, especially since they were more competent than men. It took a while but women soon began realizing the smartness of men was a myth, all we could do was drink and fantasize—the actual labor had to be done by women, and then their heads changed from wanting to marry doctors, lawyers, Indian chiefs, to wanting to become doctors, lawyers, Indian chiefs. Now women don't even marry, all they want is our seed. Liliana says let's quit this place. I won't let go of her hand, I feel uncomfortable with all these high school buddies as does she. Outside the sunlight hits us square in the face, I put on sunglasses she doesn't seem to worry about the ultraviolet light. We pick up our conversation where we left off more than thirty years ago. There are no cafés around so we find a bar *Café Purgatorio*—a dive bar with no blue shirts, frat boys, or wannabe hipsters and walk down the three steps to the entrance. I think the others must be jealous the most beautiful woman at the memorial service walks off with me—where was she when I was sixteen? I'm always surprised to find out how vain I am, it still means something to be seen with the prettiest girl in the room. I recall when some news reporter interviewed her on the street about her views and she said to him I have no idea all I do is ball. They didn't have enough nerve to put that on the tele. She talks. I listen. She tells me about her career moves, her apartments, but nothing about her love life, her children, or her family—maybe she's celibate? Being too beautiful is a curse for some women especially when young and older men abuse them and they think they are mature enough to handle it, and they're physically mature but not psychologically mature to handle the pain that comes with uninhibited sex and drugs. I laugh, where were those sexy women teachers abusing young men when I was growing up—I could have been the man. I even met the ex-husband of one of those sexy teachers years later at some party and told him I had many a wet dream because of his wife I thought he would like to know what his ex-wife meant to me. Now my imagination is black, but at one time it was strong and I could always hive off it especially since most women were never like how I imagined them, except Liliana. Now we're going to have something to drink. Even though she looks like a businesswomen, and businesswomen like businessmen have to be the most boring people on the planet, all they can do is calculate, underneath she is still an artiste. Would Jeff be pissed if I go with her? One more fuck! An adventure, only I hate adventure, I get no pleasure from leaving my routine. Instead we sit at the bar. The collapse of modern women is they no longer have time, but today Liliana has time and we can have a conversation—you can't have conversations with modern women anymore they never have time. I feel my member moving to the side of my leg. Luckily I've become less embarrassed now besides I wear dark pants now for when my body betrays me, so it can less likely be seen—Liliana is intelligent what I always liked about her, she's no dumb ass from the Midwest and recall how I followed her home one day—now they call it stalking, and saw her sitting around the table with Jeff and thought I should be there—how come everybody has a home to come home to except me. She reminds me of our first date together without Jeff, and now I feel uncomfortable, I wondered if I would see her but didn't want to recall everything. How we "accidentally" met and spent the day together—we bumped into each other in Central Park and she asked if I would spend some time with her and we hung out together. The damnation of modern woman is they no longer have time to do this, always so busy. I was still living with my parents then trying to get out of my room all my high school friends had gotten on with their lives, I was still sleeping in the same bed as I was raised, when Liliana and Jeff invited me for Thanksgiving—why even today Thanksgiving is my favorite holiday, there she was in their living room talking to me, not merely an appendage to Jeff, while Jeff was in the kitchen cooking, for her getting dressed up meant putting on a new pair of blue jeans, and she was reading to me the paper she was writing on Aeneas thinking I might understand it because I had been at war. I actually did Aeneas starts out as a decent man who saves his father and son but ends up killing his enemy who is begging him to spare his life, that it's not only a story about the glories of Rome, which is how she saw it. Only I got smashed afterwards thinking everybody in the whole world is happy but me and woke up somewhere in the middle of the street my head killing me, my body shaking, as some anonymous stranger has dragged me out from the gutter where I was sure to be hit by a car. The kindness of black men. She now recalled how she wanted to strike out and hurt Jeff and used me as a weapon. I certainly never told him we spent the day together but I'm sure he found out. Once I did tell him that I wanted to sleep with her if that was okay with him. But he/they didn't take that seriously. Why should they take that seriously? But Liliana said she was offended that he wouldn't stick up for her and would have let me if I wanted to. She wouldn't have known the difficult time I was going through, even if I did attribute extraordinary sensitivity to her, she saw me as honest, logical, loyal, a nice puppy dog— all a lie, she was the one who wet my dreams at night, that I was scared no longer knew how to live in the world where there was absolutely nothing I could do: it was impossible for me to find my place when I couldn't live without orders nor with them either. My uncle told me that it would take time, coming home from war you're never the same as when you went in—war is not like the movies and when people tell you grow up and get over it, they have no idea what they're talking about, and that I should take all the time I need, even if it takes a lifetime to forget what I've seen. That's it! I didn't see anything horrible I was a sniper. No dead prisoners, no ears of Viet-Cong, no destroyed villages only the loneliness of children and the good works of those who tried to save them. I hardly met any Vietnamese except for the children of the parents I might have killed and those who did my laundry and served me drinks. I could understand my grandfather's malaise he had survived four years in the Great War where he actually had killed people and saw them and his buddies killed but what was mine compared to his. I was a short-timer. My war would only be a footnote in history compared to his or the suffering my parents had in the Second one. All wars are unique, he said, victors are states losers are individuals. Liliana puts out her hand to mine involuntarily I add mine to hers, eating turkey that Thanksgiving our knees rubbed and I took it away—easy is the road to hell, getting back is hard. Progress! Usually I describe progress if I can read something now I couldn't understand when I went back to school, but then I knew so little it's not a fair comparison, and after going back open admissions started, which meant I could go to a city college for free, only the teachers were boring and the students insolent and a Faustian bargain was made they pretended to teach and we pretended to learn. We didn't even read works like *Faust*; in fact we did hardly any reading at all, and there was no intellectual chatter among students about ideas only grades.

I remind Liliana that she was the one who told me to take the professor not the course, sit at the feet of a good professor they are rare—how right she was! and take the most crazy sounding courses they are ones that are the most fun—the Faustian images in Plato's erotic dialogues—Plato as poetry. City University was going into the sewer with these unqualified students that all of a sudden it had to educate because it no longer only got the best and brightest but all of us New Yorkers who managed to graduate from their high schools, yet Liliana reminds me that she did some of the initial essays for me because there was no ego involved for her until I felt guilty of her doing work for me and started writing myself—and about that time when we heard a loud crash in the bedroom and when she went in there was Jeffrey his hand bleeding and a hole in the wall; he was so angry that we were spending so much time together but he wouldn't say anything, we had to spend the night in the emergency room—he was so jealous that I enjoyed writing intellectual papers (being with you) more than doing his anti-war stuff, which usually consisted of me stuffing envelopes or making phone calls, while he did all the planning. It was more fun going to the theater with you, discussing ideas with you while working on my Masters in Philosophy. You were the only one who supported me in that, even my parents had given up on me by then. What I remember about those days is she had such beautiful white teeth and now they aren't so white. Hey I had thick hair down to my shoulders now the barber takes two seconds, so don't compare— aging is a bitch, or as my uncle would say don't get old. Liliana even told me she loved rubbing her hands through my hair, all my strength was in my hair and even if I don't mind aging I don't like the physical decline—yesterday while running for a bus (I suppose my final death attack will be as a true New Yorker, running for the subway or bus) it looked like I was falling all over the place and kids laughed and a woman yelled slow down mister, don't do that to yourself there's always another bus, ha! My gait must have looked funny. Was it Liliana I met on the subway once in my thirties— the bloom of youth, after we parted and we both agreed we liked not being in the thrall of sex even if we couldn't use those words? Probably whom else would I have such a conversation with? Then instead of going on our separate ways, we both stopped what we were doing and spent the afternoon together. Then I wasn't surprised that she would do that there she told me she finally realized that Jeffrey was the only man who truly loved her—I admired her but Jeffrey loved her it was Jeffrey who actually cared for me, love is caring for another, but now she doesn't recall saying that even if it's tattooed across my chest. The closest I've come is to see a mother's smile on seeing her firstborn son—you can't miss that look—that's one of a kind, and in my memory that was the type of look she had for Jeff and I emblazoned it across my chest. Liliana doesn't recall saying it but accepts it as true otherwise why would she have come to Jeff's funeral. He has meant nothing to me, she said, for a long time, a youthful dalliance and afterwards we went our separate ways, I saw him on the street once, nearing forty, and wondered what did I ever see in him but I saw a ring on his finger and it would have destroyed his marriage and I didn't want to do that to him. Besides he was fat, letting himself go, no I couldn't go back into the same pitfalls I had as a youth. But if he never came back into the city maybe it wasn't even him. It took me too long to extricate myself from my marriage, but my juices were flowing and with him it could have been quick, a zipless fuck, but I didn't do it—modern maturity, I guess. And I wouldn't even have thought of it as cheating only an occasional rendezvous that would have kept both of us happy. But I remembered how I cheated on him and how it hurt him and I didn't want to do it to him. It was before the AIDS epidemic when women were experimenting with emotionless sex, aping men putting scalps on their trophy belt. Instead I stayed celibate for a while. Me too, one night I tired of having sex with strange women and for a year, with only occasionally missteps, did I stay celibate and enjoyed not waking up in strange bedrooms, I tell her. It was easier than I thought even if countless women told me a man who cooks isn't a man, and Galina lets me cook for her. I refused them all, or most of them, and enjoyed my early morning solitude with my books and my writing. College never touched you she said, but reading certainly did, I loved the way you would read to me. We would spend countless hours in your uncle's apartment and talk, we could spend hours talking to each other and never run out of things to say then I'd go back to Jeffrey's place and write it all down for my dissertation. He was in jail by then and somehow we felt bad being at his place so we went to yours if I recall correctly, after your uncle died you inherited his place glad to finally move out of your childhood bed. An iconic image I tell her. Closing my eyes I think it was ludicrous imagining she was the one who always got away. The barkeep comes over, we order vodka, she takes hers with a lemon and ice it goes down smoother that way she says, when the barkeep asks me I say straight because I know no other way: Cheers! Prosit! A lover is different than a wife; maybe if I had married her I would have cured myself of her—why can't I strip away this veil that separates my vision from my thoughts? How many times have I been through this never leaving going away by inches refusing to think saying half-baked thoughts, writing for something, anything, clarity never coming but with each foray slowly peel back this opaque vision. Home from 'Nam I thought I did right serving my country (what does that mean?) doing my duty, no weak Jew for me, yet no girls greeted me when I came home in uniform except to spit at me, except Liliana, who wanted to understand me, it was in my dreams that I started having doubts about the war, before even Jeff and Liliana and the anti-war movement. You would never have guessed from his death that he was this big radical not this cockamamie conservative, he always said thank goodness for the secret ballot these guys have no idea who I vote for. I tried explaining to him that the enemy knows no bounds and we have to fight them over there we were on the front lines, etc. the same lines now being used all over again against another enemy—our army is only for defensive purposes the other side has hostile intentions, we are decent not aggressive, the new normal i.e. security at all costs. Can I believe I actually believed that stuff that they hammered into me as a child? At war I did wonder will I ever have a chance to grow up, i.e. have real love not whorehouse sex, why are they doing this to me? At first I thought it was weakness, and I vowed never to show weakness and I started drinking to shut the voices up, such harpies, but now that I stopped drinking they come in the middle of the night only then if I could pass out into dreamless sleep could I be rid of them—I felt they were trying to get through and I could feel myself fighting them off each morning waking in a cold sweat and a headache a mile long and couldn't wait until I got some more drink in me to calm me down—indeed I lived with the constant buzz, I didn't know who I was, my self was stolen from me, even when I let my hair grow I couldn't look at myself in the mirror—when I moved into my uncle's place, after he died, he had a mirror on the medicine cabinet and full length one behind the bathroom door and if I turned the cabinet mirror on an angle could see my reflection backwards for eternity but still couldn't find me, there was no self all I saw was confusion and this good for nothing staring me in my face. All compassion had left me, it was difficult to speak, bullshit yes, politics yes, sports yes, but words, truth I couldn't get them out. Why Liliana is so important. Now I understood a little what my father and mother had gone through. Their world destroyed they had to start over again, yet my world was the same, interestingly they had to learn a new language, my language was the same but my thoughts and feelings were no longer the same. I became rootless, rents were cheap, food was cheap, and life was terrible this wasn't what I expected back in the world. Only with Liliana and Jeff could I talk, Eileen my ex-flame, my high school girl friend said I wasn't the same person, unhappily married now, a double silver wedding ring as big as a house, her husband had bought it for her so that he could buy himself a sports car she told me, getting laid every night, she said, we couldn't even have a conversation, she wanted to pick up where we left off, I didn't want to go backwards—drink was all I knew except Liliana and Jeff. They kept inviting me to their place, she took me to see *Jules and Jim,* my first foreign film, it was difficult I had to remember what I had just read—it made me think we were like that, only in fantasy of course, I could never have spoken the words of a ménage à trois. Was that when Jeff slammed his fist into the wall? Could we have done that, tried it? Only in my head. Silly reality why couldn't it conform to my fantasies. Ask the communists they realized reality only works by force silly freedom never follows a preordained path. How long did it take me to learn that? Still learning? When I open my eyes after my first sip of vodka, Liliana is still here, and I smile now not even remembering how to order a drink. I wanted to live with her; I never wanted to live with her. I wanted a life not going through the motions of a life, all that solid melts but I wanted to stop falling. Seeing Liliana is bittersweet—the power that causes powerlessness. After drinking I went onto seduction seduction is a fine way to avoid living, it blots out all memories, each seduction was the first one each one the promise of eternal bliss—the giving of pleasure, until women started doing the same thing to me and I got tired of being the scalp on a woman's belt. When I called America a fascist country my uncle said I didn't know what fascism was, America is a wonderful country if you can pay you can get it done he would always tell me on our car rides to Coney Island as the car broke down—here you don't have to worry that the government is going to kill you, there are no metaphysical questions here. Ask Afro-Americans I should have responded but didn't know enough history. But he would have responded that it wasn't the Negroes that freed themselves but whites that freed them. But the Emancipation Proclamation was only a political move. Yes but this is a generous country this new land and they avoid all religious questions by a wordy religiosity making them political so that they can be compromised—only in the old Muslim empire was there such freedom where a Christian, Jew and Muslim could have a place of worship on the same street and mingle together without the fear of violence. I didn't know enough history to even know who the Ottoman Empire was. What other country came up with the Northwest Ordinance he asked. Didn't know that either What? If you become a new state in the union you join as an equal probably America's greatest political move. What about manifest destiny? Aha I learned something in school. Manifest destiny was our god given right to be bordered on two oceans. No manifest destiny we steal the Indian's land and claim it's God's will. How did you get so smart? I read. That stuck with me. And his prophecy proved correct, he was the only one I ever heard talking about how communism would fail because of no freedom. Everyone talked about the inevitable doom of capitalism but my uncle said the dictatorship of the proletariat was a dictatorship and throughout history all dictators fail. How come you only casually introduced me to him? You met my parents I thought that was enough. Is the world going to tumble down if I utter a truth, he would have known what was going on and I was too ashamed to tell him? Or was I a jealous lover afraid he would want her. It's easier to smile and lie. I can see why Jeff was delighted and yet in pain when she left him. Did he stalk her? She reminds me of her life meeting Jeffrey falling madly in love with him, fucking him to death afterwards only meeting married men so there was no chance of a relationship just sex and if a relationship develops it's the same old pattern of intensity detachment then abandonment, even as she aged and had children. Now she complains children can choose who to live with the mother or the father and what looks good on paper is devastating for the child and she too has been abandoned by her children only she doesn't call it that but letting the child feel its oats, sometimes living with the mother, sometimes the father. My daughter had this fantasy image of his father and I thought only by living with him could he be cured of it. Still it must have hurt, I realized. Where's Jeff to enjoy her suffering only he wouldn't want her to suffer, at least that's what he would say aloud. He didn't abandon his daughter even when he put a tattoo on his arm he made sure there was space for his children, even when she went through her rebellious stage, boy was I pain then, Allisson said to me. But he made sure I got up to go to school on time, even if he had to spill water on me and no matter how angry he got in the morning with me for carousing all night he insisted that I go to school the next day. Tolstoy once was asked what the meaning of life was and by then he was an old man into spirituality and vegetarianism and he said the only thing that matters is non-violence—he didn't raise a teenager. My uncle told me that my grandfather too believed it until called up in the first war which was more horrible than the second because in the first the unbelievable happened no one really thought it would happen and there he was in a trench and all his former thoughts left him he was so caught up in the moment and he participated in the slaughter of innocents, the greatest slaughter ever until the next war and nobody still knows the reasons why. Mr. Wilson's fourteen points were still worth fighting for but abstractions led to too many deaths. I know what he means Liliana says, we started off the twenty-first century with a bang—innocent people die at the Trade Center because the beast Satan has to be destroyed. These guys have grand thoughts and not as dramatic as working to pay off a mortgage. But it was the first time since the Civil War that we actually had men and women die on our soil from fighting usually we fought them over there on other peoples' territory. My uncle had asked after I got home do you think you made up for your parents' shame in not being able to fight. I didn't understand what he meant my parents were victims because they were Jewish. I was so flummoxed by the invasion of Iraq I only hope my uncle's old adage holds true that you can't fight a hundred year war anymore, that people may be supportive at first but after four, five years they get sick of it and sue for peace until the next time. There's always a next time remember we were talking about a peace dividend after the cold war and now we have a hot war against fundamentalism. It was a short-lived discussion Liliana says. Adventure is important she says, jobs, rent, lovers are boring compared to adventure, she says, even women love to ape men now in war adventure, she says. I have confidence now, I had fear then but how did I do it then? Luckily in war the enemy had few weapons, later on they had more, but for me it was essentially an unfair fight—like Achilles we couldn't be beat, we shot, bombed and killed with immunity and I realized how I had gotten caught up in the moment so I couldn't just say No or even I rather not. Our men were in trouble we had to interdict, I didn't even know the meaning of the term, why I'm now so solitary is because I am too easily influenced—whoever gets to me last, only by myself can I do no harm—years of analysis were needed for that. Back in the world only with Jeff and Liliana was I not afraid to speak—nobody really can understand unless they've been there but at least Jeff and Liliana listened to the occasional words flowing from my lips. And once I started I couldn't stop, I had been silent so long and only those who had been there could understand and everybody was against us, but it was only from the moment I began to speak did I comprehend what I did. Visiting the *Shoeshine* project had influenced my behavior but not too much, I still was sure we were right doing America's will—my country would allow free elections and the people to rule themselves, it was only in discourse and study that I began to understand how we were considered occupiers. My mother was correct when a schoolteacher accused me of being a leader of the bad boys, she said, he isn't a leader he's only a follower. Once I was rejected for jury duty because the prosecutor thought me a leader who would influence others, I burst out laughing. He based that on the poetry I was reading in the jury room—Catullus, jerk! Sometimes I can reduce my feelings never eradicate them, why it's better to be solitary—I rather not, but not necessarily follow my intellect, like now I can't up and leave Liliana even though I know I should—a little more will lead to temptations that I won't be able to resist but I want to resist, the more we chat the harder it is to stop and it will only lead to no good yet it's good to feel with such intensity again, I didn't know I had it in me. Have I learned anything? Nobody learns anything except the young who think they can. You can't dip twice in the same stream! But it is fun trying. The barkeep refills her glass I'm still nursing. Liliana says your Greeks if their gods really loved a person they gave him a quick death. I say you Christians will keep them alive forever with your life-saving equipment and if you made a living will they'll find lawyers to break it. We laugh. Since Jeff introduced us and we could always banter and laugh together. Once when we met on the subway she woke me up, I couldn't believe my eyes like a mirage in front of me we rode a few stops together before she got off and I went back to sleep and then wondered was it a dream. Once in a moment of desperation my father suggested I be a rabbi, the only people he knew who never worked. However when God didn't answer his prayers in Auschwitz he had given up on God. To assert my identity after coming back from war got circumcised and now believe in God every other day. Then he suggested auto mechanics, chiropracting, marrying procreating unmindful that there was anything different. They were more hurt when I didn't marry Eileen, my Gretchen? after high school, I even assumed we would marry when I got back after I got over my wanderlust for adventure—luckily she made it easy for me (unfortunately not for herself) when she met someone else because she was afraid of becoming an old maid at twenty-one and he needed to be married to avoid getting drafted. I never thought of her again until she called me up saw me and wanted to meet. Moments earlier her father had died in a car crash and Jeff and I were the only ones she knew from the old neighborhood, her girlfriends all had left her by then and she didn't have new friends and she wanted something to hold on to as she walked the old neighborhood, like me sitting here drinking with Liliana now. She was wasting away in a marriage but there was nothing I could do. Funny how the past grabs you no matter how hard you run from it, Liliana says. She puts her forehead to mine it feels good.

Luckily my past wasn't my whole future, you can bend it a little, shape it a little, twist it a little, like a stick in water when you see it it's not actually where it is, the water reflects it, the future isn't cast in stone and I didn't follow my impulse to be her knight in shining armor and lead her away from an unhappy marriage, my first foray into freedom: not doing what my impulse suggested I do. Liliana said I owed her nothing she chose that life. And I wasn't punished by a burning silence like my parents who saw evil and its peak but couldn't speak about it; my uncle suggested I find a language to describe my thoughts, feelings, when he happened upon me as I was walking and insisted I go to the theater with him and explained to me that a life of the mind is more important than rolling the rock up the hill every day, i.e. fight the repetition of life, working at a job just to make a decent wage—you have to work, he said, but you also have to learn to think, he said, your mother and father's lives were destroyed by a barbarism unknown in the world a craziness that overtook mankind where you didn't know if you would be alive the next day and after a while you didn't care but you don't have to live their kind of life, you could or could not use your potential you are still young and have opportunities here, especially since you got your adventure out of you already. Opportunities, I felt so old like my life was over already, and I wasn't even thirty and he's telling me I'm young yet do something with your life learn to think. My dark hair was turning light, I could see patches of baldness, a gray streak in my sideburns and he said I was young—I was developing the face I deserved, which I now have in the autumn of my years. But he told me he was going to Florida for the winter and I could live in his apartment. It's time you move out of your parents' place. It was good to get away from the Bronx; the gang wars were increasing the Irish against the Italians, against the blacks, now the Puerto Ricans were getting into the tumult. In New York we welcome strangers into the neighborhood by beating the living shit out of them and you can't even choose which group you belong to it's all determined by the block you live on. I once had fury in my fists, could even taste the blood in my mouth, usually not my own, and words had no power over me but now it stopped, I didn't want that life anymore, something caught up with me, it wasn't knowledge and it wasn't belief but I no longer wanted that type of life. Still sometime the fury would emerge in me and I couldn't keep it under control unless I put myself in a situation where it wouldn't be allowed to emerge. What a woman can do to you, I thought, even if he had no idea of the fire raging inside me, but my uncle did and said I was no longer a prisoner of childhood and didn't have to live in anger of my parents' shame. But I missed the pleasure that anger could evoke in me, the difference now is it doesn't fill me up anymore and I no longer fight authority figures everywhere—the teacher who said my presentation is weak, the army officer who said I have to fire lower, I tasted blood in my mouth now it's foul, even if I still sometimes become weak and succumb, usually I don't get myself in that situation: except here I am seeing Liliana again who gave/gives me so much pleasure and pain. It's not too late to step back I tell myself, as I rub my forehead against hers: we won't run away together I'm too rooted in this life, she probably has a husband and children somewhere, then she asks why did you ask Jeffrey for permission. Didn't you realize how insulting that was to me? What pissed her off is not the doing it but asking permission to do it? I remember Jeff explaining how she rolled her eyes at me when he relayed her request to her, the rolling that was laughter not hesitation unlike the women who came after who didn't even twitch when love was being offered: You don't know if a man can be a good friend unless he can be a good lover, was the mantra when women too slept around. Then I couldn't stand being a piece of meat. But what Liliana liked about me as I aged is that men become distinguished-looking while women get fat. That was before women too got into exercise. And she said now older men are sensitive not like young bloods who want only two things they also want mothering and there are plenty of women who can be mothers, she says, but I wasn't one of them. Get up and walk away a voice in the background is saying, what are you trying to prove by being with an old flame that you're tough, you can take it? Can't you remember walking down the street spotting her and you prepared your lines, life is excellent even if it was in the toilet and before you even realized it your brains were in your feet and you crossed the street to avoid her, almost getting hit you didn't care all you cared was that he wouldn't honk and she sees you: then you thought the car will hit you she sees you die and will wear black forever, except she wouldn't even realize you crossed the street to avoid her and she was the cause of the accident. In that one moment I learned more about love: my body was in pain my soul in pleasure—my body had a will of its own. Is there such a thing as coincidence? Not only did I think it was coincidence that I almost bumped into her but also there had to be a god or at least a place we go after we die. It was pleasurable imagining her at my funeral hovering over me my shade coming up to her telling her not to be sorry and to go on with her life, meet someone else until my magnanimity was taken away by the realization that there would be no more me to take pleasure in my magnanimity or her guilt: there's no such thing as her guilt or me as a shade. So I didn't speak to her because she was out of my life and I didn't want to be disturbed by her, then I realized I was no longer a kid where I had to prove myself, I could run away. Like in a basketball game if one guy scores on you and you finally stop thinking you must take it to him on the next play—ah maturity, how come I don't have it anymore? Thank goodness I'm not this wise old man more wizening than wise. Lately people have been sirring me to death, what did I ever do to deserve that? But thank goodness most who do it are really dissing me I like that better than respect, like the young black alpha males throwing snowballs at me from behind, all I wondered was did they do it because I was white—and feel more at home with these kind of people than those who take me for a wise old goat. It's my emotions that still give me the first glimpse of how I feel but thought sometimes can douse feelings like when I see a pretty young woman I have to remember I love souls more than bodies and even their youthful perkiness—fully fledged bodies but half baked souls, don't turn me on as much as a mature woman's body and soul. Liliana was the older woman who led me to the pleasures of love. She helped me get out of myself, we never became one but with her aid we became three unlike my mother and father who had me to restart a family that had been destroyed by the Second World War. I couldn't unite what had become broken. Right around then my uncle had his fatal heart attack on the Columbus Circle subway station where he was making his way to the Sheep Meadow in Central Park, he always loved to sit there dream and laugh, especially when New Yorkers would say this is open space—he had seen the Russian steeps and knew what open space was. I recited some of his poetry at the funeral service. I stand and excuse myself, one of the reasons I don't drink so much anymore. There are very few places to go in the city and I have taken to doing it behind a tree—this city doesn't care about the elderly or the young only those in the prime of life. What killed my uncle was probably climbing up the flights of steps to get out at Columbus Circle not the ride itself, he insisted he wouldn't stay trapped in the house and twenty years later at the exact spot where he fell they had a party for the five-hundredth anniversary of the discovery of the West only nobody came and the party was called off. I laughed. My potted plant was still there the one I planted for him as a memorial to him after the police officer showed me where he fell. The first graffiti, even before *Taci* had spray painted his name all over the subway stations indicating the decline of New York because the city wouldn't clean it up hitting rock bottom when President Ford told the city to drop dead. He had taken me to my first play, also paid for my grand tour insisting I go see some of the world even as my parents said it was a waste of money. My uncle was the one who took me into the city, if you live in the boroughs New York is always called the city, my mother was afraid for me pinned a dollar bill to the inside of my shirt along with my name and address lest I get lost and didn't know my address. And when I did get lost, seeing a skyline I was unfamiliar with it simply meant I took the wrong train, and at the next stop went to the other side and found my way back. They could have tied me up, blindfolded me, spun me around in circles and I could still make my way on the subways. I am a New Yorker. In my car I always get lost. Not bad for an eight year old. I knew how to get around the city all I needed was someone to help me cross the big streets. My uncle also wanted me to go to college otherwise he said you want to continue to fight with your mother. Do you? No. Then you have to do well in high school so you can go to some college outside New York otherwise you want to stay and scream at her. I didn't understand what he was talking about but fooled him and joined the Army instead. Only my uncle was allowed to visit me when I received leave. He was the one who taught me to read the classics (the books I should have read in college) and when I got home again all my buddies got their girls—too bad. The Army at least got me away from home even if I hated home and became homesick, which I didn't understand. When I was home he took me to the grand opening of Lincoln Center and we saw *Danton's Death*, more spectacular than substantive; my uncle explained how a good idea went awry and how freedom's precious and you can't murder those who disagree with you because when you devour your own you devour yourself as well. As usual I didn't understand what he was talking about and he explained Trotsky to me—I had always heard of Trotskyite as an epithet or that Fanny, Jeff's mother, as a young girl had seen Trotsky walking the streets of the Bronx in exile, she always said that he was a tailor and would talk anybody's head off for a half hour with his spiel about politics but nobody understood what he was talking about. He explained that Trotsky had fought for more freedom but was killed by Stalin. After the play we went to Germantown (Yorkville)—my first *Konditorei* (pastry shop) with its cream pastries, chocolate cake and strudel, dark roast coffees and hot chocolate and we discussed serious issues with his buddies, even the waitress had read the play, it seemed all his old cronies had either seen the play somewhere else, or had read it, and they discussed it like it was a contemporary event—boredom and sexual frustration, I could relate to that, Eileen never let me get beyond 2nd base, my balls constantly ached after being with her—but the idea of doing something creative instead of always waiting for adventure to happen to me never dawned on me. I return and recall having a Sacher torte because they didn't have cherry pie and a dark roast coffee because they didn't have a cherry coke. I could see how having a conversation in a café was different than having one in a bar, sitting in a café, relaxed civilized, not getting drunk or stoned allowed us to have a conversation and I wondered why I never went before. Easy, there were no cafés in the Bronx only candy stores and bars of course. You had to learn to drink and eat slow, not gobble your food down and be done before you finished, in order to let the conversation linger and listen to what the other said, and you had to leave a big tip because you lingered at the table a long time and the waitress could be making more pocket money if the table was constantly in use, but here nobody seemed to rush you. One gentleman complained that he couldn't afford to leave a big tip (he had to put his son through college—really he was cheap) and I saw my uncle's class in his leaving a bigger one,

I always recall that when men these days take out a calculator to divide each portion of the meal and to make sure they don't get cheated. The night was young and I had never been out so late with my uncle, he didn't even tell them he had a nephew. Do I exist if his friends didn't know I exist? A Babel of languages was spoken in the café, I immediately tell Liliana, reminding her I took her to that café after we saw *No Exit* but the stream was not the same and by then Yiddish, German, Russian, Rumanian, Czech, Hungarian and who knows what else from the center of the universe as my uncle called it Czernowitz—the most cosmopolitan city on the planet, the capitol of the world, had passed into oblivion—I never heard of it you said, but she recalled the newspapers on the racks, the window alcoves and the darkened wood walls, I told her and most of the old geezers were already dead or had migrated to Florida, and President Wilson in his fourteen points, surprisingly because he thought he was God and God only needed ten, had broken up Central Europe after the war to end all wars that laid the seeds for the next one. Wilson never understood what some of these old men were now being forced to understand how boring it is to live only with your own kind, as they are now stuck in age ghettos in Florida. These men surprised me by getting so excited over a play ready to fight over an interpretation that Danton was like Trotsky one who made a revolution only to see it stolen away by Robespierre or Stalin, that you need them to seize power but once you have it of no use when the victors want to exchange one form of dictatorship for another. I was living in history and even when we were there we did discuss *No Exit* how life changes when you live alone in your room where you can do anything you want—too bad you can't stay there all the time, to how your behavior changes when somebody else comes into your room, and the whole thing goes crazy when you are in a group. Hell is other people Sartre said but I was too lonely to realize that and needed other people then, now it's a different story. These names were all ancient history back then to me but to them Trotsky, Stalin, Hitler, were alive and Stalin especially this ex-seminarian puritan really believed Russia was the third Rome after Rome itself, Byzantium and then Moscow. Both Stalin and Hitler needed to destroy everything in their path—especially God's chosen people not as an accident but as a culmination of their messianic beliefs. Why the French are more civilized, Liliana said, they have charm they think you have to live with other people the Russians and Germans only want to kill them. This wasn't history I was taught in school, I said to Liliana historians never mentioned this was a European civil war or religious war of cosmopolitanism against fundamentalist—the whole damn fight is by those who want to be free i.e. sexuality and those who are afraid of the body. Sound familiar? The whole thing now with Islam is the same thing, women who want to display themselves and men who want to keep them barefoot and pregnant, she says. It seems like we masses are never allowed too much fun unless it's controlled by the state, or religion, none of these guys smoked pot I say. But they read, thought, Liliana says, were alive to the world, unlike our leaders who are only interested in fucking as many people as possible. With condoms I hope. You heard the religious right, AIDS is God's revenge on modern day cosmopolitanism. And in the ghettos today young men seem to take great pleasure in needle punctures in condoms to get young girls pregnant, and girls still think they can trap men by forcing them to be fathers. Still when I finished my Sacher torte I missed my cherry coke also my hamburger steak, fries and coleslaw, what I usually had after a bout of drinking when the munches came on me. Still after this I didn't often go to the *Konditorei* even as I was changing into the being I wanted to become and when I brought you the conversation was nowhere as intense as that first time with my uncle, and slowly those cafés went by the wrecking ball as the owners of *Kramer's*, *Geiger's* and *Mocha's* moved away and the old men and women died or moved to Florida. Unfortunately our new generation didn't have that basic knowledge to take over, I say. Liliana disagrees, they have passion, she says, and without passion, knowledge of the past is not enough you are condemned to repeat it, but these youngsters today are optimistic in a way we weren't, a much more hopeful generation. You were of the generation born after the war—a beaten generation, she continues, (privileged birth, I think) false optimism your parents came off a DP list they came here sponsored by your uncle, not a new generation who could start over and so they never talked the past to you it was too horrible to contemplate not like now where the young understand their past, she says, and it's not a bad past with the victory of the Civil Rights Movement, Anti-War Movement, the Feminist Revolution, but they are not interested in history only the effects of their past and they are tolerant of others who are different. Age became me when I realized I was no longer listening to music because it was played too loud interfering with my thought. Another old man who goes to bed early, Liliana says, you're playing right into their stereotypes. I laughed but it's true and if you don't think you don't read and if you don't read you don't learn to think. And if you don't learn to think, she says, if you don't read poetry, how typical, you don't know the Greeks, the Romans . . . the ancients, I say, those who had to deal with the issues of rage, anger, rape and didn't believe that Christian love could save them from doing wrong, they knew what was right and still couldn't control themselves and did wrong, and realized how passion can overcome you. I created a monster, she says, because she was the one who got me interested in thinking about the ancients. My old feelings are coming on strong now I think I shouldn't have left with her: what am I trying to prove I can take it, I'm mature now and can control my feelings—the Jews and Christians were right avoid or succumb.

Yes but it's good to feel again to see that I'm not this dull boring old man, regardless of what those high schoolers said to me yesterday, hey old man you're going to get a heart attack running like that, my sex drive is diminished but not dead and it doesn't make life easier to get through as the ancients thought, I keep thinking I should be doing it more even when I don't have the desire—now at least I don't have to go out of my way to get it, still never controlling it, zipless fucks and violent fantasies, it would have been okay except for those dreams; my uncle grabbing me by the collar saying don't think because you came back from harm's way you're going to be alright, you're not, you have a callous streak in you that you never had before, your gentleness is gone. Fuck you! Hopefully I said that to myself. You drink and smoke like the goyim, I never heard him use that word. You don't want to appear weak, you're like your grandfather after he came back from the Great War my mother said he was never the same person and your grandmother wouldn't have married him if she knew he would turn out like he did, she finally left him and had an affair (my grandmother had an affair?) with a school teacher which humiliated him, he could accept her leaving him but having an affair with a schoolteacher a shirker, a repressed homosexual who wore pink shirts, I remember my mother telling me of him telling her no wife of mine is going to have sex with a man who wears a pink shirt. My grandparents had difficulties also? I blamed her for breaking up our home but now I understand she said then that she wanted a gentleman not a rough house; a man is not one who puts his foot down on the accelerator anybody can speed, but it's taking your foot off—go slow, my father never re- covered drank himself to oblivion. Your grandmother went into psychoanalysis. Freud! No not Freud but one of his disciples and when the Nazis came the schoolteacher quickly realized this was not the place to raise a family and migrated to America with me, your mother still living with your father wasn't as fortunate. My step-father had enough *sechel* not to negotiate with barbarism you get out of its path, my step-father wanted to go to Palestine but my mother wanted no truck with a primitive country and they found a home here. I didn't even realize he wasn't my real grandfather, my biological grandfather died in a concentration camp of typhus, this step-grandfather, the only grandfather I knew and who I would steal coins from his pants pocket was a gentle old man—my grandmother was dead before I was even born so I never even visited her grave. We have no history of the past in the States; I now visit it when I occasionally go to my step-grandfather's grave. I thought it might have been nice to live in the past, the golden age, but my uncle grabbing me by the lapels, and the lapels were wide this was sixties clothes, I laugh now if only I had kept my step-grandfathers suits and ties, I could have been in, but in the fifties thin lapels and ties were in and I laughed at his big lapels and ties, my uncle told me there was no golden age we always live in the age of bronze, even if before the first world war the Russians thought they lived in the age of silver, he told me that I had to get this rage, this anger out of me, instead I got drunk again that night. I met Jeff on the street talking to some girl and she was telling us she was an athlete and we laughed and she said do you want to fight, and I said no we rather race and offered her a head start but she refused and we ran to the corner only I fell by the wayside gasping for breath—how quickly it leaves you I couldn't even make it to the corner, Jeff at least made it that far, of course, coming in second to her. The next day I started analysis—the modern wager that I could talk about my difficulties, my parents couldn't because their pain was so horrible (there were no Holocaust support groups in those days) my pain could be made bearable theirs could not, only to leave it a mere decade later when I realized Freud misunderstood Laius—the father, he tried to kill his son twice once when he sent him away and then on the fork in the road before he got his comeuppance.

No wonder children from fucked up homes (i.e. me) are afraid to leave they think it will all fall apart once they are gone. When the family is bad it's difficult to leave. Still I could not speak, I had it all yet I had nothing; I couldn't articulate words afraid that if I said what I felt the world would collapse. I wanted my solitude but couldn't be alone when alone wanted to be with others, walked the streets looked into apartment windows, wanted bookshelves full of books, paintings on the wall, and a woman, didn't want to be so decadent, wanted that more than anything, refused to believe I wanted to be so ordinary. There were always two conversations going on within me, with others who I couldn't enjoy being with, and with you explaining to you everything that was happening to me even if everything was phony to me. I felt tired all the time, started taking naps in the middle of the afternoon, even started going with you and Jeff to anti-war demonstrations, only to be with you, I had no interest in those zoos. But I quickly learned not to carry a sign because you could never put it down and nobody would take it from you and you ended up schlepping the thing the whole march, half the time I didn't even know what it said. I could start a sentence and by the middle forget what I wanted to say, not really, I would say it to myself and it would sound so ridiculous that I sputtered the last part away only to come back to it moments later when you were talking about something else, you know I would put myself down so much that it always came out in other ways, and I would just stare at your teeth, your teeth were so pure, so white, a ray of light would be on you so that my eyelids would shutter. And you expected me to pick that up? Somehow I thought you were the only one who could see through my false bravado. I remember your feet were in the gutter even if your head was in the clouds. You brought more men into the anti-war movement than all of Chomsky's declarations. A pretty woman showed me the fruitlessness of war. I didn't even know you heard of Chomsky. My analyst asked why I couldn't say what I wanted and I sputtered something and luckily I made a vow not to quit after one session or I would have never gone back, even when he said you've had years of repression in you they can't be gotten rid of in a moment, there is no magic wand, you have to make a commitment. I gave it a year no matter what which turned into seven then ten. I learned that I didn't have to go along where destiny drifted but could try and lead a rational life even if I had little control over my passions and went into poetry because I realized my failures in everything else could be considered okay if I'm a poet, even as he wondered you keep saying you want to be a poet but you never write a line of poetry. What I liked about poetry is poets don't talk the way things ought to be but the in between nature of our lives when we know we should do something yet we do the opposite. I knew I shouldn't be around you but I couldn't leave you. You came into my life too soon or not late enough. I'm no longer the wild man, in fact analysis has taken much of the fight out of me— divine melancholy, serene resignation, and my mother was wrong meeting a good woman wasn't going to get the craziness out of me. One moment I would be laughing the next tears would be flowing and I couldn't figure out why—false sentiment I couldn't get my thoughts in one place. I remember going to see *Woyzeck*, a play about the common man, because you were busy with Jeff one night and you were angry at me for going without you but you did say you were proud of me for actually going to a play by myself. You were also surprised when I actually started going to movies, cinema, as you called it then, in the middle of the week, but there you insisted I not see stuff we might see together when you took a break from writing. But it took me a long time to understand this and talk about this to my silent analyst. But we did talk about it together. I started reading even if I fell behind in my courses—the good books were never on the curriculum. Yes my teachers gave out reading lists but nobody read them but you would pick out books for me to read. School limits your imagination, I realized I would have to find my own way I wasn't learning anything at school and you were my sympathetic friend with whom I could have a dialogue, even if what was most important couldn't be said, there was a hole between loving and saying I love.

Solitude and sexlessness are good for the old not me even as I no longer feel desire daily, the passion in my loins is still there, but not nightly and when it abates gives me some freedom; I haven't thought about Liliana in this respect in quite a while. Looking across at her she's almost finished with her second drink while I am still nursing my first, I can see why she has a double chin—that and her big ass, which means she no longer works but stays at home, are the only clues to the aging process, gravity pushes everything downward unless you work at it. Galina has a tight ass. We promised each other we would be there for each other but lovers' promises are written on wind and running water. When she wanted her freedom I rang the bell with a ferocity I never knew I had coming to her place and seeing a boy's name on the buzzer I wanted her to know I was coming even after she told me it was only for protection that she didn't want to be seen as a single woman living alone—sure it made sense but like women only putting their first initial in the phone book everyone knew it was fake. After dinner which didn't lead to sex, why should it I said so naively to my analyst when he wished me good luck, I had no idea that's what I wanted the first time we saw each other after we agreed to part after Jeff left prison. My hands flew in the air for supplication, but to whom to what? thunder and lighting did not come there was no magic man behind the cave manipulating the shadows on the wall. But there was a terror within and I had to get away, I couldn't take it and my analyst said I did right thing by leaving not playing at being a man that could stay the course—one of the few times he actually spoke to me. That's when I vowed not to see her again for a year, ha! Only later, much later, did it actually succeed, thinking if I don't see her there will eventually be an end to my depression even if it takes five years but if I continue to see her the end would never occur. At first I thought I gave up pure intensity for boring marriage but this is a slow simmer while Liliana's is a hot fire—with Liliana I thought I found my other half, with Galina we became three, each individually and us together. Still I was determined to stalk her, but only in my mind, since I didn't follow where she moved until the advent of the internet and you could find anybody but by then I realized I could have never written or loved if I had stayed in that intense state. But there was nobody I could talk to this about, women see marriage, the family, and children as the holy trinity and men only know cheating not loving—getting laid that's all that counts, why I had a difficult time being alone with men. Most of my friends are women. My drinking ended when I awoke one day wondering where I was and couldn't re-call the previous night, shivering, shaking, having a headache my teeth chattering while I tried to cohere my thoughts—all I could say was veteran and people would give me a look of understand-ing but they understood nothing. I tried catching myself but kept falling couldn't grab onto anything to hold myself up, wanted to see Jeff but he had ran away to Vermont even as Liliana had saved his apartment for him to come back to. A phone rings I know it's not mine Liliana says, it's from Jeff's daughter she wants to know where I am and that she wants to see me and ask me about her father, she gives me an address that I know, somehow Jeff has kept this apartment all these years. He's a New Yorker after all not giv-ing up on a rent-controlled apartment. He must have sublet it all these years. She's pissed that I didn't stay at the memorial service but she couldn't leave has to make sure it runs smoothly but still wants to see me. I imagine this is the first time in her life she's play-acting adult and likes it, you only feel like an adult in birth and death situations, Liliana says. She still can't stand children and says she won't be coming. Is Allisson thirty? I do quick mental arithmetic older, closer to forty I think. Married? I know nothing about her. Why all of a sudden is she interested in me? Feelings that I thought I put behind me all of a sudden are coming to the surface even I don't want to get sucked into them, I quickly tell myself even if it's for a few moments okay enjoy them now you are mature enough to free yourself from them—you are free aren't you? No more lurking, courting, and stalking—the word makes all the difference in how we map ourselves, i.e. freedom fighter/terrorist imperialist/liberator—Liliana is oblivious to my distinctions she's now onto her third vodka. She has no interest in going with me to see Allisson so there is an ending to our time here. Ours is a relation of two, not of a third person even Jeff's daughter. When she broke with Jeff she broke with me. When she broke with me she broke with Jeff. The barkeep offered to refill my glass but I still hadn't finished my first, she brings me bottled water instead, I don't want to leave with a headache thinking I still might want to write some notes later tonight—everything for poetry, I was surprised Liliana didn't switch to pot, after all she was the one who first turned me on before I dropped out to become this puritan aesthete I am now, advocating a freer life but an intellectual one— the bottle of *Lethe* comes only I no longer forget and look closer at Liliana see she is wearing a straw hat, when did she put that on, making her face look rounder, softer, and my memory sinks down to my pants—it's going to hurt again at the end of the day. Jeffrey never should have left New York, his life was never the same up there, he must have only been bored and lonely, nobody truly understood him, she opines. All I could feel is my ancient flame alive once again; be careful I say you're only going to get hurt, I can control it, you can't control it. I enjoy her company: loss and recognition of loss is important—my dream the night after I received Jeff's missive on my voice mail—I made a decision to live without her in order to begin to learn how to live, a life that isn't lived but fraught with failure. There is no failure in art, I tell myself, art is sometimes shitty, sometimes less so, and yet now I am looked upon as a genius they look all aglow when I say poet. No longer is my art looked upon as an escape from reality by friends who have nothing to do all day but read the *Times* cover to cover, instead they see it as giving me something to do. Now poetry captures the silences between heartbeats: between doggerel life and life that has to do with thought. And nobody says anymore oh, do you teach? Can thinking be taught? Only you can call yourself a poet? Except when I put it down on my IRS form, they got a kick out of that since I made no income from it and took a lot of deductions from it, but as Galina said they didn't arrest you like they did Brodsky and when asked who said you were a poet and when he answered God, they deported him. In America I was permitted to call myself poet, even if I never called myself a poet again lest I run into difficulties from the Internal Revenue Service. Liliana was an early influence; even if she was against the war, she listened and led me to reconsider my beliefs—women were good anti-war recruiters and I loved looking at her white teeth now yellowish and when words left her lips I couldn't catch all of them until I saw tears flow from them. She now says she's sorry she never had a child with either Jeffrey or me, one love child is better than any other type of child. The children she did have were more for the men in her life than for her sake, all they did was ruin her life, they certainly ended my marriages when the men expected me to be the only caregiver—kids, kitchen and church. Children not made from love can only be vestiges and can give no love on their own, which is why so many children today are divorcing. They think it's because their parents divorced not that they were not conceived in love, if I didn't have those abortions those children might have had a better chance: The one in me when Jeffrey was in prison but it wouldn't have been right for him to come home to a child conceived by me, because we were too young then to be straddled with children. The ones I have are products of useless fucks. Still she doesn't want to see Allisson and see how she turned out, even if Allisson wants to see her—you cannot relive the past and it will only bring me sorrow. I walked out of his life, the only one who truly loved me, I always had boys I knew how to flirt, make eye contact, smile, see if they had something, but usually they were blank, except the ones who only wanted sex, believe me I liked that, I loved to ball, remember. I remember. We were the first generation of women who could do so and I took advantage, but those silences, men can't talk, it's that their brains are bigger than women's but emptier, look at this new generation of men they can't do a thing, luckily women are free to explore other options. And she laughs relating her story of how one morning her car battery went dead and she went looking for a charge and the garage mechanic says that's not for a woman to do. While for me under the hood lurks a monster. When we were in Greece and wanted to go on a skiff the guy wanted to show me how to do it, Galina laughed, and I said that's women's work, she liked to play with stuff but Charon thought that's not lady-like only men run boats even if she liked to do it and I didn't, even if I didn't want to be on the dinghy. Still he wouldn't let the charger out of his sight. Foreigner? No typical American male still thinks men earn a living and women stay home and clean. I almost came late and who expected that they would start on time but I saw you and knew when I did you were the reason I came. She didn't give people a chance to schmooze or is the whole world run by digital clock now. You know it's more impressive than a typical watch but not necessarily more accurate. She then takes out a cute modern pocket watch a complete watch giving time, date, weather, cycles of the moon, like a star-trek communicator—a modern version of an old pocket watch. The barkeep asks if we want a refill, Liliana accepts, I hold back, Liliana laments that there are no more free comps, and smiles, she used to get free complimentary drinks from bartenders (male) or strange men offered to buy her drinks until women started becoming barkeeps and more women started entering bars, she recalls signs that said single women not allowed in the bar after midnight, and she remembers how sorry she used to feel for old ladies sitting at bars all alone, now I can be one of them, she says. But you will never be, I tell her. Somehow I used to imagine that these old lades had wonderful lives and were living out the last years in penance for having loved too much, now I realize they were old lonely birds who never wanted to watch a man die, a shame, women had to marry then and only older men then, better younger like now, but then you still had to take care of them, better to live alone. How she could drink that stuff is beyond me. Her mother could, I remember, but she probably doesn't want to be compared to her. Even now she hasn't lived in one place for fifty years like her mother before her. Does anyone live in one place anymore? My uncle could go anywhere in the old Austrian Empire and live but when he left Czernowitz he only wanted to go to Berlin, Galina only thought of getting to Moscow, me I only wanted to live in Manhattan. Me too, Liliana says, I only moved outside for the *kinder*, the schools were so bad in the city that I couldn't do that to them. The good schools, forget the bad ones, all they did was discipline, drill, exam, test, quiz, written, oral, hours of busywork homework, bored the kids silly, wouldn't let them run around, didn't even take the children to the park during the snow and school teachers never read books, I found that out to my dismay, how can they teach if they don't read poetry, novels or plays. Sounds familiar I say, if it wasn't for my mother's brother, my uncle I never would have known there's a world outside, he insisted I go to plays with him, my parents thought theater a waste of money, in my home we had no books, no paintings on the wall, my uncle was the only one I knew who had possessions that were only beautiful not for their utility value. Was he gay? My gaydar wasn't as keen in those days. Whenever he traveled he made sure to send me a picture postcard, the only mail I ever received. Once when I got into a fight with some punk and beat the living shit out of him. You? I was a terror, anyway this guy tells his father who calls the police and my parents didn't know what to do scared as they were of the police and called my uncle who made sure I had a lawyer, one of his card playing buddies, and when the judge tried to throw the book at me, this was the judge who was suppose to be my friend, it wasn't an advocacy hearing but a protective hearing, but he was an Irish Judge and I had hit an Irish boy, but my lawyer told him I was a straight A student (a lie) and that the boy came after me with brass knuckles and I was given a JD card. How quaint? But it worked I didn't have to go to reform school, but I was threatened with bread and water and I was scared. Then my parents moved out of the old neighborhood to a new old neighborhood, where I met Jeff we were classmates until he went to a special high school for brainiacs while I went across the street the one for dummies. Education has undergone a transformation since the sixties, she says, then at least we had a world of literacy, now students don't even have a capacity to read they know about the different food habits of cultures but no understanding of civilization, the flattening out of culture—Marcuse was prophet even if when he wrote about the one dimensionality of life life was multiple. I can see why Jeff wanted to piss them (his parents, his guidance counselor) off by not wanting to go to college, it was a terrible school only interested in testing, never taking a child to the theater or opera, but my uncle explained to us that it was a way to get away from home but we decided to go into the Army on the buddy system only the pressure from his school became too great, imagine they had a hundred percent college attendance and they weren't going to let him spoil it. But at least it got me out of the Bronx. When Jeffrey and I moved in together he still would go to dinner at his mother's and only spend weekends with me for about a year. You Jewish boys and your mothers! But I remember loving you dark haired Jewish beauties so exotic, with thick dark curly hair over such pale white skin like you've never seen the sun, and always wearing glasses always carrying a book, you had a spark that's what schooling is missing today is this spark, this desire to learn not just get good grades or do whatever to get a better job. My uncle explained to me he was rooted in the Empire but feels rootless in the States, where he lived in one apartment, until he was forced out, since he came to New York, even if he traveled around the Empire he stayed put in the city. Hitler changed his beliefs made him become Jewish when he wanted to kill us like lice, he had said, and now considered himself an urban cosmopolitan constantly trying to figure out his destiny because the other had defined him: the Germans made me a Jew, I could have been killed as a lie for Hitler, a human being changed to vermin and I was choiceless in the matter. It defined me as well only years later in analysis was I able to realize I enlisted to show I wasn't this coward Jew. I never could make articulated choices even as my uncle tried to stop me from enlisting and not become like my parents and that I should do better than them, he even offered to help pay for college, but I didn't want aid from my uncle. In America he said you can escape your roots, in the old Empire you couldn't even if in the old Austrian Empire you could travel anywhere (everyone spoke German) and feel at home anywhere most stayed close to home. Liliana answers and I didn't even realize I was speaking aloud, that here you can simply change your clothing and you're no longer like your parents, when we wore jeans and went braless, no

make-up, we changed the traditional look, I can recall young girls
getting dressed up to go to class while the rest of us were in jeans
and a tee shirt. The Dean actually gave a speech that we shouldn't
wear pants if we have big rumps, but it proved the old ways were
dying. Some woman actually wore a mini skirt and everybody, I
mean everybody, both men and women glared at her for actually
wearing a skirt above her knees. The Administration called a meeting banned mini-skirts and jeans except no teacher would enforce
the ban on jeans and so by default the old ways changed women
would no longer be ruled by fashion, there was no more fashion
police. Progress? I loved looking at women in high heels and short
slit skirts. Male Chauvinist Pig! Hippie! The interesting part of aging is not getting older but remembering what you once liked, she
says. I reply it's not being able to stay up all night and get up early
the next day. Even if I need less sleep now I still must sleep. I liked
the new order but pretty quickly the old order reasserts itself, you
wake up one morning with a hangover you know you can't keep
on going like this, you turn thirty and think it's time to get a real
job, you decide to look up from the trees and see there are no jobs
in philosophy so you switch to logic i.e. computers you become a
programmer, good paying jobs that pay so much you have to own a
home to not pay so much in taxes, then the Restoration comes and
you meet a man who would look good in the home, says he can fix
things, of course he never does, so he moves in with you once you
become pregnant only to leave when the children get old enough
to be on their own but you become too attached to the home to
leave, buy him off, meet another widower, marry him, dump him,
and find yourself alone at fifty, liking being alone with your books,
which you never have time to read. Now that's progress! You were
always a Pollyanna just as Jeffrey always said, no it's what I ran
away from my whole life a house, kiddies, backyard, crabgrass, and
that's what I ended up with, now women don't need men for rais-

ing the child just their seed, that's progress. Where would you have been if you didn't have your uncle to show you another way? Now we live in the age of information only it's advertising not knowledge that is being transmitted so nobody understands that they can make choices. Money buys out all choices, all anyone wants now is money. Can I quote you on that? I was already quoted on the news. We smile. They didn't use it, I say. We were recalling when she was asked on a woman on the street interview what she thought about Watergate and she answered I don't know anything about Watergate all I'm interested in is balling. Needless to say they didn't run that spot. But now news runs better when Castro was taken seriously ill the newscasters immediately rushed to Jersey City and asked anti-Castro Cubans about his condition and unanimously they said he was already dead and the Cuban government was hiding the information—now news doesn't even let fact get in the way. They no longer even allow information to get in the way all they want to do is fill up airtime, and then television switched to old photos of Castro to supply the images. At least you let them know you weren't interested in Watergate and had other issues on your mind and world affairs was no concern of yours only interested in how it affected the individual, not the "objective" world they portrayed as news, in which each moment is the same among any other as if it's always the same century in every week. History is the individual event, Liliana says, and when it gets caught up in the world event there's only hell to pay, she says. The complicated affairs of the world means lying what nobody wants to make public—Jeffrey always felt honestly his position and they ate him up alive—he thought he could reason with them and they ate him up alive. But in public affairs each event has no connection to the previous event his years as a prisoner proved that, he even dropped out of law school he couldn't stand what they considered truth, he finally saw Law for what it was, violence. No one told us we are simply prisoners of our time much as our parents were prisoners of theirs. Not your parents, I remind Liliana. She agrees in the Midwest it's three meals a day, and Church on Sunday, she remembers coming over to my parents' place New Year's Eve and how my parents ate in silence, which I considered normal, but which she said was strange after we left, I was never so scared in my life they simply sat there obviously they wondered why we were together, then I tell her my mother was always frightened when the toilet flushed somehow reminding her when she was in a concentration camp and a guard threw a woman into the sink hole and she was drowned in her own feces, she told me her house was always full of people that she had to get away, they said grace before meals. I told her she didn't have to wait at our place. You weren't used to such monotony. She had wanted to meet my parents, Jeff knew better, the only visitor my parents ever had, the only company we ever had, was my uncle and he didn't come too often, mostly to see me I guess, and when I came of age, and coming of age in New York means allowed to ride the subways by yourself, I would travel to my uncle's shoe store in Spanish Harlem until he was forced out for being white in a black neighborhood, he would have been killed in the Harlem riots except a black old women saved his life when looters, or freedom fighters came by yelling we have to get white exploiters out of our neighborhood, and she said you can't hurt this man and somehow he wasn't hurt, or to his apartment on the West Side. Since he was a bachelor they had invited him to holiday meals but even that became too much for all of them. Liliana said she understood more about me when I told her that story on the roof; she had taken the TV dinners out of their aluminum tins and served them as if she cooked the whole thing herself. My mother was shocked she wore jeans, jewelry and sneakers and that she wasn't afraid to be with a man who wasn't her protector (Jeff was working and she didn't want to be alone New Year's Eve) and that you used to walk the streets late at night, even as you told her women have been liberated and no longer need a man to escort them everywhere at night. I recall Jeff telling me how when she stayed over his house the first time without hesitation she slept in his bed. Nowadays girls are no longer such feminists, my daughter insists when her boyfriends sleep over that they sleep on the couch, at least the first few times, out of respect for the mother, before she takes them into bed. Then I remember, thinking it must be fun being in a relationship and being able to do different things than him. We went on the roof to see the fireworks and we could see the dome of the sky it was a crystal clear cold night but could only see fragments of the fireworks while every apartment in the Bronx was tuned to Guy Lombardo playing *Auld Lang Syne*. Your father and mother don't dine, she said to me then, they swallow taking a mouthful and then another before swallowing it down with soda pop. You guys were finished with a meal before you even started. You were horrified and said to my mother this isn't from a can is it? Where else would it be from? I didn't even know such a thing as fresh vegetables existed, not can bought, until I was in the service. No she said these are fresh, meaning she just opened the can. What she didn't tell her was that Max the grocer had let her in on a little secret that dented cans were the same as regular cans only customers always wanted non-dented canned vegetables and she was proud of her shopping skills in getting dented tins at a discount. I thought you would fall back into your old life; you had no job, no place to live, and no girlfriend. I couldn't go back you had showed me another way even if you didn't mean to you had opened up a new door in some mysterious way—to tasting life not full blown cynicism; easy to see now when you served me a tasteful meal with wine instead of my usual frozen TV dinners with soda. Your Thanksgiving dinner started me on a path that I wanted more of and I was smart enough to realize that—usually I could only accept what I was accustomed to everything else seemed strange. Tasteless food! Now I wanted to taste different foods, which meant a different way of life and at least my uncle lived to see me trying, it was embarrassing enough to sleep in my old bed but that too was only a metaphor my father had commandeered my bedroom and I now slept on the couch and in the morning my mother would wake me and force me to go into her bed so she could clean the living room. That must have been pleasant? I didn't mind moving but having to close that damn couch was difficult it was too heavy for her but I did it with the secret pleasure that at least I wasn't sleeping in my old bed. You were sleeping in your mother's bed replacing your father, my analyst said. I didn't think of it in those terms only that I was getting a few more hours of sleep. Fraud's therapy! She laughs. You and my analyst had a field day with that but all I wanted to do was walk except I no longer could stay in the old neighborhood, I was even mugged when a kid comes up to me and asks the time and like a fool I look he catches me off guard and takes my money and watch. A little *pisher* I almost laughed in his face, bastard mugging me in my neighborhood. You were lucky you were mugged in the seventies not the eighties in the crack epidemic where they didn't kill people because they didn't hand over their watch quick enough, when crime got out of control and you couldn't walk the streets safely anymore, where women had to take a taxi home at night it became part of our budget. Then I started jotting down random observations on paper napkins and you suggested I carry a journal but to carry a journal you needed a book bag and you gave me one, which I carried with me until recently, and if you carry a journal in a book bag you might as well carry something else as well it's too big just for a journal, so I started carrying books to read along with my journal, even if I never carried books or a book bag for school, I had no idea what I wanted but knew what I didn't want to be drawn back into the old life. My mother kept complaining when I brought a new book home where are we going to put it don't you have enough you haven't read all you have, and your life was so foreign to me I didn't know how to reach it. All I could think was that I had to find a stupid job that would bore me to death but at least I would have somewhere to go, some money in my pocket and then some girl would see me as a good catch and magically transform my life and I wouldn't have to spend time in gin mills. It was you who suggested we go to off-Broadway plays together instead of drinking. I never told you how I used to walk past your house hoping to catch sight of you through the window or just out for a walk at midnight. That's okay I would consciously walk past your place hoping for the same thing. But I did see in my old girlfriend how easy it is to ruin your life become your mother and ruin your child's life. Solitude besides being lonely allowed me to break away. Brave talk for a man sleeping in his mother's bed. Only until my father died then I knew I had to get out even if my analyst said now you're trapped you have to stay with her I knew if I didn't move out I would be trapped with her forever. You figured that out? No my uncle told me I didn't want to live with my mother, but my analyst at least gave me ten more minutes. I could tell the world how to live but what I couldn't figure out is what I wanted, at least analysis gave me somewhere to go four times a week. If you're a Freudian you have Freudian dreams, a Jungian Jungian dreams, a Reichian Reichian dreams and if you don't believe dreams mean nothing but in dreaming the imagination is released not bound by sensory inputs. While you were into the feminist revolution I was trying to come to grips with the spirits that haunted me. It really was shell shock, Liliana says, you didn't want to admit you were weak—American machismo, after all you had killed and seen men die and that has an effect on you. The spirits of the dead come back and haunt people even if we live in a modern age where we don't believe in ghosts, they exist, I know, you couldn't have a meaningful relationship with me it took you forever to loosen up and I doubt if we would have even connected if you weren't Jeffrey's best friend at first you could barely talk you were so silent couldn't put two syllables together always hiding behind cynicism and sarcastic remarks, putting everything down, I remember being surprised how you took to that beautiful painting of twenty-nine representatives of the state surrounded waiting their turn to be guillotined the thirtieth head already in the basket—the revolution eating its own that you insisted we go back the next day and the day after you couldn't get enough of that painting then found out the *Assassination of Marat/Sade* was playing and you actually called me to go. I called when I knew Jeff would be out. Then you went to the library and read the play, actually wanted to cut out the pages you wished to read and carry with you, until I told you you don't do that to library books and you actually went out and bought your first book from which you ripped pages out of so you could memorize lines. You surprised me, she says, besides me no one I knew read except what was required. The demise of culture! But you kept going back to see the play, reread the play, became engrossed in subsidiary material of the play somehow that play was invigorating to you. It was the first off-Broadway play I had ever seen and you were the only one I could talk to about it, I felt funny talking about an intellectual activity, not sports, girls, or killing. But I remember you refused to write a paper on it, you were in school by then, saying you didn't want to ruin the experience by having to write about it. No matter I was afraid that the teacher wouldn't understand or laugh at my literary pretensions. That's when I first started carrying books in my book bag, I say. I was the one who got you that lovely book satchel for your birthday, even if you were afraid to use it because it was new. I really started my serious reading after that, novels, plays, poetry, changed my life, sometimes I'd be so engrossed in my reading that I missed my subway stop once went all the way to Brooklyn before I realized and I'd either turn around or walk back. That's when I realized I wasn't learning anything in college and instead would read any book I wanted and did minimum work to pass. Hey you were better than me all I read in school was *Archie* comics and Jeffrey showed me *Classic Illustrated* comics for the synopsis of the major texts we were suppose to read. Ah what we did in high school. What you did Jeffrey says he was a reader in high school why high school was so easy for him. Yes in college he had a girl friend in high school I had one. We laughed once at that, he reminded me when I gave Eileen an ankle bracelet for her birthday she smiled but looked disappointed she expected a ring. A ring, I swear that never even crossed my mind. You the leftist knew nothing of the dreams of girls. I remember being surprised Marxism had something to do with the Soviet Union, that workers paradise. My uncle was the only one who said that workers paradise will fail, everyone else talked about the inevitability of socialism but he said freedom always wins out no matter how long it takes. His friends all thought he was crazy. All old leftists. Trotskyites. Spartacists. Anarchists. Gays. Jewish avant-garde artists, cosmopolitans, all workers who believed in the coming revolution but it wouldn't be like the last one. All who hated America but could live nowhere else but America. By pure chance a Hungarian Cafe opened up a few blocks from where my uncle lived up on Amsterdam Avenue and this was before the neighborhood changed into the Upper West Side i.e. wasn't in vogue, near fortress Columbia, Columbia students hardly ever migrated off campus, it was considered dangerous, except to the West End Bar, all around was considered ghetto but for him and his cronies he could go there and play chess, kibbitz, and speak German once again. I know he loved that place and his last words might have been pawn to queen four, he always had told me to get your pieces out early except the queen and control the center, he loved positional tactical play, and after he died I started using his openings, as my analyst said I was keeping him alive within me. It was my job to break up his apartment and luckily I got most of the stuff out before the super got in and threw the rest of the paintings out, the furniture, probably kept the television, that was new I had given it to him the year before, but I had books, some paintings and had managed to get the piano moved earlier. I thought he died broke and I would have to pay for the funeral, but I found a bankbook stashed away with money to pay for his funeral, and to my surprise this old black women shows up who at first I took for his cleaning woman but then realized she was the woman from the Harlem riots who had saved him from being considered the white devil as blacks were determined to drive white store owners out of their neighborhood by breaking windows, stealing, calling him honky, and finally Jewish exploiter. She was the one who told me his shoe store has been empty for years now. Finally when he was robbed at gunpoint instead of buying a gun to protect himself he simply closed the shop but apparently had kept in touch with this lady who had rushed him to the hospital. Her name was in his address book and I contacted everyone in it to let them know about the funeral. As they lowered him into the grave I thought I inherited this old lady and I have to visit her once in a while and never saw her again. My uncle would wear a sports jacket, button-down cardigan sweater, trousers, dress shirt and tie to our family affairs, and that's what I went out and bought for his funeral. None of his friends came, he truly outlived his time and had few friends left, even those at the café only knew him by sight they weren't his true buddies, that must have been the most difficult part of old age having no friends left. On his tombstone I had chiseled "The descent into the underworld is easy. But to retrace your steps to climb back to the upper air—there the struggle, there labor lies," from the *Aeneid* his favorite poem. I spoke to him in the funeral home all by ourselves the night before the funeral thanking him for the grand tour, and for him telling me not to be like a mute animal when I came back from 'Nam. Talk about it don't become like your parents living as if you're dead they had faced the unimaginable no matter how horrible your situation is you must talk about it, the difference between humans and animals is that we can talk, mute silence doesn't help you, you won't be considered weak if you get help. He suggested one of his cronies who was a psychiatrist (he had roomed with him after the War while he still was in medical school) but I wasn't ready for that then and he didn't push it said when you are ready don't be afraid to speak about it. Besides going to a psychiatrist on Park Avenue seemed crazy and I wasn't crazy, even my mother said that. Only later did I go but didn't ask him for his psychiatrist's name but found one only when I couldn't stand the emptiness anymore and needed someone desperately to talk to (trust) but stood mute each time I tried to express my feelings to you—and those dreams were killing me, a train going off its tracks then spiraling out of control twirling up in the air and landing in the river. And when you asked me what you would change in the dream if you could, I looked at you uncomprehending, how can you change a dream—it is what it isn't. Not change the dream you said, what would you do in the dream that was different, the internal not the external. It never even entered my mind. My rage was getting out of control and I couldn't calm down you even said I dressed disturbed, torn jeans, sneakers, tee shirt, but usually I would walk away before trouble became too serious but all of a sudden I was getting into fist fights, I scared myself, that's when I decided I have to get this under control I can't do it by myself and when I started it was painful I wondered what bullshit am I getting myself into, but little by little the irritation ended a new desire took over me. Gently very sensitively Liliana places her hand over my hand, unlike the time when Jeff was showering and I was napping on the couch she came up to me and started sucking my cock and me half-asleep wondering if this is real and she saying don't worry Jeffrey takes long showers, and me trying to get her to stop, still not sure if I dreamed it or it was real. She says that must have been the time you lost your innocence when you realized what you did—I didn't know if she meant 'Nam or analysis, and now life for you has no more spring. Not true I think, spring left when she left, but analysis certainly helped get a handle on it even if I had to overcome my fear of sounding weak, her caressing my hand feels good and I'm surprised how much an old flame can do to you. The demise of my sex drive is grossly over-exaggerated. Oh how I hated being a prisoner of sex liked masturbation much better, used Liliana as my fantasy masturbation object, now here the memory is coming back to haunt me. I still don't need *Viagra* as long as I can conjure up Liliana. It won't be the long slow climb to death via drugs, but detoxed and in control, but how will I know times up and I have to end it, will I be able to take control? I always wondered when would it be time to go to the undiscovered country, I, not me, will have to do something not hang around dribbling food down my mouth, maybe I can get back with Liliana until we part, which we must, do it correct this time and commit suicide that'll teach her, only she wouldn't know; the ultimate irony killing yourself over a woman and the woman doesn't even know: No act of kindness however small is wasted, I think, as I pat Liliana back on the top of her hand. I remember telling myself that I should take up the piano once again, hating it as a kid because it interfered with ball playing but now that I have one, but it stood as a monument out of tune in my apartment for years until Galina came along, I think that's what brought her to me. Unfortunately I didn't save his old satchel from the landlord's insistence that the place be ready to rent by the next month, even if I had paid a month's rent in advance to clean it out, and instead finally decided Liliana's satchel wasn't new anymore and used it—I always feel uncomfortable using new stuff, like I don't deserve it—even now hesitating to buy a ten-dollar bar of soap whose aroma I like, shouldn't I simply use the cheap stuff. But at least sometimes I win those fights with myself now and say I deserve a nice-smelling soap. Then I think I'm like my uncle hardly any old friends left, and I'm comparatively young, until I met Liliana again, maybe you just run out of the need for friends, or at least friends who can't have a conversation. She's still caressing my hand and it feels good, I feel like a babe in her arms, I have no memory of my mother being that gentle with me and when she passed I was the dutiful son and buried her but only my friends came to her funeral, she had no friends ever, at least in my lifetime. I buried her and forgot her. It's on the day of my uncle's death that I light a candle in his memory, I smile thinking of this. Why are you smiling? Liliana has such sharp eyes. I explain that I am thinking about my uncle, and she explains that means he's still with you—where the past crosses the present is a dual moment one thought upon reflection, an intertwining of moments which lasts for seconds but where we not only live in the now but also the past. When young the future dominated all my thought now I hardly think of the present let alone the future, looking across at Liliana I see her smile, her teeth are still white, only not as white, but her face still lights up a room—she could eat me up or better yet go down on me, which she was one of the first to do even if it's commonplace now and as if she could read my mind says young girls do blow jobs now at the drop of a hat because they don't want AIDS and want to be sexually active, but mature women want it in the arse. The blush comes to my face that is if I could see my face, even if my face looks different each time I look at it in the mirror, which can hardly be seen over the liquor bottles in the mirror behind the bar. Poor woman finally someone she can talk to and she feels my embarrassment. She hasn't been able to talk all these years so I promise myself not to let my embarrassment ruin the conversation even if I'm old-fashioned and not into lube and tush. Homosexual culture: changing fashions, changing fashion changes culture no longer are boys masters of civilization, fashion demands to be worshipped and homosexuals create fashion, changing the functional to the beautiful everyday use now becomes attractive. At home we never used the good china unless my uncle came, he used his good stuff everyday. I could always tell when my uncle was coming my father climbed up on the chair and brought down the good china—good china bought in *Alexander's* not *Woolworth's*, my uncle had bought *Hutschreuther*—a forty-piece set and my mother wanted to know why he wastes his money on china when he eats alone. I don't eat I dine my uncle said. And when I asked him he said food tastes better off fine china, of course, I had no idea what he was talking about, food is food, but now that I dine off his set I appreciate his taste. He was the one who taught me not to be prejudiced and that I can have red wine with fish or white with meat, a good bottle of wine goes with everything, like good furniture will match with anything you don't have to get a dinette set or a bedroom set, don't let conventions spoil your fun. It wasn't Jews who brought the world culture, i.e. a written record, rather it was Gays who challenged functionalism with beauty—love against force, the Law (anger) that lurked beneath all governments was the violence of a boy subculture unbeknown to most because it was disguised as valor, bravery, God and country, seen for me the first time I read Svevo, who my uncle had said was the best "undiscovered" novelist, the model for Bloom in *Ulysses*. And then he goes and gets me a copy of *Ulysses* in hardcover, my first hardcover book. Liliana smiles says her summer semester abroad was in Rome but we never read Joyce he was called a sissy and not appropriate reading for young girls, and she recalled thinking okay I'll read him when I finish school but never got around to it. But she remembers coming into my place and seeing a copy of Svevo on my dresser, and she didn't even think I knew who he was let alone read him. Her hands are completely removed from me now and she's drinking again, my god, how she can guzzle that stuff down, I feel the echo of her gently rubbing my chin and wish it would continue, I can't ask her to continue, but I touch her arm instead. It's pleasant to the touch, and I hope she doesn't remove it, and recall when we did it more roughly, more furtively but still with a profound sense of gentleness. At least I think I recall because I can't remember doing something so shameful, yet I know we did it even if I don't want to recall it. Jeff was my best friend and I knew it was wrong but somehow convinced myself it was okay to do it and each time said it would be the last time until the next time. She's a free woman, they've broken up, it's not as if he doesn't know, it's in the family. I like that reason best. After each moment I would totally forget that we had done it until next time. Your analyst must have looked at you as a cash cow, she said, he could buy a *Ferrari* with all your guilt. Now even as I realize I shouldn't have done it with her I realize I had to go through those experiences to become who I wanted to become—the anger in me had to be released if I was to become gentle—or as Jeff said to me then at least I would have put up a fight in a Nazi death camp, now if the commandant said put the cigarette out of your mouth as they were going to shoot us, I would say, do it, don't cause trouble.

Liliana has that superior smirk of one who hasn't been in analysis and believes she'll never need it and she was/is certainly superior to me especially when I first came back from war and suicide was never far from my mind, especially after a couple of my buddies had already committed suicide, one in particular I remember I was so jealous of him because he came home to a wife, a child, a home in the suburbs and he had this picture perfect life on the outside, and one day blew his brains out in the car. All I could feel were things,

later I could put words to them, anger, rage, fury, while Jeff and
Liliana were living calmly, even if she did say to me don't worship
me I'm not living this perfect life you seem to imagine I'm living.
I didn't know what it was to live calmly, except when I went up to
Montreal during the Six-Day War . . . to get away from me, Liliana
interjects, telling everybody that I wanted to enlist and fight for Israel and everybody thinking me this good Jew, whilst in reality I
only wanted a free trip to Israel—the promised land. Up there I did
meet a Canadian girl in *Ben's* and noticed how they lived a gentler
life than we in the States, first time I heard that term not America, and maybe the United States wasn't the greatest country in the
world, she introduced me to more Americans, i.e. draft dodgers,
who seemed to live a nice communal life of friendship, drugs, good
meals, adequate necessities not grandeur, unfortunately the fear of
the long winters scared me off, and that I had started analysis and
had promised myself I would give it a year at least before I quit
no matter what. Maybe now is the time to run away again, youth
certainly wasn't this golden age and before old age, illness, disease
slow me down maybe I can do it; this thought is a pleasant one and
I make a mental note to remind myself of this late at night when I
can't fall back asleep, maybe I can dream about it. Never made it
to the Israeli embassy after I met that girl, we just had fun for two
weeks and then I came back to the city. I must have had the only
analyst who didn't take a vacation in August. I'd still rather not be
young again, and if I had to relive my life would shoot myself even
now I see myself standing apart—not from Liliana, but from everyone else who I would never let get close to me until Galina came
along. I always missed the moment, the abyss is deep like a child
standing on the fire-escape looking down from the third floor to
the ground below afraid of falling, wondering how you get down
to the ground, then wondering what his parents would think if he
jumped. Liliana looks at me not at me through me says she never re-

alized I was so complex, more likely I thought you were this dumb working class kid who only could talk sports, and drink, and went to bed with whores like any good soldier boy, all similar not the same person but all the same values afraid of strong women so you hide behind a veneer of masculinity or stayed high so as not to deal with reality. Yet the last time I went back to the old neighborhood I felt so out of place that I couldn't wait to leave, quickly grabbed a taxi downtown and had an exquisite lunch at a most expensive eatery with a bottle of champagne, where I had made sure in advance there were waiters not waitresses and unfortunately didn't know a place where waiters wore white gloves. How uncomfortable I became in the home of my youth. When you took me to *Jules and Jim*, I say, I saw a different persona of man. She doesn't remember seeing that with me. We went to a lot of films together because Jeffrey hated going to movies and then there were a lot of places in town that showed good foreign films then, now there are only multiplex's that show twenty movies you don't want to see, and neighborhood movie theaters have been swallowed up. I haven't been to a movie in ages, she continues. We went to the *Beekman* in Greenwich Village, or the Village as you called it, and I was always afraid of beatniks, I say. One even picked me up once but I didn't go with him because I knew what that meant: drugs and sex. How did you know? I just knew, of course, I didn't know only believed I knew. I remember walking along the streets where the *Masses* was published and even *Dissent*, and thinking these old fogies haven't a clue as to the new revolution, years later to find out most of them were FBI informants. More FBI informants than old radicals left. But I did listen to some Ginsberg poetry even if I found it wanting. I thought the beats wrote poor poetry because it wasn't based on any vision only gut feelings. You did say you wanted to live in the Village. Never did, oh once, for a couple of months at a friends place but it was too noisy and no parks I liked the West Side better. But at least you could have today because of economics children stay at home longer or because they're so broke with college debt that they can't afford to get a place, so many parents want their children to go to college because they think it gives them a good start in life, and if employees were required by law not to ask if you went to college, like they are no longer allowed to ask if you're married, with children, or your religion, all of which correlate with good work skills, I bet the student body would decrease by half, but as long as colleges keep raising tuition parents think it's important for the children to go. Wouldn't it be cool I say if one year parents placed a moratorium on college applications just said no or I'd rather not, tuition would come down in a flash. You're a good sixties person she says, college is useless, she says, most middle class families now are only concerned with college costs. I hate you; you're going to make me defend college. For that one person who gets to read the *Aeneid* otherwise nobody reads anymore, they might as well burn all textbooks on the college walk, thinking is so vilified in academia now. Tell me does anyone read poetry now? You were a late bloomer and college gave you a chance otherwise you would have been forced into the world of work without being able to think and would have rolled that stupid rock up the hill for fifty years without a smile on your face then retired and wouldn't have been able to recall what you did all those years. I never thought of it that way, but it is true children postpone adult hood longer now. Not only that they don't throw off their parents values like an old cloak but actually believe what their parents tell them—but then jobs were plentiful and rents were cheap, now the young have the freedom to explore other options, we are products of our situation. Bullshit, Liliana says, now we have mid-life crises and start over both men and women just do it later that's all when we can hurt more people, that's all. I thought youngsters start their mid life crisis at twenty-five, I say. Make-believe ones, she says, you can only hurt your parents at twenty-five, one little knife in the back before they slip into dotage and they still can help you financially, but at forty or fifty, you can really do damage to your parents, your spouse, your children, and if you're lucky yourself as well. Why I didn't want to reproduce? However that decision isn't made by men—when I turn forty I want children—it would be me or somebody else, even if she denied that—and one day she went into the doctor's office feeling weak and rundown and soon the nurses and technicians were hugging her—imagine that at my age, she said, and nine months later I was a father. Luckily you can't stay a child forever and finally when I was out of my parents' house, working odd jobs making do, life was cheap, when I finally found my own place had to make my own dinner, do my own washing, clean up after myself, I decided I better marry. Only women no longer wanted to do these things either so I had to learn, even learned sewing when I got pissed at tailors charging me so much money to sew on a stupid button. At first I used women to help develop a taste but finally decided I have to find out what I like—what paintings I want to put on the wall. Only what I didn't realize at first was that my life wasn't getting better I was making the same old mistakes, only disguising them better because I was more sophisticated in language and thought—still fighting the system the protagonist and the chorus like in a Greek play the chorus stood behind me, still getting into trouble, fights on the job instead of the gin mills, with my landlord instead of women, still walking the street late at night always doing things thinking I could magically transform my life not learning how to wait, grow, then they happen and the pleasure is in waiting instead of hanging out on street corners, finally even having affairs with married women. You know Jeffrey didn't own me, we were together and apart, and we each had our own life. After I left you I said I wanted no more to that type of existence and bingo back to the same thing,

I couldn't help myself always sabotaging myself continuing to do the same things I always did, always frustrated, always scared afraid I was no longer the kid but condemned to be average not this poet I wanted to become even if I had not yet written one line of poetry. I couldn't write because I couldn't find my pen, the paper wasn't correct, there was nothing else to be said, until one day I wrote and wrote all night long exhausted myself that I almost convinced myself that I was a poet only something inside me said I had to do it again the next day to truly be a poet. Oh! The next day I had no interest in writing only drinking. But then I saw you again and I wanted to say I was writing poetry. Is that when you rang the bell so persistently? Three times! I didn't answer the first time because I knew you'd be a beast, the second time because I thought you would be half beast half man, but when you rang the third time I knew you were human, only you would come at me like that. You forced me to confront what I had become and I started realizing that easy is the way that leads to hell getting back that's the trick, as my uncle always said. You started doubting all the lies you told yourself? Maybe I was self destructive not the other is doing it to me maybe I'm doing it to myself. My dream of how I imagined myself to how I really looked, incongruous, blinded by the light I am riding toward Jeff and fall off a donkey the donkey speaks watch it you're going to fail in the act but I was blinded by the light and hop back on and rode right off the cliff then the jackass says anyone could see you were going to fall and I think why couldn't I have a dream with an eagle and thunder bolt,—then my analyst interposed himself between my thought and act and I realized that I would/should explain my act to him, in the beginning of course I took the easy way out and kept silent but then realized this makes no sense if I'm not talking, i.e. showing my anger by sleeping in the session even if felt good. Remember I had to learn not to do what my impulses told me to do, that became my freedom not to do impulsive things and then create rational reasons why I had to do them instead I could do what I didn't want to do. Then a loud noise penetrated the bar from the outside ratatatratatatratatat, dig we must, as the sidewalk was being destroyed outside the bar. Liliana suggests we leave but instead I said let's go to a back booth that could drown out the sidewalk drilling somewhat, as the barkeep said nice music for drinking, and as we walked over to the booth I realized she didn't want to leave either. Usually she always had to be someplace else if we ran into each other on the street. As we moved to a booth the drilling stopped but not to worry this is New York more would occur. The Second Avenue Subway line is still incomplete more noise is expected—the definition of modernity the destruction of old neighborhoods into public spaces where nobody goes, showing off the power of the city, state, or national government by building functional complexes with no particular style and not caring for individuals who have to live, work or pass by these monstrosities. I show her my uncle's pocket watch, I've become more antediluvian the older I get, his pocket watch is my prize possession except that it doesn't keep as good time as any cheap store-bought digital watch and it costs more in upkeep than buying a new one. But I started using it when I became embarrassed that I always looked at the time because I had nothing to do with my hands as if I had to be someplace, now that it's in my pocket it's like I don't have a watch. Do you still carry my briefcase? she wondered, since I'm carrying only a book in my sports jacket. I did until recently when I was searched in one of the police checkpoints to see if I was hiding a small nuclear device, and the clasp wouldn't open they were forced to break the lock. They sincerely regretted having to do this and said that they are not liable for damage to my lock resulting from this necessary security precaution but I could fight it in court. What an incisive mind he had? She. Then she asked what is this? A book? I know it's a book but are you a traitor? Luckily it wasn't in Arabic, I would have never gotten out of police custody, and it took over an hour as they checked the book out saying I graduating college and I never heard of this book, so now I no longer carry your book bag around with me. Do you think you fucked up your life? Liliana asks. A good question I don't know but if I had to do it over again would mess it up just the same, maybe not the same way not try to repeat my errors but I know I'd still mess it up. What I don't say is when I look over my life all I recall are the moments we were together. What I do say is when I was sixteen I looked backward not forward and said if I were thirteen I would do it differently now I'm too old to change, played basketball differently, shot more, played harder, practiced more, gotten better could have made the team maybe then a college scholarship, now it's too late and then I was only sixteen. If I could have gone to school earlier maybe I would have found books earlier. College was a total waste. You're now rereading the books you should have read in college but that your uncle and I told you to read, I told you the good stuff wasn't on the curriculum. It's difficult for me to imagine how stupid I was, a failure now because I have no interest in the material world but poetry moves me lets me get up in the morning without thoughts of gloom and doom. You were a guy you could do things, I was daddy's girl trapped by gender, young women weren't allowed to do anything but be cutesy sex objects to dashing boys in white armor I laugh now at one of my high school beaus who expected me to wait home for his phone call while he went gallivanting around town (drinking) and expected me to shine on his life. Little fucker I felt so good escaping that life. I learned quickly if you don't go by yourself you never go. The reverse for me in high school I only went in group-think. Yeah I probably didn't go to movies by myself back then but then there were no serious movies in Cedar Rapids only cornfields. But in New York I could go alone even living with

Jeffrey, especially after we moved in together and he became old, what is it with men once they live with a woman they become their fathers lying on the couch in a tank-top tee shirt watching football never wanting to leave the house while I wanted to see films, plays. He never liked serious films or off-Broadway plays and boys couldn't go with me if I weren't their lover. At first I too bought into this crap that I needed a chaperone, needed to be protected, by a man, but at a woman's college I learned to be independent. I couldn't make my escape right away but I planned it early, two years at Ames then a summer in New York, I figured my parents would trust me enough by then, then I finished up here. I remember you were the first independent woman I knew. No makeup, always wore jeans, braless. What smoking pot did for me allowed me to see the phoniness of bourgeoisie life. I remember your comments on my *Aeneid* essay insightful, concise and I was surprised you seemed like another of Jeffrey's dumb friends i.e. working class boys who probably had no sisters so didn't know how to talk to a woman. You were the first person to take me to an off-Broadway play and I'm the native New Yorker. Living in the Bronx doesn't make you a New Yorker; you hardly left your neighborhood all you knew were Broadway and only musicals at that—you missed the golden age of Broadway theater because you didn't even know it existed except that it was expensive or for out-of-townies. I remember talking about it afterwards, that's what surprised me, we used to see something then what's to say but know you wondered about this character was it done correctly, that director's choice even pissed when the director had changed the meaning of the author's words. You always complained modern playwrights see women as these empty receptacles not like Antigone, Medea, or Lysistrata who had minds of their own. Shakespeare is excused because only young boys could play women's roles and he couldn't make them too sophisticated young boys couldn't play those roles.

Education is a dangerous thing. It allowed me justifications for my intuitive thought to see the world differently. I already knew the world was a crock but thinking proved it to me; the fear of men that women could be raped or worse made pregnant unfortunately almost became a reality in the eighties when crime became so bad and the city became less safe and the old ways came bouncing back. Luckily I was in the city in the sixties when you could walk the street alone at night, besides we women were into karate by then. It was Jeffrey who always wanted me to call lest I be lying in a ditch somewhere—men do that to control women. When I first came to the city my parents would call me daily until I finally convinced them to call only twice a week, but that was only after I moved in with Jeffrey in my senior year. Anything to get out of the dormitory. My parents never called when I was overseas, we didn't even have a phone only my uncle called and relayed the news. I even called my uncle from Berlin on my grand tour, he was the only one in the family I could talk to, even sent him a photo of the address of the *Renaissance Theater*, now a supermarket with row after row of empty shelves in East Berlin, where he saw a performance of *Faust* in 1932, the centenary of his Goethe's death, with his steamship ticket to America in his pocket. He understood my thoughts without as much as me saying them and he insisted I spend the summer in Europe after I graduated college so as to learn other ideas, or as he said let the serpent of knowledge bite you, and that I had a moral obligation to live to my fullest. He was worldly, Liliana said. Don't be a jackass live for your own sake not for your parents' or anybody else, he said, he'd seen so many useless deaths he didn't want to see one more, he wasn't impressed with the desire for money that seemed to be everywhere in this culture and said you talk of wanting to be a poet, talk is easy, the thing is to do it not just talk about it—childhood is over. He was the one who forced me to confront my fantasies and wouldn't allow them to become

reality—trade-offs weren't for him, if you were going to do something do it, don't lollygag around, too many people get sidetracked
when life gets in the way. I remember thinking easy for him to say
he's old and can look back but I have to live through it. What I
hated about my grand tour was being taken out of my comfort
zone. What I remember most about East Berlin was the humiliation at the checkpoint where the young guard who searched every
crevice of my body, pointed a Tommy gun at my chest, I wet my
underpants, and wanted to know what I was doing in East Berlin,
he didn't believe I was only a tourist. Everything was shabby, yet
I recall thinking yes, yes, but they have family, interesting friends,
read books, sit around the dinner table and have intellectual discussions, not like in capitalist America, saw it all through the lens of
ideology. I realized I hated traveling and only did well rooted in
place—in one place where my routine was set—where I could get
up every morning and know where to get my coffee from, where
to go for walks, have a window sill to write on, where I had a
comfortable chair to read poetry from in the morning, listen to
my radio at night, feel at home speaking English and the change
of culture, i.e. feeling uncomfortable in Berlin wasn't only because
I was Jewish, I also felt uncomfortable in Vienna and Budapest. I
needed my routine. All these interruptions in my daily life forced
me to change myself in ways I did not like. I was not a happy
camper and cut the tour short, suppose to stay two months left
after three weeks, wanted to find the cafés my uncle frequented
but walked the wrong way and couldn't find any of his old haunts,
never even making it to Prague, feeling great to be home, even
as I said I couldn't stand America, when the customs official said
welcome back I smiled yes, and as the bus pulled into the city I
said to myself I can only live here. I look at Liliana, you only knew
me before not after I became who I had become in some ways you
truly don't know me but in others you do—underneath all these

layers is still the scared little boy who wonders why he's scared even as he says hey I'm not a kid anymore. When I see my reflection in a store window I wonder who that is looking back at me it usually isn't who others see me as and I can only see my true self now looking in Liliana's eyes. Why did you want to go to Germany anyway, your parents couldn't wait to get out of there? The thing to do, should have done my junior year abroad maybe then it would have been okay some structure, but I was too cool to do whatever the college suggested we do, and actually it didn't suggest we do it I'm not even sure if it was an option. Why not Paris? Baron Haussmann, the Robert Moses of his day, had destroyed all the little streets, nooks and crannies, with his gigantic boulevards long and straight, demolishing neighborhoods like Moses did to the Bronx. The communists, the fascists, the capitalists all had the same idea destroy native quarters like the Alexanderplatz in East Berlin, which my uncle claimed was the heart of Berlin then an ugly boulevard with absolutely no people walking the streets, even had an ugly TV tower, now ironically the most expensive real estate in Berlin as the capitalists are trying to capture some of the glamour of the Weimer Republic. Unfortunately like much that is going down in downtown New York now with its lack of charm, all technology, straight lines, no play on light and dark shadows, paved over—no more magic cobblestones that rose up to form a fortress, after the *Stonewall* (Gay) riots, now all paved over with tar—as usual I feel at home nowhere but can only live here. But even here you can't walk the zigzag way anymore avoiding wide streets it really didn't matter anyway crime had gotten so bad that you had to force yourself to walk on well-lit streets or not go out late at night, now I'm slowly starting to remember my joys of walking the city streets and getting lost in the city once again, especially now that Harlem is safe to walk off the cross streets even as new Harlem is destroying the old Harlem. They too are having their gentrification and new high rises are going up totally transforming the neighborhood as blacks say whites are moving in really not realizing how many blacks are now successful and buying. When New York became bad, became crime and drug-ridden, you had to worry about the other guy and how quickly we began to take that for normal and even now when the streets are relatively safe again I hesitate in some neighborhoods, even if I am slowly coming out of my shell. In the bad old days of high crime, drugs, and filth, if there were no children playing on the street and no parents watching them I would never walk down that block. Now neighborhoods are changing again, and the poor are being deported. Progress! We now are the Baron Haussmanns and Robert Moses destroying the old, the uniqueness of our city for the geometric straight line—uglyification! she says. We build in straight lines up and across and destroying our city, but at least I've lived long enough, I think, to observe people at one of the mega-lopolis projects bitching that their views are being destroyed, their empty spaces being violated because of new big buildings next to them even if my uncle isn't around to say hey you bastards destroyed my old neighborhood with your urban renewal and I had to leave, sorry it's taken you forty years to suffer a similar fate as mine. Of course when President Ford told the city to drop dead we all suffered while he pardoned tricky Dick and some poor black guy got twenty years for possession of two ounces of heroin. I actually refused to budge on that one, Liliana says, when I was on jury duty I was the lone holdout even though he was guilty as shit I didn't think he should go away for life while Nixon stole the constitution blind—couldn't do it! You thinking of leading the masses? How did they let you on jury duty anyhow? Cut my hair, wore a dress, little white gloves they thought me this nice conservative young lady. I laugh also because I wouldn't have voted guilty and put some drug dealer away for twenty years, but last year when some hooligan was caught carrying a gun, a concealed weapon, I didn't hesitate to send his ass up river. What do you think he was going to do with the gun, steal from the rich and give to the poor, no pistol whip some old lady. You were in the revolution while I was learning how to live but didn't know what the verb to live meant, still really don't, to exist, yes, to live, no, except I know it's not political. Still it was ridiculous that a young black male spend so much time in prison. Progress, they're all there now. But I didn't put them there. If you come before the criminal justice system you're guilty, Kafka knew that. I refused to be part of it. Remember we met at *Nedicks* near the courthouse and then you suggested we go to Chinatown for lunch, she says. First time I had sweet-and-sour pork, first time I ate pork, washed it down with a bottle or orange soda from *Nedicks*, I say, I loved their orange soda. Was that the golden age? Na just an age we lived through, always far in the past remember Jeffrey was coming back from prison right around that time, I must have been thinking of him when I insisted the kid be let go. Not let go, he probably had a new trial and another jury convicted him. Remember there is no innocent in the system. I remember that boy had never been downtown before this was his first time out of Harlem, I couldn't believe someone living in Manhattan knew nothing about the city except the few blocks where he lived. That's how *McDonald's* and *Burger King* made a fortune made every store exactly alike so these ghetto kids would feel right at home and not be afraid to go in. Didn't you go back home right after that? I remember passing by Cedar Rapids right along route 30 before the cross country highway system was complete and we drove through Iowa thought I might look you up but didn't have enough guts when actually there, thought about it the whole trip and afterwards why I didn't do it after we passed town. But they did have a good steak house and I kept imagining you would walk in and we'd have a conversation. When you didn't show I became too shy to call. It was only temporary; I was now too much of a New Yorker to go back. When I got back my friends couldn't believe I lived in New York, all they knew of the city, what they called Manhattan, was *Kojak*, the crime shows they saw on television. But back with my friends most married the streets folded up at night and all you could do was drink or watch cars racing. My high school friends were now married with bay-bies (it was time to get serious and have bay-bies as one of my high school classmates said) pot-bellied, smoking, sounding more like their mothers every day, we had nothing to talk about. I wondered what the fuck I got myself into, even the ones who smoked pot considered it a hard drug—the others thought one puff you're hooked for life, I thought I fit right into the stereotype big city kid corrupts small town kids but many of the younger ones had been smoking at school and were no stranger to harder drugs. One even made a play for me grabbing me by the ass and throwing me up against the wall, I remember saying don't laugh it's just young blood the problem with boys is they have to learn to zipper their pants, but I had to escape again you can't go home once you leave I felt so out of place in my home town. You didn't even know who I was? I was surprised we hadn't spoken since Chinatown. But you came and again claimed me for your own. I wanted to stop. But didn't stop I was again only a ghost of myself, a mirage, why did I ever go back to you, I wanted to see how low I could go but it wasn't me I was an observer in my own life, I could watch myself watching myself but it was only my body the real me was off trying to write poetry, even as my analyst said no the real me is back with you. Life was elsewhere. Now Galina asks if I didn't do enough crazy things in my life and had regrets. No way. Remember we went out and bought a dinette set and you wanted plastic because it was what your mother had, she says. Formica, I say. And what is Formica but plastic. Except I didn't know it and instead you insisted upon wood, we schlepped up and down Third Ave. looking into thrift shops before you found the right one. I was surprised because I thought you had (who made that a rule) to buy a whole set but you found the perfect wooden table, which we carved our names and date underneath, then we went out looking for chairs. Playing house. I even remember the paper was delivered and I would read it. Knew every conceivable opinion. It didn't matter what I was reading I was reading and didn't have to face Liliana at breakfast. However if tested on what I read would surely fail, I couldn't even keep the name of the lead in my head from the first to last paragraph. Horrible writers, journalists, Liliana says, I know they muddle up all thought, how you could read that crap surprised me. Newspapers destroyed writing as TV destroyed theater. How come after we stayed together we didn't even go to the theater? But I did learn from her how to read books, she did get me hardcover books, and after you have hardcover you couldn't go back to paperback, unless you carried it on the subway. And I am always surprised when a woman starts a conversation with me on the subway about some book I'm reading, so much so that I kind of started to expect it, and would get angry if a pretty woman didn't start talking to me about a book I was reading and even sometimes consciously closed the book so they could see I was reading a serious work (poetry, novel or play); and if I had a good conversation wouldn't even run across for the express but stay with the woman, usually they were older, and continue our talk. I remember a woman comparing Pynchon to Dos Passos. I should have followed her home. You could tell it was summer that's when I would read Pynchon or Dos Passos. Nice old lady, as usual I was surprised she chatted with me, and afterwards looked for her around the area but never saw her again. An opportunity blown. She was reading him in a book club, and later when I had to help my daughter find a college went around to different book clubs in the city, all only populated by women, nary a man in sight, and choose a small liberal arts college that the majority of women attended, at least their was a spark of education left in them; once in a while somebody from a state university was there, but I never met one from the city system. Probably from those all girl schools, they really did a good job educating women but most had to admit men when women didn't want to be segregated and now the schools suffer intellectually as a result. I laugh, my daughter wouldn't even think of going to a school without boys. Hey we've fooled women for five thousand years that they are inferior that men could talk abstractly that women could only feel, now all we have left is the physical. She doesn't smile at my attempt at humor. I shudder at my old ingratiating ways that I now should suppress seeing that the only purpose is to be liked, or as my mother would ask, did they like what you wore in school today, not did you learn anything in school today. I would come home from school exhausted, defeated, useless, if there is a hell it better be populated by school teachers, and I would sit in bed all night listening to *Radio Unnamable* staring out the window to all hours of the morning, while Galina, as I found out much later, in Tbilisi, Georgia in the former but then real Soviet Union, was doing the same thing, listening illegally to Willis Konover's jazz program on the Voice of America. She had hooked up an antenna from her window over the roof to catch the clandestine broadcasts. Only hers was more serious nobody bothered with me, her grandmother had been given an order by Stalin's henchmen to move out of her apartment (her husband had already been shot in the Lubyanka prison) her neighbors telling her not to give the paper the order was written on to the police when they came to move her because who knows then where she would end up and like a cheap melodrama totalitarianism wanted to look legal the police didn't force her out without written authorization, and she ended up staying in her two rooms with one gas burner in a communal apartment where Galina was raised. The closest I could come to imagining that was when my parents went to the country for one summer and we lived in our little room and shared the kitchen with a big stove and refrigerator with strangers. Galina had said to me privileged birth—born after the war, and Liliana responded geography is destiny. After hearing Galina's story I no longer felt sorry for myself, no longer was I envious of others when she had so little, luckily she had her music which allowed her an escape route. I remember you had a Pollyanna way of looking at the world. Liliana interrupts my thought process, you were also envious of my life style even when I mentioned you should not be: I was confused, rebellious, scared wasn't sure what I wanted you thought because I was living with a man I had it all—and that was so shocking then and so commonplace now. My mother thought Jeffrey was living in sin, but I imagined you guys sleeping arm in arm in a single bed. It was queen size I needed my space. And I realized it would have been terrible to bring a baby into the world when the world was such a mess, and also because I was so confused. I wished I had your strength of character, even if you were so confused, you knew more what you didn't want more than what you wanted, and at least you weren't living with strangers. Except for one another. In analysis all he kept harping on was my mother wouldn't even listen when I wanted to talk about you, only my lack of relationship with my mother, that in surviving a concentration camp she saw life as death, he refused to go into the political. Or that my father was never around, always working, and that summer we went up to the country, he stayed in the city during the week only driving up on weekends and after the first or second weekend never came up until Labor Day he enjoyed his solitude so much. Now I am somewhat like him enjoying solitude, ersatz solitude, but only in the family situation not by being totally alone. Alone I was too scared to do anything, and at my weakest point met someone thought okay it'll be nice to be with someone—I never felt so alone after my mother was in that coma, my father was already dead, my uncle died a year ago, and here was I all alone in the world and you had already disappeared from my life, I couldn't find you anywhere and I wasn't sure you'd even realize what I was going through, I had someone to cling to at night. Your desire for happiness, your fear of loneliness kept you from being a great poet! I thought it was because I wasn't Gay? I didn't know how to go on. I kept hoping you'd show up even if I had nothing to say to you, I stalked you but only imaginary, walking streets I thought we might bump into each other, like the time in Cedar Rapids, what are the odds you'd pop into the steak house. I would have called except I didn't know how. All fantasy on your part. Jeffrey and I never truly did it again after he left prison. Don't destroy my illusions doing it every night in a single bed. Did it like married couples on weekends then bi-weekends until we hardly did it at all. All I see is you and he happy while I couldn't even get out of bed in the morning. I jacked off all the time to the image of you. You did? Did I say that aloud? No matter how many naps I took I couldn't refresh myself and each chore was an obstacle I wondered if I would have enough strength to do it, like going downtown to buy a stereo, I had to break it up into little parts, get out of the house, grab a train, walk to the store, purchase it, carry it back to the subway, walk home, nap out of fake exhaustion, let it sit in the box for a few days before Jeff came by to help me set it up. Yet as I did each piece I realized how easy it was but still couldn't put it all together. First thing I listened to was Bartok, then Webern until I finally got around to Shostakovich string quartets, I would sit in my room, really my father's room by then but he only slept there, lights out, only the neon light of the stereo and some colored light bulbs I had turned on, listening. I think now that Galina became mine when she saw my uncle's piano in my place, she loves to sit and play hours upon hours even with her shoulder injury she keeps going, and I love to listen to

Schumann's *Kreisleriana* in the morning and Beethoven's *Moonlight*, *Appassionata* in the evening. Meanwhile outside a war was dragging on, soldiers were dying, politicians were writing books that they said would stand the test of time and Nixon cornered like a rat in a trap went down. You forget Liliana says that women were also now insisting upon a life outside the home (off our backs!) redefining the difference between masculinity and femininity i.e. women were no longer going to be passive. (I loved it on my back, I loved when you climbed on top of me, I loved making love on my back.) Yeah my mother actually wore pants, can you believe it? That's when I knew the woman's revolution hit home. It wasn't the pill that changed women's lives as much as childcare; women weren't forced to stay home all day with the little kiddies. Yes, I said, and women thought it would be a better world because women believed in cooperation not competition, but the dominant values prevailed. You just can't proclaim you're free. I'll drink to that. She would drink to anything. We had to destroy the old ways before we could build new ones, only the old ways didn't crumble so easily and we became afraid not afraid in our passivity but afraid to overcome our fear and we settled for ordinary success albeit at times without a man. In our new age the old patriarchal family is dead but we don't live in a matriarchy either (ah I'd love to suck at the breast of mother goddess—my mother didn't even give me her breast when I was born everybody was into bottles then) who knows what's coming it's so confused right now, maybe this is the new order, and the cop was correct in stopping you and confiscating your *Reluctant Fundamentalist* we are now at the end of western civilization, the breakup of the family changes everything not the grand issues like war and peace because when the family changes the culture changes as well. Now all we have is me, me, me, the rise of the individualist with no concern for the other, not even for ones in our family, look at the homeless, the aged, the young kiddies, nobody wants to take them in—no more group solidarity, like the women's movement once said we are inseparable, we not I. How come nobody likes freedom, I say. It's not freedom she says it's individualist caring for nothing but your own needs, no responsibility for your fellow man, i.e. the capitalist ethic and believe me I know about that. You were successful? God was I? Hated every minute of it but I was too good to walk away and got used to too nice a life style to want to give it up and be poor again. When companies started giving bonuses if we finished our projects on time I finally had to say I needed time to spend the bonus but I fought too hard to escape a mother-daughter relationship I wasn't going to be no school mom to a bunch of sniveling undergraduates, instead became mother—unless they wanted to fuck me, to a bunch of sniveling adolescent boy wonders. These young men saw me as their mother-confessor because they couldn't share weakness at work with other men, and they certainly couldn't tell their wives, and they just had to talk especially after a scotch or two. I never had sex with men in the office but when I needed it it was easier with married men fewer complications, single men always wanted me to darn for them. You really knew how to hurt your mother bringing home a nice Jewish man that you were living with but refusing to marry, you could have brought a black male now that would have done it to her showed her real contempt. Never thought of that or I would have. She liked Jeffrey mind you but all she wanted was grandchildren to spoil, but she raised the wrong daughter for that. She laughs, I told her I didn't know how to marry, even now I don't forgive her for ruining my life but at least I've come to terms with her. Lend me your cell. She does. Here call her tell her you forgive her? It doesn't reach down that far. What does death have to do with it? You weren't the only one struggling with your mother, Jeffrey came home from prison at the wrong time, the feminist revolution had been in progress for a while now and I couldn't go back to the old ways, and Jeffrey was the kindest/gentlest man I ever knew. But I was suffocating under his gentleness, at times I wasn't the same person in the morning as I was in the evening and he expected me to cook dinner (I had vowed never to cook a meal for a man again) and he thought he had to get a job to support me, and he now wanted a family. It's interesting after a radical break with our way of life we more than anything want to get back to normalcy. How else could a shmuck like Harding have been elected president? He looked presidential. Ah the good old days when presidents were real leaders Polk, Grover Cleveland, Harding. My mother never taught me how to sew I would lie to the men lying with me except they would go around so disheveled because they couldn't even sew a button finally I had to give in and sew buttons on their shirts, trousers, then they came to expect it. Do I have to prove to myself I can take it? I should have fled the first moment I saw her. Why should she upset me so? Did I actually go to Jeff's memorial service to see her? She means nothing to me now, she meant nothing to him even if she meant a lot to me then. All she does is stir up old feelings it shows I'm alive that I'm not this boring old man even if I don't see myself as boring, everybody else probably does, around her I have a life even if I never had a life with her, she brings back a flood of memories and stirs something in me that I rather forget, my uselessness as a young man when I would waste time staying up to all hours of the night—before I realized creation begins at dawn. I am not proud of how I acted to Jeff. Cheated on a best friend, losing a best friend, how many best friends can you find in this world? Since Jeff none. Now I have no one to talk about this with. He ran away married had a child, divorced, married again, had more children, separated, the modern epitaph, and I can't speak truth to them about Jeff and me. He may have wanted to go back but you can't go home again. How many women did I see years later but it was never the same.

Liliana is the one I feel passion for convincing myself it wasn't because she was Jeff's woman. I am my own person I wasn't Jeffrey's
woman, she says. But I was Jeff's best friend. She still makes my
skin tingle, and I can't do something else when her smooth skin
rubs against mine now allowing me to kiss her, did she kiss me
back. It happened so fast I can't remember, but her skin felt like
cracked shellac. Not so smooth up close. Haven't I dreamt and
dreamt of wanting to meet her again and already smooth is absent
from memory. Touchy, touchy, doesn't last only memory lasts yet
I can't remember without touch. At least she didn't give me her ear
to kiss, as some women do who are not used to kissing as a greet-
ing. Usually American women can only be lovers or spouse-mates
with men. Like men who stiffen up when you try and hug them.
Here I go again thinking it would be fun "fucking up" my life by
running away with Liliana. Where would we go? What does that
have to do with it, we'd start over. One problem we'd end up the
same way. Besides I can't leave the city. And now Czernowitz is
some backwater town in Romania no longer a cosmopolitan city
part of the Austria-Hungary Empire, where Jews could always feel
at home because German was spoken everywhere. One more shot
at glory? This image never leaves you; even if this was my last year
it could show God has a sense of humor. But no I can't something
holds me back—fear, sense of responsibility, but I kept thinking if
I only saw her one more time I could explain all to her. What is
there to explain? Everything/Nothing. Even my poetry seems pale
in comparison to her, why my poetry is weak is that I don't feel
strong enough, don't have it in the soul when it counts. Yet I can't
do it any other way, all I want is my solitude, I'm only happy thinking not doing. She's talking now, I should listen even if I will never
see her again I will continue to look for her—like moths to a flame,
Jews to *shiskas* I'm drawn to her. Can I learn from any of this? Can
I use it in my poetry? Why poetry always fails it can't get to the

essence because the essence shifts depending upon my mood, the time of day, my health, the world situation, even if not as miserable as when they came for you in the middle of the night—geography is destiny. The other side started it we have to defend ourselves, we need room to expand, to grow, the enemy in our midst, what other bullcrap all human craziness because we never like to leave well enough alone. Did I kiss her on the lips? I can feel her lips upon my skin. Her skin isn't as soft as it looks she has a sharp aftertaste. Maybe it didn't happen? Couldn't have happened I would recall it better. I can recall the teddy bear my mother put in the washing machine when I was three and it came out all shredded and torn but this I can't recall. Jeff why did you run away? Now I'm ready to start life even as I realize I would do it the same way all over again, that I would constantly walk the streets to try and bump into her and allow her to trigger memories that there's nothing to be done about it but to accept it, I certainly won't learn from it. Jeffrey must have felt vindicated, she says, out of the clear blue, committing suicide the night President Bush announces excuse me I have no policy, I'm embarrassed, I can't admit my mistake do you mind dying for me? Bush, Nixon, Johnson all willing to send other people to die to show they're tough and didn't want to appear weak in God's name—in his name everything is permitted. Bush's second election proved you could fool all the people all the time the issue was who would you rather have a brewski with, not the war. My words must have triggered something in her or her own words got her thinking and what she thought about was us. It doesn't make sense that he would kill himself after what the president said, he probably didn't even hear it. You don't commit suicide over foreign policy. Even our generals didn't do that instead bided their time till pension then became television commentators, an interesting career change, none of them denounced the president and then burned themselves on the lawn of the pentagon. No longer do I read books, she says, I gave up being a member of a book club when work became too much, never went to the theater, she then tells me she switched from computers (logic) to financial analyst when she saw how much more money they made. Then I was knee deep in the system, had to buy a home so I didn't have to pay so much taxes it kept sucking you in, made a fortune had a big house, car, and never much liquidity all on paper. When the company pays you so much money, they own you, granted, a nice way to be owned but still owned, only salvation I had were mini-vacations to recharge the batteries, otherwise I literally worked all year long 24/7. I had a home that could have made *Better Homes and Garden* if I was ever there, then when I had children I thought for the *kinder,* better they have a front lawn, schools were better out there—what a joke, it's like the sixties never existed—the days that changed my life forever were no more, I had to work hard to make up for the time wasted changing my life. It worked, I say, women now perceive the world like men. Except I thought the sixties had put a crack in the world, before and after, but the crack sealed and it's the same rotten world only now women can participate in it, not as passive elements but as active decision-makers in making the world more rotten—but at least I knew for a moment there could be a better way. Yes we never realized the sixties was but a moment in time not time itself. The only big difference is that now I did it without a boyfriend, sitting in that big house one day I realized this is one of the few times in my life that I am without a man and that I could stay home on a Saturday night not have to have a date, of course, I made sure I worked on Saturday night so I wouldn't feel that I was a loser. The new knowledge I thought I learned slipped right through my fingertips as the old ways kept coming back in, the difference between my mother and me is that I knew I would work while my mother stayed home and made lunch for all of us, even my father would come home for lunch everyday, while I paid a fortune for a modern kitchen I never used. Did you . . .? NO! There were no dolls in my house: I didn't put Barbie dolls, Raggdy Ann all over the place. I had modern art on the walls. But dolls aren't as bad as I thought when my children played with them I saw they interacted with them didn't become passive creatures even boys now play with dolls, called GI Joe and X-men and it's the same idea aggressive play which is okay by me. I bet she moved to get away from me, she knew I would never follow her there, I hadn't taught her a thing, history hadn't taught her a thing, she didn't learn from history, there is an undercurrent running through history that goes back to caveman days no matter how bad and miserable things are and we're trapped in the old ways, for moments you can come up for fresh air. She laughs has another shot, I suggest a pitcher of wine so at least I can keep up with her but her anger simmering beneath the surface is bubbling over now that she has a chance to talk to a compadre. We thought we were creating a new world but the Restoration came with the election of Reagan and the world went back to its old ways. In the sixties we were breaking away—creating zones of freedom, now the only zones of freedom created are little enclaves where the police are afraid to go and drugs and violence run rampart from the state, the family, the church—art over life, now we're all trying to be good little mamma's boy's churchgoers and supporters of a global state.

It is not an accident what we did and the way we did it. We are talking about the sixties the way my uncle talked about the Weimer Republic, did anything happen afterwards. If it did I can't recall, Liliana says. I used to read *Worstward Ho*! in the subways in the bad old 80's when the city was broke and the subways weren't working and we'd be stuck between stations forever, and a preacher man would be shouting from crack to Christ, a thousand people die each day imagine this is your day and you are trapped in a subway, or the train wouldn't come, nothing much happened before either, I say. It was fun to see things had always been worse and that they never change. Since when did you become so smart you had potential but you certainly weren't into books when I knew you? That was when I changed, I say, thinking I'm glad she actually is able to see this change in me, as she again puts her forefinger under my beard and looks me straight in the eye, if only she said down. Either way my penis was up. She brings back the visceral in me, I can see why I would lose it in front of her—if I could I would keep her at bay, but I don't think I can do that. It feels nice to feel again. I would dream about this but now it's taking all my strength not to become involved, caught again, to see her pass by me like this means I still don't lead a humdrum existence, but I've spent a fortune trying to teach myself not to follow my impulses—analysis didn't make me a better person only gave me more words to make excuses by. If only a philosophy of life? It did, literally I was able to get out of bed in the morning, now it can be done quicker however, a quick fix, one pill will make you whole, unfortunately I say egotistically you need more than that. Why? Wouldn't have had to go through all that pain. Jeffrey stayed in his sleep state, Liliana says, and I'm now getting used to her reading my brow, what do you think dropping old friends and running away to Vermont marrying the first young thing until she got some *sechel* and couldn't stand his moods and left, means? She now even speaks Yiddish. Then another wife, more children, he couldn't stand the silences, being by himself, prison really did a number on him so he led a life of hiding in plain sight, running away from himself, never had a free moment again because IT all would come back, his running away from himself. And he probably had no one he could tell his story to, up there they all saw him as this successful married man and father not the scared boy who wants to change the world. It's a miracle he didn't become religious. Then he wouldn't have to think at all just pray. His library had only books on the issues of the day, he no longer read for thought, he still read newspapers, liked to hold them, knew every conceivable opinion because he had none. You refused that type of life. You wanted a life of thought. Aren't they always there besides me, who else am I comparing myself to. Certainly not with the truly great. The names of those in their lives fought for life; the sixties imprinted more meaning in life then I was prepared to admit, we agreed we were going to change the world not become part of the world, imagine educated people now don't go to the theater, never to a movie or at least never see a foreign film, never open a book. Remember you took me to *Ivan the Terrible* and Jacques Tati's *Monsieur Hulot*, I didn't know what to make of them they were so different but I knew they were profound. Now I'm fearful of renting them lest they lose their aura on the small screen and change the taste in my mouth from a profound experience to a banal one or worse maybe they weren't so profound and it would destroy my illusions. No. Isn't it lovely how we don't remember the same things. But I was surprised that you actually came with me to the cinema Jeffrey wouldn't and he suggested I call you and I knew you would feel uncomfortable but he said it was okay he wouldn't mind if he didn't have to go to these foreign films, he disliked anything that took away from the struggle, as he said, and you actually agreed to come with me that surprised me I figured you for one not being able to be with a woman unless her man was present. Maturity! Yea! Jeff called and asked me to go he didn't want to see that crap. And that's how I got interested in Russian history. I couldn't believe you knew nothing about Stalin, Trotsky, and the Gulag. We never talked about that stuff at home or in school. I didn't even know Trotsky lived in the Bronx until once Jeff's mother said everybody pointed him out, said he really wasn't a tailor but a revolutionary in the old country and she was impressed even if she didn't know what the word meant. I remember buying *The Russian Revolution* but it stayed on my shelf a long time before I had enough courage to open it because I was afraid it would be too difficult for me, I always thought I can't read this stuff, it's heavy, but once I started I was charmed and started debating questions with him—it was like reading the ancient Greeks who had no Bible so everything is open to question—all I believed wasn't true not even close. You grew a beard. Jeff shaved his moustache so I grew mine, so we wouldn't look like the Bobsy twins. Then I saw in it the first few strands of gray, maturity, old age, that's not what I said but what I whispered and you said I looked like a Marxist intellectual with my beard and my wire-rimmed glasses. And your fisherman's cap! At least you finally got rid of your white socks, she says, you always reminded me of the farm, boys from the sticks who would wear white socks with penny loafers. When I came home started growing my hair long to be like everybody else. Style of clothing then determined who you were or who you wanted to become, suits for the conservatives, chino pants, white socks and penny loafers for the jocks, dungarees for hip men and women before dungarees became a fashion statement and Levi's became jeans as fashion designers started charging an arm and a leg for them, women wore minis men bell-bottom suits then money got into the picture and clothes became expensive, except we found flea markets or antique shops that sold old clothes. Now my daughter goes to a college where women dress for class—skirt, blouse, makeup jewelry. I remember boys from Jersey would come into the Village trying to look hippie and pick up girls but their clothing would always give them away, it was always a little off, the collars too wide, the shirts too expensive, they had to find other ways to appear authentic, remember boys wearing wigs to simulate long hair. I remember the army saying it was okay if they did it during off hours but got pissed when men wore short-hair wigs during their short-term service. You would wear a tie-dye shirt and tie, to show you were part of no group. Now I

only wear a tie because nobody else does especially to dinner parties. Then it was easy to tell where a person stood by the clothes
she wore, remember we went up to a friend's house and she had
on her serving robe and you said let's get the fuck out of here. No,
I say. Now you have to listen to a person an artiste is not one who
simply has a beard. You mean you have to produce. It's much easier
to make the claim, I say. If I had enough guts I would wear a cape
then the world would know I'm an artiste, *Saks* had this sale on
opera capes and I actually bought one, full length but don't have
enough guts to wear it except on Halloween. Maybe as a shroud!
Thank you. I did wear it once to Galina's concert, but it was with
Russians so I didn't look out of place they're all aristocrats in their
soul, especially before the whole thing collapsed. Now of course
their main enemy is gone, the State, and many of their artists are
still working but they have nothing to say, especially the poets. Still
their stuff will be read after all the academic trash is forgotten their
stuff has substance, Liliana says. You ever read these Russian writers? I don't read anymore. Their descriptions of the totalitarian state
will last long past the academic treatise or historical analysis even if
poorly written or exaggerated because they have the ring of truth
to them, the State gave them such good fodder, she repeats herself.
You are modern, she continues, since Aristotle everyone knows
that poetry is more serious than history poetry deals with universal events history with what happened. There are no clothes for a
poet, even if there are some for pseudo-poets, and the only way
you can tell the difference is by what they read, see, paint, psuedo-
poets don't read poetry or anything else for that matter, have no
conversation and in this age of inner exploration say useless things
to garner sympathy or show how they overcame hardship all to
hide themselves so they don't even know what they really think
and to find their thought you have to dig under layers of bullshit. I
force myself to look beneath the surface only the con artist has per-

fected the authentic self because they have no skill nor knowledge no product except themselves and so never doubt. The ones who never doubt are liars; only those who uncover layers of themselves while talking to themselves have a chance at finding truth, I think. Can I quote you? I think how many times I've had this conversation with her, first in letters, later when I wrote my poems to her and even later poems via e-mail that somehow never reached her. It's easier now being fooled, she says, now you could become good at it and even fool yourself—working long hours, weekends, two jobs, driving to and from work anything not to have to face yourself, always busy, and if you're lucky you can buy yourself time away from yourself—time isn't money it's organization so that you have no time to be alone with yourself. Where I live few people walk so you never see a stranger on the street: man is truly a stranger to man in the suburbs. When I first moved in and actually went for a walk one night, late at night, the police came by stopped me two, three times wondering if I was drunk, lost, a hooker it finally made no sense to even leave the house without a car. So I went nowhere unless there was a purpose behind it, never a stroll for the sake of thinking, walking for the sake of walking, you can't drive for the sake of a drive too much traffic. I laugh, I was surprised you even came for a drink with me usually nobody has time anymore. That's why women now carry business cards if a man is interested he'll get back to her. I want something between her and me the bar stool being too uncomfortable and the noise outside is getting louder the barkeep had the courtesy of at least not playing loud music, and we should feel lucky because now it's usually kept on all the time, and loud also, to disallow conversation only chatter. We move to a corner booth where we can't hear them drilling, constructing, destructing, blowing leaves around, trucks backing up, car alarms going off, car horns honking at pedestrians, pedestrians cursing at car drivers, unfortunately near the juke box and they have huge speakers but at the other end of the room so we only have the little speakers of the juke box to contend with. Imagine being below these things like when I moved out and the upstairs neighbors kept blaring their stereo all night and the thumping on the floor would never let up. And as typical New York neighbors you could ask them to be quiet, you could hit the ceiling with a broom stick nothing would get them to lower their speakers—(if I could create a machine that you could put on the ceiling just making noise you could make a fortune in the City with so many people wanting to get even) the noise of the thumping, the end of a bus stop where busses kept their engine idling, the major cross street where cars would be jostling, honking, and if I was in the kitchen area I couldn't even hear the radio in the living area—it was a large studio and I stayed refusing to admit this is crazy, besides if I had moved back home I never would have left, I was in a prime location in the Village but all I could do was walk the streets at night because it was so noisy at home and I didn't want to move in with roommates all divorced, divorcing men who wanted friendship while I needed my solitude—rents had started moving upward and I knew I'd have to find a place, but for the time being was stuck. I bought rugs to cover the wooden floor, closed the windows to keep out the bus exhaust, used the air conditioner all year long, a wonderful first place, stayed about a year before I gave up on the Village and moved back to the West Side, besides they had Central Park even if it was dangerous then at least on warm days I could walk near the perimeter until it became safer. I remember big blank white walls and I had to find paintings to decorate the place, no reproductions, no posters, an artist girlfriend had told me to support artists, get what you can afford and like, and I learned about the Russian Avant-garde—the first generation of Russian artists escaping the Soviet Union being taxi drivers, dishwashers, supers, but knew they were artists and didn't let the real

define them. I still wasn't getting up early usually because I didn't
sleep well the night before so I couldn't write poetry in the afternoon, until my uncle said that excuse no longer works when you
reach thirty-four. If you don't start now you never will. At least
you were finally out of the Bronx, Liliana says. Only physically, I
would spend the weekends there to be with my mother. But you
had a place to go home to that's an important step, now youngsters'
stay put. Different times, now some want to be with their parents,
parents are their best friends. Parents aren't your best friend they
are the Law, if they are your best friends we really have moved into
a different world, she says. What is important about leaving home
is meeting all these new people, too bad the young now are post-
poning adulthood by not leaving home, she says, we met people
who were doing the same thing as we were trying to do starting to
live life not become a continuation of their parents. I wanted to live
which I wasn't living when I was at home, I say. It was like I was
an exile finally allowed to taste freedom and freedom has a taste,
it tastes like fresh bread from the bakery across the street where I
would get my croissant and my coffee in a bowl. The French influence on the city. And no matter how far from the Bronx I moved
I didn't let the distance get to me and would go back every weekend lest my mother be alone until I started seeing more plays on
my own, cinema on my own, the opera, who would have thought
I would do that, poetry readings and slowly drifted out of the or-
bit of the Bronx. Still no writing! You were letting it germinate.
I went in search of myself. I had no discipline—writing requires
discipline you'd think poetry you just sit down and in one burst it
comes but only thoughts come lines come only when you do it
daily. I thought I could be a poet without concentration just let it
flow but upon rereading I saw that it was in rewriting that thoughts
actually came together. Brodsky (where I met Galina) told me that,
it was cute I wanted to talk about what was going on in the So-

viet Union, the dialectic of being Jewish and Russian as applied to the KGB, or which was the more murderous group the SS or the KGB but all he talked about was the difficulty of translating: what word do you use to describe a young woman in St. Petersburg, he didn't like lass, I suggested cunt, pussy, he said too strong he wanted a translation of Russian slang of the fifties into American slang. Here we had the greatest poet of the century and it was like a Monty Python sketch, where they have Marx, Lenin, Mao and Che, the greatest revolutionaries of all time playing a gong show where they ask them questions only about football (soccer). Finally I said in your poems you don't want to talk about the irrational as if you can legislate the irrational out of existence, but we in the West know that the irrational returns. It was fascinating being around these Russians who believed so strongly in art and if their husband had been an artist in Moscow they would manage their careers, and their mistresses, but become empowered with feminism here in the States and wouldn't play second fiddle. Galina divorced her physicist husband when he couldn't find a position anywhere here and wouldn't become a taxi driver, dishwasher or super. He could have become an American high school teacher they were willing to wave the language requirement but he couldn't stand American teenagers. Also that was around the time the New York Public Schools were going through a terrible financial crisis and only the worst of the worst became schoolteachers. Can you blame him? I go over to the juke box thinking all it will have are bebop or doo-op but I see it is connected to the internet and can play every song ever recorded (i.e. the long tail) and I play *The Dybbuk* for lyre and shofar, Galina's masterpiece and the waitress comes over and says the machine only accepts two-dollar bills, which I don't happen to have on me and Liliana walks across the empty bar to get some; I am seeing her sashay across the sidewalks of New York and men always smiling at her, looking into her eyes, wondering if she would be a good lover. She was. I never looked at woman's ass only their eyes. I recall how she would always stare back at men unabashedly look into men's eyes until they turned away or made contact, as if the eyes were the window to the soul to see which men she thought looked interesting and who she would start a conversation with, and it usually wasn't the glib boys who would throw off these gratuitous compliments about her dress, her eyes, her teeth, but shy men who had a difficult time conversing with her, she would always end with I would like to see you again. She comes back with a two-dollar bill, I play the smooth sound of the lyre punctuated by the haunting melody of the shofar. I imagine she stopped picking up boys when crime became great and you had to be afraid of the other guy, would she pick up her old habit again now that the city is becoming safe again. Now I won't dare smile at men old habits have replaced the new and I never had as many men as you accused me of. Besides men my age are so boring that I can't even have a conversation with them, they have no more interests except talking about their illnesses. And women young women these days act as if feminism is a thing of the past and they expect a knight in a white horse to rescue them and carry them away. She sits down orders oysters and a martini for lunch, at least she's not drinking the hard stuff and I get some wine and realize I'm going to have to pay for this, did I bring enough cash, then forget it, I'm having too much fun. Forget my love of solitude we are picking up where we left off over thirty years ago which surprises me since I don't even do that with male friends anymore. Liliana recalls when she first visited me in my apartment and brought fresh flowers, I was surprised I never had flowers before, plants yes, she had given me her avocado plant which I promptly forgot to water and it withered away in my parents' place, she said don't worry these will wilt soon you don't have to water them but simply enjoy them and watch their life cycle. I loved their temporariness how they would start as buds, blossom then wilt all within a week. I enjoyed each stage, surprising myself, but I was finding out not only was my body undergoing a change so was my mind. Who would have thought I would like fresh flowers so much that every week I would get in the habit of buying some and would enjoy their beauty like I had been doing this all my life and feel a void when I forgot to buy them? I was impressed Liliana said. And now Liliana says to me what I kept saying to her when she was talking about home i.e. Cedar Rapids this is home now and we were both right, the city is home and I wouldn't go back and neither could she. That's when I started carrying her briefcase around with me, always had to have a book as the trains began to stop running even if at first I was too angry to read eventually I learned how to read on the subway while the train stopped between stations or I was on the platform waiting twenty, thirty minutes for the train. If at all possible I would walk. But what book did you carry up to the Bronx? she wants to know. Maybe Thomas Wolfe, I was into the dramatic then, starting to read then, no longer this cynical kid everything was a crock, the world was full of phonies, and I alone knew the truth like I imagined in those anti-war parades and the Left had stock in the bus companies. Analysis, reading, getting out of my parents' apartment left me with time that I used wisely in walking, smiling at girls, and even starting to write, mostly jingles and immediately realized, how I did that I do not know, but I immediately realized I had to get out of advertising because it was ruining my thought and I couldn't do serious work by doing frivolous work in the afternoon, I couldn't forget it as soon as I came home. I had to keep my writing special and not ruin it with trivial stuff even if it paid decently. While you were quitting your job, Liliana retorts, I was working late in the computer world, which meant going to bars at all hours while waiting to see if the program would run and then relaxing over a scotch, I became a real good *Pac-Man* player. I loved that game, first computer game for women not all this macho killing. At first I gave them lots of quarters but by the end could spend the whole night on one quarter I was that good. I never talked the melody of larks and cuckoos, or the dome of stars when I wrote, I say, always the sounds of the city, cackling of children, pigeons and sparrows drowned out by car alarms, garbage trucks at all hours, rain puddles washing the dirt away, the cursing of junkies, the glassine envelopes down on the ground, the absence of old ladies at their windows, but never computer games, never understood them. You weren't bored and had nothing to do for hours on end and the only place that was open was a bar. You no longer could walk through parks at all hours of the night or unlit streets, condemned to wander routes where only people traveled, I would feel a rhythm and compose lines of poetry that I would revise later making it into a coherent mesh. Stop it already, stop it, I know you blame me for Jeffrey's suicide and are being too polite to say it, you want me to take the blame all by myself. My denying only made it worse, she was convinced the only reason I wanted to come with her was to blame her and that I really did blame her for his death. I could never be so clever as to think that unless she explained herself to me she was guilty. After all it was over thirty years ago but that's outward time for him it was going on everyday, I think, and think, as Liliana reminds me, when Jeffrey said you bastard you ruined my life by sleeping with Liliana, I thought he said I could go to bed with her and was giving me permission. And she was pissed thinking he could give permission. He must have thought about her daily but she refused to be seen in a bad light, she wanted to justify herself but to herself, even if Jeff was depressed from that moment on, she claims he used that depression to manipulate his life and not to have a life and hide behind depression in his public persona. He was a big boy who chose the kind of life he wanted to live, he didn't have to run away. At the time I saw it as moving. No he had to escape so he wouldn't see me again and he would never see me because when he ran away he had no intention of returning nor I of going up to see him. He used depression to hide his self from himself. I know about that thinking of my drinking using that as an excuse not to do anything, it's so easy and convenient only when you look at yourself in the mirror can you get up enough courage to face yourself. Except he went to prison, I say, and that too must have been an awful experience—getting raped, forced blow jobs, a white kid was an easy target, he had told me that in confidence but now there was no reason to keep the confidence any longer he was dead. She doesn't believe too much in the real, Look I was down after he left it hurt me so much that I vowed never to go with married men again, it was wrong, and I didn't want to hurt another woman the way I had been hurt I never should have had an affair with you, true Jeffrey and I weren't married and it was all fun and games that is until I broke his heart. I would come home from my secretary job, which he wanted me to quit, but I didn't want to be dependent upon him, which is what he wanted; all of a sudden wanted a child, dreamt of me being pregnant, he'd watch television all night and I'd go to bed earlier than him because I had to get up early the next morning, and on the weekends do the laundry, iron his shirts and wonder what the fuck has become of me. When I couldn't take it anymore called you again at least I had in you someone to go to a play or film with—Jeffrey was happy in his despair and I was becoming Jefferized as you said, catering to him, feeding him, while he sat in front of the television in his undershirt watching football. At first I thought it would be take some time coming home from prison but he kept it up, he didn't clean, he no longer fixed anything around the house, I had to pay to have an air conditioner installed because he wouldn't put it in, and he was good at that type of stuff unlike you. And when he got that job campaigning for his cousin he was depressed that it didn't bring in enough money to help pay his share of the rent, then when his cousin won didn't get him a job like he promised, i.e. the city was going broke there were too few patronage jobs around. In school we were equals but how quickly life changed, and all I could find was secretarial work, me with almost a doctorate. That's when I looked up from the trees and saw the forest and realized I better get into another profession. And it no longer was enough to shock my parents by living with a Jew; that was fun for a while but once you get to be thirty it loses its shock value. Then there were the fights, I never told you about all of them because I thought it might upset you but when we went to a play or a film he would get so angry we'd fight half the night then he'd beg for forgiveness and blame it on his depression and then we'd have make-up sex, that seemed to be the only kind of sex we had. He was a young man who lived like an old man, but what did I want? That was the question, was I to be this scared little girl forever needing a man who couldn't even go to see a film without a man, women said I should join their consciousness-raising groups, I laughed, being with women they said was good, but I had gone too long to all-women's schools to always want to be with women. Besides I knew how to manipulate men, kiss, kiss, in public, and I would kiss them and they would kiss me back and then they were like a little lap dog—the kiss was a tether that they weren't going anywhere. I was a coward we were both leading deceitful lives together, him with his anti-war activities me being afraid to be by myself—inauthentic lives lacking any seriousness. You were the ideal couple for me. If I dreamed I dreamed I could be like you guys together, unmarried, doing good works, while I struggled to get out of bed in the morning. We were faking it, phonies, even if you thought we were this ideal couple because we had this apartment by ourselves and our place became the unofficial clubhouse of all you Jewish boys who still lived with your mothers, remember how you'd come home late at night and wake your mother and ask her to make you dinner and she would, all you guys expected your mother to do that. Finally I had enough I remember screaming loudly one day, a metaphysical scream not a yell, not a shout, but a scream, I couldn't hold it anymore, let them think I'm mad but I couldn't have his friends come into the apartment, they were all his friends, women have no friends only friends that he had before we moved in together, his old high school buddies, college classmates, or the friends we made together, his friends, they stayed in touch with him after the breakup not me. After the scream the silences, the long silences, I couldn't speak, what had become of me. And Jeffrey, the boy genius, couldn't even figure out that anything was wrong, kept saying it's my period. I started dropping acid, I remember asking you to do it with me but you wouldn't even smoke pot with me so you weren't going to do acid, in fact I was the one who induced Jeffrey to try pot and acid, he never would on his own, and it so re-powered my thought I knew I wasn't going to be the same afterwards no longer would I have the sword of Damocles hanging over my head and I would always be high from then on even when he started his prison sentence—I couldn't leave him then, and he only had to serve three years because of your letter for clemency, we never expected that from a judge who had served in the marines. The prosecutor had selected a hard ass right wing judge who he thought would throw the book at him, but you a veteran writing that it also takes courage to stand up for your religious beliefs as much as fighting in a war convinced the judge that Jeffrey had taken a principled stand, and to everyone's surprise sentenced him to thirty-six months in prison instead of sixty. Everyone thinks soldiers are gung-ho but once you've been in combat it changes you, you somehow get a different perspective upon life you realize you only survived by chance and you aren't this great hero you thought you'd be by seeing too many movies of glorious deaths even if you liked to imagine you could see them all around at your funeral, that's fantasy not thought. The movies never capture the fear, the wetting of your pants, only the outward reactions, the adrenalin flowing not the solitary moments when you are scared shitless—killing is waiting, very little action so it's not even precise words can't really describe feelings—there's no such thing as truth of the moment because if you name the moment it's not the same as the moment before when it had no name calling it something brings it into a little clearer focus and retroactively gives it a meaning. Sometimes you can explain what happened, sometimes I couldn't, sometimes it corresponded to what actually happened, sometimes it didn't but it happened just the same. But it was true to you, she says, and your letter somehow impressed the judge so much he realized the truth of it, unusual for the Law, and the District Attorney appealed the sentence, I thought he couldn't double jeopardy and all that, but I found out there double jeopardy had to do with the trial not the sentence and a higher court rejected the judge's reasoning for lowering the sentence but allowed it to stand. I should have left him before he went in, she says, then he wouldn't have dreamt about me when he came out, she says. I say don't say stupid things. I should have left him cold he would have gotten over me and I wouldn't have had to keep that apartment three more years, only held onto it because it was such a good deal, as you say becoming a true New Yorker, but he wasn't the only one in prison. The sixties ended, but the age of antipathy hadn't begun yet, Reagan hadn't been elected yet—you knew the first day he was elected and he wore his tuxedo drank champagne at the inaugural ball that a new day was coming, the day of the dictatorship by the bourgeoisie (the Restoration). That's when I realized the sixties were only a moment in time, I tell her, remembering how the Russians thought Reagan had actually defeated the

Soviets with his build up of arms leading directly to the breakup
of the Soviet Union. Galina and all her Russian friends wanted a
victory parade down Wall Street. The sixties was a good age, Liliana says, we had spirit as opposed to now and conformity where
people are only concerned with making more, the me generation
now complacency and self-hatred reigns. Only later or sooner now
sooner they get pissed at how their lives turned out and now have
the potential to create more damage than we in the sixties ever did,
like each political leader has a greater tendency to be worse than
the previous generation, when we were young we didn't have the
potential to cause much damage even if we thought we ruled the
world, we could hurt a lover, a husband, now you can destroy a
family, a State maybe even a nation with more power comes more
damage. My great political insight, but the letter to the judge actually made a difference, the judge citing it in his sentencing of
Jeff and I was happy for Jeff but still three years in prison is a long
time, especially a white boy with integrity, and he never wanted
to talk about it when he was released, what he didn't want to talk
about I realized later was that rape is power and he sucked dick
and the authorities knew about it but let it be. And when I saw
Liliana after she had left Jeff she kept asking about him, but I knew
nothing as well, he left his old world to start a new life and I always wondered how quickly the new life became the old life. I
was on Jeff's approved visitor list so was his common-law wife Liliana but she never went to South Dakota. Some small college had
gone belly up and became a federal minimum-security prison and
to make sure Jeff was close to his family and friends the Federal
Department of Prisons shipped him off to South Dakota, totally
against all prison rehabilitation strategy where you should stay connected to family and friends, and where I was able to go only in
the summer. I thought it important to see him so he wouldn't feel
totally isolated, and he came out of prison in worse shape than I

did after my tour of duty. Psychiatrists always talk childhood, historians events, but I realized it is our first failure in the world that destroys us: Me in 'Nam, Liliana Jeff, Jeff in prison. We had deep shit hard lives but not brutal lives and were able to survive them even if we aren't able to forget them. All I can remember is taking trains back from Jeff's prison being so depressed that I would walk home from Penn Station because I needed the noise of the city streets to galvanize me and the phone would be ringing as I walked through the door as Liliana was waiting for me to give her a report. Jeff was the reverse he said prison was so noisy he now wanted quiet. So when he left New York he could only go to an imitation South Dakota, Vermont. Imagine Jeff gets what he wanted, a house right off route 7 and St. Paul with a white picket fence, a pregnant wife, a car, even a dog, he must have gone crazy but wouldn't admit it to himself. Now when Allisson asks tell me about my father what am I to say? Should I let her know how much he hated that life? Because I would hate it does that mean he would? The slow part of the shofar is now playing, Liliana says this is beautiful she would like to meet her, it's where the dybbuk enters the soul of the individual and fills the heart and soul of the individual and the individual can no longer live a rational day to day existence, now God is beyond the reach of the scientific—the lyre comes in now. Liliana says she's celibate now and it's good to be free of the sex drive, the last few years I have actually had real relationships with only women, no more zipless fucks for me and I never was into lesbianism and I would like to meet your family. Wouldn't my daughter be surprised to think I had a life and is not just this boring daddy who only loves his coffee and morning time to write. True I don't read the papers but in every other way am a boring man. It's true my wife has trained me and I'm good for nothing but being a husband and father. The fundamental change the sixties brought about, Liliana says, is that we no longer need men to raise children and a whole new era has opened up because of it even if we didn't envision freedom in that way. The shofar plays solo, as Liliana as if responding to the lyre, says, who could have guessed when we discussed feminism the ignorance we had in all the changes it would bring and the change in the family created more problems in the culture—the lyre rejoins, the event, the breakup of the family was more important than the closure of the university, the ending of the war, the rise of black nationalism, and it isn't rational the shofar pipes in it's the eternal recurrence. It is not the God who speaks geometric truths who wins in the end. As usual when people talk grand theory all they have are limited facts not the fundamental fact of our ignorance—here the lyre and shofar play together. Did you see all the women who turned out to Jeffrey's memorial service, she asks. Only women bury us I say. Two, three families, stepbrothers and sisters, love of his life, ex-loves of his lives. And now all friends I say. Don't say that you don't know, how many times I thought about him but was too afraid to contact him, I could have been one of those stalkers only now can I admit that to myself. When the erotic force enters your life you are no longer the same as before; the piece is ending. How devious we are to ourselves, is that the piece or is it me thinking. Women are the worst, she says, hiding behind the family never able to see what we truly want. The final human liberation will be when we can truly be—finding our individuality is the most difficult thing of all. The shofar and lyre join together playing apart it's not the event but following it that is important. Who would have ever thought I could remember more about this time than my childhood? Now I'm finding an answer to my mother's silences. Her eternal waiting for me: waiting for me at lunch time, at 3 o'clock outside the school, in front of the apartment building while I was playing in the street, jumping up whenever a car came down the street calling out to me—her only words—watch it, watch it a car is coming—

she had a beach chair which she specifically bought to sit outside and watch me when she became too old to stand all day or sit on the stoop. I didn't want her company I wanted her to get a job, not for the money but to get her out of my hair. Then when I finally got her to stop shadowing me she would sit home in the dark waiting for me to come home or nap in the fetal position. She was holding it all together for me, but when I didn't need her anymore she lost it—sitting alone in the dark crying, long naps in the afternoon, waiting to give me milk and cookies when I came home from school, only as I got older would I stay out longer until I couldn't stand the cold anymore. That had to be later when the school's changed dress standards because when I was little I had to come home right away and change out of my good clothes into my jeans, I wasn't allowed out to play in my good uncomfortable clothes that always never fit me because they were hand me downs from some neighbor's child. A yellow or white shirt, always too big, a tie, finally I learned how to make a Windsor knot, pants two sizes too big, I'd grow into it, shoes with taps so I wouldn't ruin the soles. Only later Jeff took me to *Brooks Brothers* did I learn about dress-up clothing that fits and is comfortable. Liliana laughs, you took fashion advice from Jeffrey. But my habits were set and immediately afterwards would change into blue jeans, a tee shirt and sneakers. My uncle said I had to be gentle with her she had been through a lot, but that was before I was born couldn't she get over it. Why did she have to ruin my life? The greatest misery parents inflict on their children, Liliana says, is ruin their childhood it's not like we're going to have another one. I remember once when Liliana burst out, I hate my mother and I thought you couldn't say that, god will strike you dead, nor even think it before I admired her honesty. She still doesn't have sympathy for her parents; while I at least am ready to understand my mother after all she had been through but only reaching that when I had a child and realized the impotence her family must have felt when Hitler began to destroy all Jewish life. If instead of invading Russia the Wannsee conference had occurred but no Operation Barbarossa there would be no Jews left in all in Europe. My parents till the end kept their passports on the dresser in case they had to make a quick exit. I continue that tradition even if I have no place to go. I had a dream I met my mother and father and apologized for the way I treated them and felt bad about it because I really don't feel bad but I wanted them to feel good. Then I realized it's okay this is a dream I haven't really apologized to them and I didn't feel so bad. It's okay for you, she says, but my parents didn't have that excuse your parents went through a horrendous time my parents didn't have that excuse, born here everything rosy and they wouldn't let me be, I always had to conform to the neighbors expectation of me and couldn't be the tomboy I wanted to be, at thirteen all I wanted for my birthday was a baseball bat, not jewelry nor a nice dress, which of course is what I got. Our parents simply may have done the best they could but the best they could wasn't enough. So please don't tell me about rotten parents, yours at least had an excuse. And you were a boy who could do things, lived in the city where there were places to go. I never even looked out the window, I said, the Bronx wasn't the city, it was a small provincial neighborhood. We heard the shofar blowing against the wind, the lyre stroking between the breaths, the dybbuk, that imaginary body inhabiting a soul, and us thinking at least we would have had somebody to talk to. Again her hand streaks out to mine and rubs against mine, she's a good listener, as she gently massages my thumb where words itself are useless and silence is not the answer. The reason I was able to escape was I was able to expand my vocabulary to understand my feelings, my anger, my rage, resentment, and envy, previous desires that I couldn't get a handle on. Now I can make them into thoughts convert feelings into lines of poetry, if only I were queer I could have been a contender all great poets are gay, but I'm not, nothing I can do about it, men don't turn me on, all I can do is turn my feelings into thoughts, something a little weaker than before not strong enough to dominate me anymore. Poetry has allowed me to renegotiate feelings. If I had talent I could have used more colors on my canvas not gray painted all the time. The music ended but not without a long wailing of the shofar and quick upbeats of the lyre, as Liliana says while still holding onto my hand, you have to go on living as decently as you can what else can you do. Is this your philosophy of life, I ask, is this all you learned in graduate school not about your responsibility to others (boy do I see myself as this pompous old man) no longer interested in only myself. Liliana interrupts, last night I had my first naked dream ever, I was running naked through the streets but wasn't even worried I would make it to the studio, what I love about painters is they paint in a studio not write on a desk, my jeans are in my pack, not to worry I say to myself I'll put them on when I get there, but for some unknown reason check and realize I'm unprepared and decide to go home and dress because there's no sense going to the studio without pants, cut back through a hallway figuring I can take the bus in the back and it's raining out and I see a crowd of people around the bus stop but I wasn't embarrassed and walk right up, I'm naked and I'm more concerned how will I be able to do my work and be able to get back in time. I only like to work by natural light the studio has no electricity and when I'm there at night like to hold a drink, sit in the dark and listen to music but I paint only by natural light, and so with the crowd at the bus stop I see you and Jeffrey and want to talk but you're into each other and so I don't bother, then you start talking really loud then he yells back and I realize you aren't this happy couple I thought you were and you're both holding a lot in. Jeffrey says he had a heart transplant to keep the old ticker going and you're yelling don't make jokes this

is serious, the bus comes I'm about to board you guys see me, then
I wake up and say to myself okay, okay be sure you're awake or is
this part of the dream. I'm in her dreams is all I can think. Then
I say to myself I'll get my clothes ready in the morning I should
have done it last night. I didn't know what to wear to the memorial service. What do you wear to an old lover's memorial one you
haven't seen in over thirty years? You would want me to say something but I knew I couldn't, when we knew each other he wasn't
as well formed as he was to her, we could stay up all night making
love, I'd come five, six times, he would make sure I had an orgasm
before he came but insisted it was my responsibility to use birth
control. For me she insisted I pull out before hand, I recall. That's
because with you I never had time to put my diaphragm in, she
answers. How can you mention this at a memorial service in front
of his child? And I can't stand jokes yet the solemnity calls for it
because we would have been laughing, we never took anything serious always ragging on things, we would laugh together no matter
what happened. What I would have said is death is the enemy and
we shouldn't give in to it even though in the end we all give in to it,
and that he should have called again even if I didn't call him. As she
continues I think now I can get rid of my landline I don't need my
name in the book anymore either, nobody stops by and I'm pretty
well hidden. I kept my phone only for those occasional calls from
old friends but now who's going to call. Even in my dreams, she
goes on, you guys were my heroes I never felt so unprepared for
life as in the face of death even as I told myself I want to be there
to describe it not have it happen in my sleep. It's like I'm a little
girl watching them bury me and I can see all the nice things they're
saying about me, not true of course, until I realized what Jeffrey
never realized that there would be no me to watch them. Then the
first thing I did when I finally awoke was pick out this outfit and
felt better, only I changed it three times before I got it right. Do

you like it? And as I walked in it dawned on me besides you I was the only one who truly knew him, everyone else there knew the adult man not the confused revolutionary who became the adult male. The ones who truly know you are the ones who know you through youth before you start to dissimulate and role-play even as we hide we role-play only as a kid you're not so good at it yet and you can't hide behind the silences, nods, grimaces, avoidance that you can later when you can be alone more. As a youngster you need other people if even you scare them away you once told me your first poems were autobiographical only now when people ask you what you write you say autobiographical even if you can disguise it better. Writers only write about themselves just fusing them into other characters I say. Jeffrey's daughter must think she knew him better than anyone else in the world yet I venture to say she hardly knew him. She told me, I say, that she didn't know why she did this memorial service but wanted to explain your absence but I'm sure she never knew of your real presence in his life either. When I said that I saw her cringe I told her not to get upset it was an imaginary you he didn't know you anymore like I didn't know you anymore you were part of his past like I was part of his ancient history, but somehow I hit a nerve because Liliana and Allisson understood the vagaries of the mind and how you could always recall an image even if there was no actual body physically there. How many times did I conjure up images of Liliana in my sadomasochistic feelings of sexual humiliation to masturbate to? Liliana recalls walking high through city streets because we didn't want to stay cooped up, we enjoyed the intoxication of city streets, the noise, the crowds walking wide streets mixed with narrow streets, up and down different blocks being with the hum of the city sometimes even "accidentally" bumping into people other times getting out of their way, once when high I remember riding the subway alone, she says in a low voice, can you believe this the subway was packed

I stand next to a young man and rub up against him let him feel me up, sometimes, at first, they would pull their hand away but I would rub up against them once more and they'd get the picture, and then after letting them feel me up, would hop off at the next stop lest they get any ideas of forming a relationship with me. Once Jeffrey and I went down by the Holland tunnel just to listen to the car horns, the endless lines of cars and trucks, busses trying to make it into the tunnel, and we were surprised at all the prostitutes hanging there and there I wouldn't go by myself but I took you or Jeffrey and watched them ply their trade. It was a "turn on" I never appreciated, I say, I couldn't stand the racket of these cars, trucks, busses trapped in the city trying like mad to escape the city, to where? New Jersey? Remember you suggested we sell the *East Village Other* at this massive traffic jam up but nobody bought it, and kept their windows shut like they actually had air conditioning in their car but were afraid they were going to get contaminated by hippies. We tried to break through their shell but all they wanted was to escape this hell hole and get back to their wives who hated them and children who didn't know them, Liliana says, laughing, I know I became one of them. But I loved those Friday nights when we goofed on the suburbanites, never realizing that one day I would become them, when I stopped getting high and started making money. I too became indifferent, taciturn, boring saying I'm doing this for the children and using my children as an excuse for not living. How did I do this to myself? And I can't blame my first husband for this failure of mine, it wasn't his fault, I hit on him—he was a nice guy, I saw him in a bar one night went up to him and asked what he did, let him buy me a drink, he was dull but nice and I thought he would make a nice scalp only he stayed and we moved in together and married when I became pregnant, so we really never got to know one another, it's like couples who meet on vacation from different countries who speak different languages, once they get to speak the same language it's too late they see how dull the other person is. Lucky divorce became easier we parted the best of friends, I didn't want alimony, just wanted my freedom but all he wanted to do was hurt me because I hurt him and wouldn't give me custody and every inch of tenderness I had for him evaporated only later did we become friends; I was never close to my second husband either, and we never became friends, when he left we parted for good, but then I had no children by him, even if my youngest daughter considers him her father because he was around most of her childhood when their biological father left, not that he didn't see his children when the pangs of guilt hit him especially around the holidays. I even tried going back into the city but it was too late I couldn't live like that again, by then my body had become too accustomed to the good life. I didn't want to live poor again. Then this knight in shining armor comes along he had the cutest smile, the nicest hands always clean and well clipped, a frail young man an intern in the company and I took him home with me, made love to him, I should have let him go, shipped him out, instead he stayed over one night then two we read poetry aloud to each other, what a dear, but it was only a lark to him to pick up girls he acted sensitive. And this time when I got pregnant didn't even hesitate to get an abortion I didn't want another child but he stayed helped raise my two daughters, it was like playing house to him until playing was no more fun for us and one day he moved on as quickly as he moved in and I haven't heard from him again. From then on I said don't let anyone seduce you so, it wasn't even the words he said, because I don't remember what he said, but it was the way he said it, gentle, sensitive, sincere. How did kind words seduce me and before I knew it—me who prided herself on independence, was married a baby in hand and another in the belly ensconced in a house that he found because the apartment was too small for a family, I was impressed how he found a house on a cul-de-sac, plenty of closets, which surprised me when I only had one closet I was surprised at seven closets but soon all the closets were full; supposedly a good school district which is one of the myths of suburban living their schools are a hoax if I had home-schooled my children they could have learned all they learned in less than twenty-four hours that the school system took over a year to teach, and the teachers would pride themselves on having never read poetry or novels: I never read was their mantra. Suburban schools prepare students to be administrators—filing and make-believe work, not poets or thinkers. But how could one argue with all this especially after living in a small studio in the Village, it looked like growth, I was getting on with my life not fixated over the breakup with Jeffrey and I not realizing that was the freest time in my life and didn't even know it.

Fun city became zoo city, as the city itself fell apart everyone started living in fear, scared, anxious, all the time you had to look over your shoulder at the other guy and he was looking over at you, junkies were mugging and boosting, the police were afraid to come off the busy main streets, and everything began to change: I was trapped inside my home at night, gates on my windows like I was living in a prison; I became afraid whenever I saw a group of young black males, that's when I knew it was time to leave. You mean you were mugged. No only my gold necklace ripped off me, but the city was getting scary my next-door neighbor was robbed on our block and pistol-whipped, my apartment went co-op and I could buy at the insiders price and what was funny I met Gilly on Wall Street, and he had just moved out to New Jersey said the city was too scary to live now, I remember the first time Jeffrey introduced me to a black male, I felt uncomfortable especially when he rolled a cigarette I thought we'd be addicted for life; that he was this sexually powerful stud who only wanted to get into white woman's panties. True I say. Not Gilly, she says, all he liked to do

CAFÉ PURGATORIO

was gamble, smoke pot, and watch sports a gentle soul who when he made some money selling pot left the city. That's when I finally realized all my parents said, what teachers said, what I was taught were lies, pot is good for you. I didn't become addicted and I saw being under the influence I no longer was this goody goody girl who listened to her parents, teachers, but a new me who was exploring how to live on her own and that repression was bad. Later when we dropped acid we both had this vision that it changed our lives, and Gilly said if only prisoners took this stuff it would change their lives forever but the police don't treat criminals with drugs only persecute them. And when we bumped into each other at *JR Music*, we both liked jazz, we reminisced ate lunch in the park together and he convinced me to come out to his place in Jersey and just see it's not as bad as it sounds—the space, the green, and he had painted bases on the street so his kid could play ball and the travel time wasn't bad especially if you could work off hours. We were at a rent party with Jeffrey smoking weed when Gilly copped some acid and I saw myself split in two, my soul was split and laughed, imagine if my mother could see me now, living with a Jewish man, friends with blacks, wearing pants and not being suffocated by a small town atmosphere where you kept your mouth shut accepted what was your lot in life and prayed to God on Sunday, I was so glad to escape their conformity so I was a little dismayed when Gilly said this is the life, it's almost like he was close to the soil, except of course he only had a little patch of grass, and his friends were boring, silent, just like my friends from back home who married had children and only fucked the man they married. Gilly's friends were boring and silent because they had nothing to say all they could do was drink and impregnate women and I used to think my old girlfriends were out of their mind and now I became just like them. I used to keep in touch with them through letters remember them? And they couldn't write what they felt

119

only clichés about love and happiness not that I escaped my parents' place, or that I am more lonely in marriage than I was living in my room or that I see nobody stuck inside the house all day with my baby or that my husband is a lout who when finished with me left me and that they were bored out of their minds remember these were intelligent women and some even had gone to college and not just to get their Mrs. degree. And now I was about to become one of them. It wasn't the beauty of the place that got me it was how much I was paying in taxes and when the building went co-op I saw the advantage and took it: bought low sold high and escaped the city. Just as I was moving in with Galina I think and having no desire to own but thinking we had this apartment with wooden floors, one room for the piano, too bad we couldn't leave it the music room and rugs on the floor, books piled high a nook for me to read and write. Galina got tendonitis in her arms from playing so much, I remember, it was the first time she had unlimited access to a piano and she practiced too long at first. We didn't even have a book in the house but I did have a brand new car and sometimes a pencil to take down phone messages. And we'd go to a mall on Saturday night eat at *Friendly's* and hope to find one movie we could watch that I could stomach in the multiplex—forget foreign films or plays except theater in the round, i.e. musicals. And I kept telling myself how much I like this instead of being stuck in the city—I became who I wasn't. My neighbors were educated, somewhat enlightened, and we were friends but I had little in common with them, in fact what surprised me at first was this desire to live far away from another neighbor, space between houses was considered a good thing but at least when their children became of age parents let them (insisted) that they go to good schools i.e. name-brand schools away from home. A far cry from when my guidance counselor, bless her soul, told my father what do you want your daughter to marry a laborer i.e. a high school gradu-

ate, or an educated man, i.e. a college graduate and they let me
go to the University. My heroine! I never would have escaped if it
wasn't for her, she looked after women, probably the first educated
woman the town had seen since the twenties graduated from the
University of Chicago and being a guidance counselor in the sticks
was the only job she could find. I even wrote a letter back to my
old high school principal saying the school hadn't prepared me for
college and he should make changes, but I never heard back from
him he must have thought I was an apostate. She smoked, allowed
me to see her smoking, wore trousers, invited me to her home and
once we even snuck away to Chicago for a weekend to see movies,
of course, I told my parents that I was going to a friend's for a sleep-
over, they believed me I never lied before and we drove all the way
to Chicago to the old Bryn Mawr theater on the Northside and
saw a double bill of *Night and Fog* and *Smiles of a Summer Night* and
were back by Monday morning. She told me to leave early don't
wait or you'll never get out. She was the one who introduced me to
the folk music of Dylan, Joan Baez and a whole different culture.
And when I moved I was bored but safe and wasn't there much
what with working long hours and the commute—she smiles all a
lucky break I had taken a Katherine Gibbs course all women college graduates took back in the day so that I could be a secretary
and have some money and one day I looked up and wondered what
am I going to do with a Ph.D. in philosophy and found a job at a
small computer company and realized hey I can do this shit (I understood logic and mathematics well enough) why do men talk like
this is difficult and learned programming on my own and soon was
making real wages, and I started to like what money could buy—
besides my do-gooder days were over you couldn't make a dent
in poverty, and their poverty of thinking, I would see black men
everywhere with their mothers, and they were so dependent upon
food stamps, welfare, government handouts, the ghetto mentality

is so pervasive that I realized my leftist idealistic days were over, and I would get back to my thesis one of these days only one of these days never occurred. She laughs who would have thought I'd be worth over a million. My inability to move, even to pioneer neighborhoods, which Galina wanted us to do—buy low sell high, buy our apartment at the insider's price, sell it to an outsider then move still in the city but to another neighborhood that was up and coming, which some of her friends did, has allowed us to stay poor. My inability to live anywhere allows me to live among my neighbors as I drift among people rootless but only on the West Side of Manhattan. Liliana dwells. I wander. She migrated from the Homeland, I'm still searching for the Promised Land. Dissatisfaction is the human condition, the Israelites complained to Moses why didn't you let us die as slaves, even if I can't precisely pinpoint the moment it began seems to be the operating ingredient of my existence, I think, my inability to live anywhere, at least I haven't awakened on my own couch and wondered where I am or what am I doing here I don't feel at home here—that image comes to me late at night when I can't sleep and I remake my life with Liliana, even if lately that dream is interrupted by my saying to her listen as much as I love you I can't leave Galina, as if a) I would and b) can't I even have a dream in peace without reality interfering like the time she stood up to me in another dream and said I'm staying put, or did I realize she liked her condition and wasn't leaving it and only afterwards interpreted it as I'm staying put?—why do I need such reality in a dream can't I have some symbolic fun. Mine came from lying on the couch, listening to music, my pants open and my hand on my crotch with candles or colored lights surrounding me, she says. Unlike Jeff, however, I see no reason to leave the city and hope to be carried out in a pine box. Be careful what you wish for, she says. The city you loved is no longer the same it's a colder place now, more business-orientated, money, greed, ugliness lack of charm that destroyed the fabric of life, it isn't only crime that destroyed the fabric of life in the city it's also the decline of smallness, some streets are the same now as shopping malls you can hardly find small independent stores anymore; caring, charm, you hardly see fresh flowers anymore, nobody cares anymore, civility is gone, how many youngsters walk out of a place and just let the door slam, no manners, no concern for the other guy; street life is gone remember when I lived in the West Village all those street people who at first I thought were dangerous in reality kept the neighborhood safe, my car was never safer when it was on the block with all those guys who would sit on stoops all day long, gamble, drink and basically hang out, and the old ladies would sit at their windows and look out on the street, almost like a private security force and their were no muggings on that block. Still I refuse to go, the wanderer who never moves. And I refuse to go into the new chain stores, mostly because they play loud music where high school graduates are forced to work while waiting for a prince to come along and rescue them or at least get them pregnant. Their futures are written on their faces and they don't even look in the mirror to view it, a whole generation condemned to retail trade not being able to benefit from the grand progress of the city because of a lack of a serious education. And men lost totally lost no more high-paying union jobs where they could at least make serious money only the crumbs are left, which young black males refuse to take afraid they'll end up like their fathers, and if these guys live in public housing they're lucky otherwise landlords with the help of the city, and who can stand up to that concentration of power, will slowly and not so slowly transform their neighborhoods for me for the better but they will have a longer commute into downtown—gentrification is like urban renewal of a generation ago, black removal. No one is saved, she says, and many are stricken, she continues, the parable of Kafka—god will come but it will be too late for us, she says, he gave me pleasure especially after a boyfriend moved out and I could finally shut the television off. How come men only watch television? You could always find a man of mine lying half nude on the couch, right after they moved out or I kicked them out, I would still peek at the couch for a bit to see if they were lying there until I got use to being alone again. Anyone who can stay friends with their old boyfriends is an interesting person, I think, to have that ability to connect and reconnect and continue a dialogue as before is a *mensh*. I look out through the window up above and can see a deep blue sky it must be cold outside, lucky I have nowhere to go otherwise I would say I have to leave but I don't want to get away from her so won't make believe I have an appointment to wander aimlessly in the cold is depressing, yet how many times have I told myself have a plan know where you're going before you go into the cold instead of wandering aimlessly in the cold but now I force myself to stay. You can leave if you want to? When else am I going to see you again? You remind me of my mother telling me that there's now good stuff on television it's educational, and I didn't even know what she was talking about even if the TV was always on in our house, especially during dinner, it was never tuned to PBS. I sip some wine to keep the glass between us so she doesn't see the smile on my lips and if I had enough guts would ask her to run away with me. She says I remind you of your mother? I don't think that's a compliment. What my mother said about you, I say, is she's too pretty she'll leave you cold. We could run away to Czernowitz now that it's a backwater swamp of Romania and can move into my uncle's old apartment if it's still standing live comfortably for about a year or two before she leaves me. The dream I will have tonight, I'm driving on snow and ice and can't control the car and a woman (Liliana) cuts in front of me and I wonder how can she do that? how can she have the nerve to cut in front of me when I'm slipping and sliding on snow and ice and I shift into a lower gear to control the car better, and I try wrapping the steering wheel with *Tefillin* (long thin leather straps that orthodox Jews put on in the morning) only it's not very neat and then I hear Galina say your life is unraveling out of control but I am holding onto it, barely. Why not Glasgow, Liliana says, I love the lilt of the Glaswegians' accent, and women there have a custom that they don't date friends of friends, less complications that way. I make a mental note of this to remind myself to recall this on nights when I can't fall asleep. Maybe they'll help me get back to sleep or at least pass the time. Liliana probably still writes letters and doesn't use the word processor and her reading my thoughts says I no longer write only use the computer the greatest invention since the hand-held blow-dryer. I couldn't wait for computers to come into general use I was one of the first in the offices to use them, to really get into it. Oh it's me who doesn't use e-mail and word processors and still writes letters. Be careful where fantasy ends, I think, remembering a woman I couldn't wait to get into bed she was so hippie-looking with long hair, braless, no make-up on, and she deflated my cock as she took her wig off before she got into bed with me, at first my immediate thought was cancer but it was only for beauty, but I no longer could get hard I liked her hair not her. And a couple of weeks ago I tried to recall a friend's name who I had seen less than a week before and for the life of me his name was a blank and there I was driving up to Stony Point, New York up along the Palisades and all of a sudden Sylvia's name came to me yes I desired her over thirty years ago I thought and she lived in Stony Point but my friend from last week his name wouldn't come. Go figure. Liliana still has those strong muscular legs that would be nice to be wrapped around me at 2 A.M. especially now when I can't sleep after getting up and using the bathroom, I laugh. She says, it's good that you can still think like this but even better that you don't act on your impulses and realize what they are. But I realize I think nowhere near what other people think, in fact I have no idea if other people think and can barely discern what I think and sometimes think it's better not to think at all and continue drinking my red wine. But I know I will pay the price, this drinking will ruin a week's worth of work trying to get back on schedule, like when I have to bring the car in early in the morning and I get off schedule, I make a quick mental calculation: Liliana is worth it. Who else would I be able to have such a fine conversation with, usually my eyes would turn my body tilt away from the speaker when people chattered having nothing really to say and only talked for making conversation because they couldn't stand being alone—a fate worse than death in this culture and now you can't even be alone with yourself for a moment, the noise is so loud. Even people walking carry iPods so the sounds of the streets are absent. I tell Liliana how Jeff and I would drive out to the airport to pick up stewardesses, of course, we never picked up any but we did it because we were bored and had nothing to do at night. But I never liked the symmetry of the terminals the cold, cold floors brightly colored walls and chairs, and whenever I could would leave from a bus terminal, the old one at 42nd Street my favorite, I could sit and think in one of those places. Jeffrey must have taken a bus to Vermont, she thinks and I agree. He was one of the first transplanted New Yorkers who moved to Vermont, she says, now the place is crawling with them. Then the city changed, I say, and the terminals became shelters for the homeless you couldn't even use the bathroom homeless had staked them out and lived in the stalls or you would get mugged in the middle of the terminal and bus terminals became empty and only recently have I been able to resume my nocturnal habit of sitting in bus terminals going nowhere. Liliana smiles I wonder how long the bus ride is to Vermont, I stopped using them after my first bus ride back to Iowa, I just couldn't sit on a bus for over 24 hours straight, I thought I'd die,

I used to try and read Sinclair Lewis on long bus rides he would instantly put me to sleep, the stopovers, connections, it wasn't romantic traveling by bus as I thought it would be. Me, I love bus rides going up and down back roads rest stops falling asleep, I read Peter Handke, even though lately he's been writing about something not all description, and sometimes it takes me a moment to fall asleep. I remember her once taking a bus to Hoboken then hitching across country. Can you believe it? Yes I did do that, she says. Hoboken is where bums used to hitch a ride on the rails it was the last stop on the rails that's how the term Hobo started she tells me. I never heard that I said and doubt it it's true, I say. She tells me it's true but she can't remember where she learned it. She also tells me she was never groped or treated poorly by any man hitching and it was only men who picked me up and they would be my protector some even drove out of their way to make sure I safely got to where I wanted to go, they saw me as their daughter, sister, mother, never a prostitute never made a pass there real religion took care of me. I always found it fascinating drunken bums, politicians, men you'd like to shoot are yet very protective of women unless it was their own. Now I don't have guts to do it but the rednecks never threatened me and they really did have rednecks from being out in the sun so much. In the South they killed but in the Midwest, at least where I'm from, you could hitch anywhere. Lucky that guidance counselor told me the way to leave is to go to college far away from my parents, my old town, my old friends, my old church, still it took me two years to escape but I worked all the time in college to save up enough money to leave even if one my girlfriend's went to Los Angeles and got stuck in low-end waitressing and cashiering jobs and couldn't make it in Los Angeles and had to come back, I had a plan. Get the fuck out? No, yes, but get out so I didn't have to go back that's why I stayed a couple of more years I knew when I left I wasn't coming back. I didn't even date, even if I did "lose it" before I left, I wanted to do that so I could get it out of the way. Where were you when I was growing up? Don't get so uppity, she says; when you enlisted Jeffrey said you wanted to marry your high school squeeze so you'd have something to come back to. I hardly knew her and I hadn't slept with her I only did it so I could say I was married and it would make me feel more like a man, I say, that's what men did back then, marry, get the women pregnant and run off and join the army. But she had enough sense not to fall for it. My only experience was with a boy I met at a football game snuck him in the dormitory he wanted to shut all the lights, I said why I want to see what you look like he wanted to make love in the dark, he got hard instantly penetrated me spit it out and it was over and I was no longer a virgin. That's all I wanted but he kept calling like we were lovers or something and he expected me to ask him to the *Sadie Hawkins* dance, the only time girls were permitted to ask men for a date, but I wanted nothing more to do with him. I didn't even get to see him raise his cock, it didn't grow it sprung, he got it up and then boom—the Restoration and it was over. But at least I wasn't a virgin anymore even if I looked no different I knew that I had done it and felt good. I thought the sixties would live forever, she says, it changed lives, she says, it changed my life, she says, the civil rights revolution, anti-war demonstrations, feminism, I thought the country would never go back to where it came from, and then it was over. I never understood how men could like women like my mother. Not to be outdone I say my mother was worse. At least yours had an excuse. I haven't gotten that far in analysis, I say. We laugh. The only friend I truly had in high school, she says, was my guidance counselor and now I can't even remember her name; my high school girlfriends were really acquaintances that's all, not like you and Jeffrey who were real buddies in high school. Girls are so catty that I couldn't stand to be with them and I used to think it was me I had no friends therefore something is wrong with me, but luckily college came along and I met girls who thought like I did, girls with brains. And I couldn't wait until I grew up I thought grown ups know something; now I realize grown ups know nothing, I knew more when I was young than I do now, she says, and I laugh and agree. Now all I can say is I had a privileged birth i.e. being born on this side of the Atlantic when the war was over so I had a chance to grow up unhampered by death and destruction. Pure chance, Liliana says, war is no longer declared merely perpetrated. Remember that idiot Kennedy who almost blew the world to bits in the Cuban Missile Crisis she declares, thank goodness the Russians knew something about the horrors of war and backed down otherwise nobody would have had a chance at life. The times were a changin and we didn't have to live out our lives under harshness only boredom, she says. Better to live in boring times where the individual has a chance, I say. We developed the ability to articulate what we didn't know and didn't have to pass over it in silence, and that ability extended our language we could articulate it even if at first only in events even if our art was chaotic and blurry it had a more concrete meaning in that it changed lives or at least changed my life. At first it was only a confused era but it disturbed the tranquility of our elders only they never tell you that you too become elders but at least now I have a language to describe the process of thought, even if now it's moved toward the inside I never would have had it if it weren't for the sixties. Otherwise I would be like all my other high school buddies, successful, Liliana takes that as a dagger thrown at her, it isn't, and it's a revelation to me. Language may allow us to extend our misery but it's only a metaphysical misery not where we struggle to survive physically or live under severe mental conditions that we die a little each day. Look at the street kids in Czernowitz I say, living in the sewers, smoking varnish, money impossible, life short, brutal and harsh, a far cry from when it was an polyglot watering hole. She doesn't reply at first then says when we are dead we are as dead as them and there is no answer. I had it made professionally, a lovely house, two children, lovers; I made all the right choices but was a plaything of the gods. As flies are to boys we to the gods, they kill us for sport. I reach out to catch a fly with my hand but move too slow and it escapes, in fact I never catch them, except once, actually caught one killed it in my hand and it scared me so that I actually caught a fly in my fist that I immediately let it go only too late it was already dead. It is difficult reliving your life, she says, what if we had run off together would our lives have been any different? How can she say that she could have called anytime and I would have come running, I was much too shy to call her, but all she had to do was whistle and I would have been by her side. I had to find out who I was not live through a man, she says—give me the laughter of the ancients, she says, but nobody is around who can give me that all we can do is receive. I see the tree tops blowing in the wind and the moon between the empty branches, and I think that it must be deep into the night, almost like a primeval forest but realize it's the booze getting to me, I'm deep in the city not some ancient forest. I usually don't drink this much anymore especially on an empty stomach, and I usually now eat healthy—disgusting food that has no taste, all to live a little longer—I couldn't get a salad here probably only grease, a chicken-fried steak and fries, I can't eat it now for fear it will taste too good and I will go back to my unhealthy habits. Maybe you can taste it, Liliana says, chew it play anorexic and spit it out, punish your body let it see what it's missing who said there's no connection between mind and body. We laugh. But I must get some food in my stomach; it's just difficult when you're not at home. The barkeep reads my mind and brings over some lovely Canadian cheese, who knew Quebec made such tasty cheese but first she gave me an iced sherbet to dry my palate. Because we are

taking up a booth for such a long time I make a mental note to
leave a big tip, besides Liliana will be impressed with my generosity.
But she says you do good for the wrong reason, the only reason
to do good is the good itself not what other people think. She's
still cheap. When she first took me to *Hung Fats* in Chinatown for
sweet-and-sour pork I offered to pay but she said no I asked you
out, but I wouldn't hear of a woman paying and we had an argu-
ment winding up in sharing the bill, which we have been doing
ever since. Will she take out a calculator and divide up our bill?
The moon goes and hides behind a branch and I can barely see it
and we huddle deeper in our corner to keep away from the crowds.
I wonder if this is an open-seated bar and others will join us for
lunch, but I think we have the look of an assignation and no one
would dare interfere with that. Jeffrey and you were doomed to
be best friends living near each other and having similar interests
i.e. baseball cards, cub scouts, boy scouts, baseball, Hebrew school.
Even though he was smarter than me, I say, and got himself kicked
out before his bar mitzvah so that he wouldn't have to go through
it, it was only when we got into the wider world that our interests
diverged and you would have thought mine would have become
more serious not his, after all I had my uncle who showed me
a different world from our parents, our pernicious teachers, jock
friends, he didn't have much family, but he had started his intellectual (serious) reading early, and I didn't listen to my uncle until
late when I was ready to listen before that he was preaching against
a stone wall, but I always liked looking at the scar on his cheek
which when little he told me he got in a duel and I believed him,
imagined him fighting over a girl only later found out from my
mother he almost died, bled to death when a Brownshirt (Storm
trooper) gave it to him when he didn't move quick enough out of
his way. My uncle even took me to my first baseball game and I
remember vividly how the grass was green because on a black and

white set it always looked so gray, and we lived in the part of the Bronx where there were no ball fields and we only played in the street or school yards so the first time I saw an actual ball field was Yankee Stadium. He taught me that in baseball you count balls first then strikes, but Jeff already knew that. He took me to theater and concerts, when younger I would fall asleep asking my mother did I have to go. Jeff would have loved to go but I wasn't allowed to take him. Why did Jeff start reading, I don't know, I just know he loved *Franny and Zooey* and couldn't stand phonies and he made me schlep out to City Island with him, a train then a bus to the last stop, where we ate frog legs because that was in Salinger's novel, then he was reading *Lord of the Flies* before he went on to Hesse's Wolf of the Steppes. If I was reading anything it was hagiographies of baseball players i.e. Mickey Mantle where they never said he was a drunken bum and had wasted his talent away. Nothing serious. Only later when my uncle would take me to cafeterias that dotted the old Upper West Side would I listen to intellectual conversations, by then Jeff was beyond that into action, which my uncle and his cronies—survivors from German Concentration Camps, Russian Gulag's escapees from Communism in Eastern Europe, said you don't want, it would only make things worse. And then I realized they were talking about the proletariat, i.e. my father, and I knew I couldn't be on his side. Somehow I never saw myself as a worker, American brainwashing, Jeff said. That's where I can say my education began not in college which was so boring. You told me your family despised your uncle. Yes what did all his talk amount to he couldn't support a family, still he was family and they invited him to holiday dinners. And he didn't condemn me like my parents always did but wrote me all sorts of letters from whereever he traveled or when I enlisted and would always ask me about myself and what books I was reading. Books? Meanwhile Jeffrey was protesting the war he was one of the first to realize (he was reading I.F.

Stone) the Gulf of Tonkin resolution torpedoed through Congress was a pack of lies, there was no attack, no boats, no boat wakes, no boat gunfire, no torpedoes no sightings of enemy vessels and yet no Admiral stood up and said it was all bullshit. Interesting how many times we go to a preventive war except there is nothing to prevent except a politician's backside. Yet my uncle didn't criticize the Vietnam War he hated the communists so much nor did he criticize the American Educational system saying it was like Berlin of the twenties, even as he said it was Berlin itself not the curriculum, or even the early Russian educational system at the turn of the century, especially in St. Petersburg, in both places like here, they believed in equality, free love, drugs, and changed consciousness and he was glad to see it happening here in the States as well. He was the one who insisted I go back to school and I did hear Ginsberg who I confused with Ralph Ginzburg not realizing I wasn't listening to a poet but some porn publisher (a first amendment advocate) who got screwed by the American court system for mailing a magazine from Middlesex, New Jersey, Middle-Sex, get it. And I did hear Kunstler and Chomsky when they came to speak and they made sense. From there like in St. Petersburg or Berlin I went onto non-conventional abstract art, not realistic drawings or figurative paintings that of course I knew nothing about the only abstract artist I heard of growing up Bronx was Picasso and all I could say about art was I know what I like and what I didn't like with no understanding and dismissed what I disliked without trying to understand distortion, colors, patterns, and got into psychedelic posters and then brain music of Mahler from the score in *Death in Venice* even if when I went into the record store and asked for Mahler they showed me Malo, then Bartok and Shostakovich. Taste takes time to develop, Liliana says, and you were able to develop it while Jeffrey was in prison, she continues. The first sculpture I bought was a box with a gear shift saw it at a antique store, fell in love with it, wondered should I buy it it's so useless, after all what do you do with it? It's practical value was nil, but somehow I loved playing with the gears in a wooden box, it attracted me even if I could hear my mother saying it will just rot in your room. I wouldn't be bound by old rules and I saved up put some money down and eventually it became mine. I still have it except Galina doesn't like it so it's consigned to the closet. Dealers cheat my mother said. It's called profit I said. My mother said haggle, I didn't bargain, I didn't want to appear cheap or Jewish. How could she know she never was in an antique store in her life, she sees television that's how and all businessmen are crooks on TV, not like the police or the courts, or the military? I was happy with my purchase. I still enjoy taking it out of the closet and playing with it, looking at it. My first artistic purchase, and I felt proud for doing it. Superficial European culture, she says, art has to be made for use not to be admired, she says, art must spring from the divine not human intervention; we cannot lose ourselves in art. My uncle was impressed, I think, that's what allowed him to make sure I got his paintings after he passed. None are worth much in dollars but I still enjoy looking at them everyday—I try and make time to stop and stare so that they don't become mere decoration upon my walls. Which means you can't get a flat screen television, Liliana says, if your walls are covered with paintings and books, like *Quentin Durward* you're trained in the old ways while the world has changed. She explains a novel by Walter Scott who was trained as a knight in a world of guns, i.e. societies values changed. Why I go to off-off-Broadway, I figure soon they'll go like the dodo bird. Everyone thought the radio would die with movies and television and it's now stronger than ever, so you never know old forms can change and be more popular than ever. There's hope your sculpture and artwork will make you rich. I would be grateful if it's saved and someone else appreciates it. I recall cleaning out my mother's place and you swept the place clean and found my mother's engagement ring hidden in a metal box behind a loose floorboard i.e. the family jewels and you saved it and said make sure you give it to your wife one day, I had totally forgotten my mother had told me about it, and I gave it to Galina but she doesn't wear it fearing that it will get lost. The box also included old decrepit life insurance forms from Germany, old receipts in German and English, even a citizenship paper but not from my parents' even an old pocket watch bought at a drug store when they first came to the States that wasn't worth repairing. Yet my father did spend real money and bought my mother an engagement ring, it is an attractive oval shaped full of little diamonds around the center diamond, which she was afraid she would lose so never wore it. It's a beautiful art-nouveau piece that my uncle must have selected; I can't imagine my father doing anything like that. It's now in our safe deposit box instead of a loose floorboard. The apple doesn't fall from the tree, she says. That was then, at one time I actually saved my books so my daughter would think she had an intelligent father when I passed, now I much rather give them away, like my uncle did, to make sure they have a good home. No matter how much I wanted to be different from them I end up similar to them, will my writing give me enough strength to be even a smidgen different or is it all preordained only I hadn't the bad luck to be born on European soil during their civil wars that ravaged the planet as if they were god's creation and only they counted. It's not like me to be kind to my parents. What I always liked about you even when you wore button-down shirts is your Pollyannaish optimism while Jeffrey would sit in a dark room waiting for the apocalypse. You thought feminism was a phase not the end of civilization and you were correct people came out of it with more freedom, with more opportunity with more variety comes more freedom and if it stays around long enough will become accepted. It destroyed old ways, I say, as Jeff said, but it brings about new

ones in its wake. Like the family she says. Yes that venerable insti-
tution the family, did you ever think the Greek playwrights were
talking about fucked-up Jewish families. All unhappy families are
alike, she says, misquoting Tolstoy's famous opening line—the best
opening line in all of literature. We were among the first to see
the play *Hair* where both men and women went nude on stage
and the world didn't collapse. I even saw *A Streetcar Named Desire*
where Stanley went around nude breaking dishes for no reason just
to be controversial but the director said it was for "artistic reasons".
The play, like much of American theater i.e. O'Neill and Miller
are now historical curiosities. Now nudity is considered normal.
Everything is normal in this culture but some stuff sticks others
don't. Spoken like a true poet, she says. Take the meaning out of
everything, culture is always dead but revising itself, new forms of
entertainment that replaces the old but it's only when there's war
that individuals lose freedom probably why governments like war
to keep the masses down. We don't have total war only skirmishes
that are bad enough to oppress some of the population, there's no
such thing as peace, leaders always find reasons for war to keep
individuals quiet. Now that women are no longer trained in self-
sacrifice, are not ready to do all for men, men are upset. Women
now talk about their own happiness and the only way to shut them
up is war. Unless you were caught in the Trade Center I say. Even
so, she says, it's not the victims who demand vengeance, she says,
women still want to talk about their own happiness no more repet-
itive housework or having to think what to make for dinner every
night. Happiness is never an easy thing to achieve it's easier to realize how corrupt the world is and if you put your needs last at
least you have an excuse for being sad. You take no responsibility for your life blame it all on capitalism as if communism ever set
women free. It takes time to develop notions of freedom sometimes
even more than one generation but we're not allowed to have that

much time for developing ourselves; now there is neither total war nor total peace but it's in these peaceful periods that freedom can develop until politicians, generals, clergy, and others can't take it anymore and bring back the militaristic order. Only now women partake of it also, I say. How many men have I dated, she continues, who all they wanted to do was take me camping so they could show off their skills—be the boss, skills that are not much needed in the modern world, i.e. to make fire by rubbing two sticks together, know which way moss grows on trees, but I would usually fool them since I loved to hike and would walk them into the ground. I remembered our disastrous hike in the wilds of New Jersey where I finally couldn't take the outdoors anymore and said, let's spend the night in a motel while she wanted to sleep in a lean-to. Yes and you were wearing red underwear I was impressed you knew about colored underwear only gays were wearing them in the sixties, I thought for sure you would be wearing all milky white tucked in like your mother raised you. Ha! What she didn't know was that I ran short and had borrowed Jeff's and after she liked them so much switched. Me I love to walk in cities can't stand countryside, and now she agrees. And now I can walk all over the city again now that it is safe again, it's fun getting up at two in the morning and not being afraid to walk outside your apartment. In fact I love walking off the beaten paths of Central Park until I force myself to realize hey it's all artificial (man made) but at least safe for now. On a hike you have to concentrate on hiking in the city besides looking out for the other guy you can have a conversation with someone or like me now so in my head that I never truly see where I am, I don't look at a sunset, or a shadow from a tree, or a blue-green sky unless I'm with Galina and she points it out to me, usually by interrupting me saying where are you now? then look. The biggest change in my kind of woman, I say, is that they all walk only for a reason now; you can't simply go for a walk with them anywhere unless they have a place to go. And they never have time to sit and chat. Liliana looks at me. But only you, she says, otherwise you are correct I had no time to waste walking with men. I always liked it when men left the house to go for a walk, except in the suburbs hardly anybody walks, but now women do it as well as men, a small increment leading to a lasting change. Walking gives us freedom outside the home away from spouses, children into friendship and a window onto the world, now we no longer have to be home to supervise homework or put the kiddies to bed, usually we still have to make breakfast, true freedom! She points to me and I don't make a joke, which is easy to do because I remember making so many sly comments about early feminism even as I supported it because I couldn't quite accept it, remembering listening to my mother say when you finally leave home I'm going to go to school and learn a trade and get a career, all talk because she never did it, she couldn't have lived if she weren't supported by a man. Now all I see are women going to college and men selling their bodies i.e. getting low-paying physical jobs rather than go to college, uninterested in culture—how will they become poetry readers of the future? It's good to be able to have a conversation again, even as I became whole with Galina I missed having repartee with Liliana, someone who I could converse with not have to explain myself to with someone who is not a native speaker or who uses incomprehensibility as an excuse for making one repeat and repeat until you get tired of it and you have limited conversation just attempts at understanding. Besides she's not talking about her career aspirations or how the United States is running amok over the world—imperialism is the highest stage of capitalism, claptrap I hear from immature leftists, who now whenever they criticize the United States somehow bring Israel into the picture: The Zionist conspiracy. Do you realize the Jews purposely ignored Muslim clerics who helped Jews escape Europe in World War II in their

Holocaust museum? So what? So they can preach hatred against Muslims! But it's fascinating to listen to someone of intelligence say that we are pissed when someone does to us what we have been doing to them: i.e. 9/11. I'm a legitimate target, she says, and all individuals can do now is kill civilians, there are no more purely military targets armies don't fight armies anymore, only we do it with great patriotic fever remember how we all marveled when workers hung a battered American flag on top of the rubble that was the World Trade Center. Could Hollywood have scripted it better? In fact all we now know are images scripted from movies. And all anti-war movies are shut down in production in this great wave of patriotism—the last refuge of scoundrels. We didn't discuss reasons for war only talked of a smoking gun being a nuclear bomb and lucky for you, she says, then corrects herself, and says for women as well because if a draft is enacted I imagine they would have to draft us women as well now that we claim equal rights, now the army doesn't have a million men it can call upon, only those who barely graduate from high school or who need structure in their lives or want to test themselves looking for adventure, not to mention those from broken homes, and they just can't kill them as easily without having replacements. I add children of immigrants who are grateful to America. She's thinking Vietnam I realize, did I think like this at one time? Impossible me, looking for adventure or to prove Jews were tough, I couldn't have my reason was pure: communists were evil. That's what happens when you begin to study, to think, Liliana says, to become aware, you realize there are no unselfish motives you begin to doubt what you've been told, you start to look behind your foolish thoughts—that's when life starts to become interesting and when I started getting scared, she says of herself, so I immersed myself in my work, she says, then in my house and my commute, she says, so that I wouldn't have time to think anymore, and when that wasn't working I would get up

FREDERICK MARK KRAMER

early and jog, she says, all to make sure I had no time to think about
what I was doing—had a nanny raise my children (I could afford
it) rather than engage with them, never went on class trips with
them, never got involved in their play, dreaded taking them to the
park on Sunday, of course I would find work to do that had to be
done on Saturday, only Sunday was my dreadful day, home alone
with two children even if they were spaced far enough apart that
I didn't have two infants at the same time. Images come back to
me of Jeff's new-found friends, reformed hooligans, who he would
spend all night with gambling (cards), smoking, drinking, the most
uneducated savages I ever met, who had no interest in books, art,
music, poetry, people I started to realize I was trying to escape
from. Their women, i.e. high school girlfriends remained stuck in
the baby doll version of adulthood and couldn't leave the house
except with their husband but were willing to bed me (at least I
think they were, how do you know if you actually don't go through
with it?) to get even with the men who robbed them of all illusions
yet they couldn't break free—especially after they had a child or
two and no employable skills. I was good at masturbating to their
images. Thank goodness I'm through with that now, she says, it
doesn't grab hold of me like it once did—bedding your lover's best
friend, I did learn that was wrong, she continues, even if you think
it can work out everyone gets hurt in the end, she says. I thought I
bedded her not she bedded me, learning in the future changes the
past, who says time only goes one way? Now I need help getting
it up, I don't need spice to make the marriage work only to make
the body work, can there be any more spice than spending time
with an old lover. You can see the difference between your parents
and me as a parent she says, you turned out decent that had to
have something to do with your parents, and your uncle, teachers,
friends even if you're not willing to forgive your parents mine on
the other hand have disappeared each running away first chance

140

they got the oldest at fifteen, the youngest waited until she could go to college but both wanting nothing to do with me. I wouldn't beat up on yourself so much I say you did your best. Sometime your best is not good enough, Liliana replies. I recall some woman, a teacher or a social worker, I can't remember her profession or name, but it was someone I wanted for a moment, saying to me your parents must have been lovely people for you to be so sensitive and gentle, and my member shriveling up—you don't talk about parents during love-making, Liliana says, her vodka getting refilled while I'm still getting to the bottom of my wine. She orders another but I can't order another yet she orders for me. I'm afraid to break the mood I haven't had a conversation like this in a long time and have forgotten how much I missed it. Nobody talks anymore, as my mother once said to me you don't talk Yiddish you scream it, that's' the way conversation has become now—why I never learned Yiddish. Mostly because people my age have run out of possibilities even as some have to do something before the possibilities run out. Yes they divorce now, Liliana says: one last chance at happiness before we die, I remember using that line on my last lover before I decided to go celibate. You don't have possibilities when you're young, she says, only old because then you know of how few choices (chances) you actually have before your possibilities dry up. You have less chances when young because you have unlimited chances like if you have many boyfriends you really have no boyfriends, she says. When older you finally have the chances to do all the things you said you were going to do when younger, not that everyone does them, but at least now you can attempt and not worry what other people say, when you are younger all you want is to be happy, have sex, get away from your parents, be like everyone else, and all your energy goes into those activities, some of my girlfriends never went to college because they used all their strength to get away from their parents, mostly into unhappy marriages and it took them time to figure that out and by the time they did stuck with babies it would take another twenty years for them to leave, luckily for me the culture changed and some of us were allowed to get out. Older you don't have to worry about being popular, famous, a celebrity, have to do something, do something, only after you have some experience under your belt can you begin to realize your authentic goals, ones that you're willing to work hard for and the others are all bullshit, and to get yourself moving and if you can do that you might be able to get through the day; junkies, alcoholics gamblers can't even do that without artificial stimuli to get through the day, other time-servers use sports, sex, another day at work—always looking for excitement, but excitement is not life only an escape from boredom, when you're young you think it'll always be like this until you reach that juncture—it's almost as if it is a spiritual puncture of your soul—the only time you can talk metaphysically, where a bolt of lightening flashes, of course, the discontent has been there all along regardless if you recognized it or not, in dreams, in depression, in your daily activities, but all of a sudden you realize you actually have to do something otherwise you won't get out of bed in the morning, even if you must get out of bed, you can't stay curled up in the fetal position forever, and because if you don't get out of bed that morning you know you'll never get out of bed again, so you face yourself in the mirror and that's the beginning or the end depending upon where you're standing as the observer, because now life no longer looks full of possibilities it only led down a narrow path and it's difficult to find another road especially if it's going to be unpaved, less traveled, now you have a restless face, and no matter what metaphors you tell yourself they no longer work and you have to struggle to get up each morning, it's here, now, that living becomes intense, when you start to live the moment not as if you are passing through it; so don't talk to the young about possibilities it's only those who won't let the moment slip by again that it will resonate, when young you decide to become dull and boring talking trade-offs, only those who have wrestled with a dream, slowed down time and began to think about what they want besides not to grow up—a favorite tactic of women (I want to interrupt and say men too, but don't) and when you slow down the day long enough that you can begin to think how you want to live instead of just living you put your life aside and learn how to live; no longer is it possibility it is life itself that hangs in the balance and that is why, Liliana says, you never heard from me again. I remember how she would awaken with a bloody nose and I realized she was fighting with someone in her dreams. Never did I realize it was me. I don't recall she says. All I recall is that you were a good sleeper like a baby. Now I sleep in dribs and drabs I tell her, no longer needing the large amounts of sleep that I once needed—we each recall different moments of the relationship. Only when you realize everything is at stake can you make the wager, she says, make the leap, she says, which might fail because failure is our lot, but failure at what you desire is more important than success at what you don't, you now make the effort because you are only interested in the moment—not like some women who can spend seven dollars on a hair dye to totally change her look. Lucky women I say, we men, have to spend far more, to get a Z car (sports car) some trollop or become homeless on our voyage of self-discovery. Mine was more serious than that but I agree with you sometimes we are only left with metaphors to describe actions, you can't name them any other way—where our language itself is incomplete because if metaphorized it's not really named only described artificially and a void exists between the thought and the action, which vulgar psychologists nicknamed the mid-life crisis. You hit rock bottom but still to climb out it has to be done with thought otherwise your reacting and you'll simply get back into the same situation again like leaving one bad job for another. Or one bad woman for another, I interject. She smiles, we laugh, we laugh together. She continues, you don't want to recreate what you just left—you can't be only as happy as your un-happiest child. You must find your desire, your passion, and that takes time there are no shortcuts, and I slowly found that out it wasn't in excitement only restraint. Hey I too found out freedom is in not doing what your impulse tells you to do. Why I became attracted to you while living with Jeffrey was the excitement even if I can't pinpoint the moment you changed from becoming a friend to being a lover. It wasn't when we slept together, that I am sure of, she says. It happened before that, I say, when I was able to phone you and enjoy talking to you not only Jeff, I say. We both didn't do well with temptation Liliana says. Jeffrey should have chaperoned us everywhere but our fun was in doing things we liked together, she says, our freedom was in doing things we enjoyed together and Jeffrey didn't enjoy them or was it in simply shocking others in that we could do things together and not be sexual with each other, but I wouldn't have told you that and you wouldn't have heard it even if I told you because I could change the world with my words but couldn't listen to myself, I had to learn to speak about myself, not my men, my job, my children. Discernment in language is the first step towards freedom, I say. Liliana agrees: you can only develop sophistication in language that doesn't hide our thought but tries to put them in relief as you age. She continues to drink. My stomach rebels, I get up the barkeep immediately points to the bathroom she doesn't want my vomit mixed in with the sawdust— I'm thinking this would be a nice place for my remains body and soul mixed together, forget about throwing my ashes over the city, besides it's against the law—pollution and all that, but how about in sawdust is there a law against that? I make it to the urinal and it all comes up—I must have read that somewhere I'm not that clever to think it up myself—last date the book was taken out was

1972 then me, there was some kindred spirit back then and we read the same novel written in the thirties—amazing novelists when finished are history while poets are for all time—this thought holds me as the regurgitation continues, someone is in the toilet but the trough is free only it's a women's room refitted into a men's bathroom that I have liberated. When he comes out I rub my head on the cold toilet, it feels good he asks if I'm okay, it comes out all mixed up, I say I won't drink anymore I can't stand the smell and Heidegger comes to mind somebody once said he was more serious a philosopher than Sartre, where am I getting this from? and I couldn't believe he said that, he as an academic philotaster so seems more profound because he used more obscure terms living in an academic cloister and also in his case deep in his hut in the woods, while Sartre's novels, plays, and philosophy displayed a more engaging wit, style—forget about Heidegger's subservient behavior to the Nazi state while Sartre lived free, that reminds me I am going to see *No Exit* again where he tries to use words and the logical concepts of language to describe our irrational condition. I flush, the cold feels good on my head—there's nothing like nausea when thinking of Heidegger, oh I get it nausea leads me to Sartre and Sartre to Heidegger, but what about having my mind and body interred in a bar mixed with sawdust? I wash myself with cold water, Liliana bursts in wondering if I am okay, I just need a break I tell her, she's sorry she didn't realize I don't drink that much anymore. We can leave if you want? And go where? I'll drink less; good conversation isn't that easy to find I don't want to let it go to waste. Give me a moment since there is no attendant to give me a towel, wouldn't that be cute in a dive bar like this for there to be a bathroom attendant like at the *Plaza*. I would pee there just to have an attendant hand me a warm towel until they switched to paper towels and now there's no more *Plaza*, I say. You want bowler hats, a stick, and starched shirt collars to come back as well, she asks. She holds my head up and asks how I made that pirouette to get away from the urinal, you should be in a ballet, she says, I laugh not even conscious of it. But I never observe my surroundings usually simply pass through them so when I walk if I don't have a conscious recollection where I parked the car (I now try and write down the street and avenue) sometimes it takes forever to retrace my steps, mentally I am somewhere else inside my mind even when I try and feel the moment. Now I'm in a bathroom spilling my guts out thinking Heidegger having an ongoing conversation with a woman I love which continued together, apart, in dreams, awake, in walking the streets solitary or in company that might last until my final day. What I love admire about Liliana is that she introduced me to all this and I've forgotten how enjoyable it is to talk to somebody about this, she introduced me to modern intellect and we conversed about it after—where my uncle tried she succeeded. With her I always had a partner to do things with she was not only my lover at the time but my best friend. Now I go alone because if you wait for the group, i.e. my wife, I don't go. Did I ever learn anything by myself? Never! Artists are not unique individuals only copycats I only learn when I get out of myself and into my creations so I have no idea who I am or what I believe only what my poems say. Liliana escorts me out of the bathroom and back to our booth.

Inside the booth Liliana orders me a *Slivovitz Fizz*—plum brandy, was she out of her mind? But it calms my stomach. Where was I? Oh yea, the moment in life when I couldn't hold in my vomit anymore, when I realized it was all bullshit, when I realized my own life wasn't a real life, I came to this moment in analysis, in reading, in living—a juncture—college hadn't touched me, life had destroyed me, my parents and my uncle, who I thought would live forever, were now dead, now only thought could save me. I could settle, but I didn't want to settle, at least now I wasn't

going out and having affairs with all sorts of self-righteous justifications, and I was working in an office making decent money
always depressed or down if not clinically depressed because I said
I wanted to write poetry but I was doing everything but writing
verse. Doggerel yes, verse no. Liliana breaks in; only those women
who didn't have affairs with my boyfriends were my friends by
then. That's how I know I became human I tell her when I gave
up being the class clown or the pretentious clown—acting serious,
go figure, I gave up being cute with others and was able to start to
be myself. I no longer even wore glasses, so others would think me
smart, let my beard grow ungainly, loosened my tie, I wanted no
more disguise, no more pretense then started discarding suits and
ties all part of another world, the world of appearances, what do
appearances matter? Appearances matter a great deal, Liliana says.
I was disgusted with going through the motions and worse being
successful at these, others were envying me, can you imagine that?
People envying me, for what, and I'm looking around seeing boring people everywhere, some who could only do the job by taking
short breaks to recharge their batteries, others who would spend
the entire summer in the Hamptons. What happened to Coney
Island I would ask? No blacks in the Hamptons comes the reply,
if it was an honest reply. Me, I wanted somehow to break from
myself and the only thing I wanted to do was learn, not to be a
student but to really learn, really understand all that I should have
been taught, of course, only in retrospect can I draw this outline
an adumbration of the moment, which only upon looking back
seems to be a juncture but while in it it was a long night's jour-
ney into thought where I was trying to calm my passions, and lead
a rational life more that I wanted one of easy virtue. Luckily I
had saved some money and realized the disillusionment of worldly
goods quite early, I became Mother Teresa giving away most of
my possessions, the accoutrements as I called them, playthings that

weren't important, and I could laugh at myself and my foibles and this helped. Not to mention you met Galina, Liliana interjects. Yes, it is easier with someone than without. I learned from her we could go onto other things. I began to realize the person I had become was not the person I wanted to be, it would have been easier if I had a mentor but I didn't make friends easily by then, I couldn't be with friends long enough and even now when old enough to be a mentor and am willing most young know more than me and refuse to listen. Which is okay, I wouldn't have listened either, while you were picking up licenses putting them in your back pocket, so to speak, because you never knew when you would need them some day, I was disposing of all unnecessary goods so as not to be able to ever use them again, I say. This mentor stuff is the stuff of dreams, Liliana says, we have to go through it alone for it to have lasting value; you no longer wanted to be part of the silly people like when younger you wanted to be in the army to show them a Jew could be tough. How does she know this? When I began to cook, I looked for long cuts, started reading in the morning, shopping in the afternoon, got into the habit of making a new meal each night instead one or two for the week. No more short cuts, only long ways. A man who can cook is sexy, Liliana says. Galina lets me cook for her. Now I start to doubt, only in false memory is there a juncture that changes your life, a decisive moment, all moments continue leading one way or another, or I could have just lain down and died, of course, metaphorically, I might still be alive but I wouldn't be living. But I did begin to learn to live means more than sensual pleasures. You were growing up! Oh how common-place that is. She said there are no decisive moments in one's life unless maybe you're six and your mother dies. Lucky you weren't a woman in the Middle Ages you would have gone into a nunnery and been trapped for life. As it is I assume you thought of the Jewish solution, Israel. What have I got in common with the Jews? I wanted to free my imagination not go to a war-torn country where I would be considered an occupier. That's why I rid myself of my car began to walk again even when the city was unsafe (of course I walked on the safe side of the streets) and would compose couplets or sometimes memorize lines of poetry to try and make them mine. Did you stalk pretty women in your walks? I would only follow older women (that looked like you) who would never look around; young women would immediately knew they were being followed and that ruined the fun, I didn't want to harm anyone just have somewhere to go. I can't keep anything from you. Occasionally I would "accidentally" end up in your neighborhood and would look up and see if I could find you, once you came up on me unexpectedly—surprised me, usually I would spot you first and would stay discreetly in the background seeing you was enough to torture myself or to jog more than I ever ran before, after seeing you I even did a half-marathon, three times around Central Park, the big loop six miles, the lesser loop four miles and the reservoir a mile and half then I ran home, the most I've ever run, telling myself now I can tell my grandchildren I ran a half-marathon even if I didn't even have children then. Childish nonsense but you only get a love like that once a lifetime if you're lucky and like empty prayers that float up to heaven while your thoughts stay below it passes but you realize the intenseness of your silliness and if you can die in that moment you're lucky but you don't die you go on and on and all the rest is a footnote after you have tasted intense love and that taste is bittersweet. Now I stop my fizz and ask for another glass of red wine, my mouth desires the taste of pure wine not a substitute for one and the barkeep brings over a carafe of red wine. Are you going to twirl it? she asks. I put my hand on the stem, lest my fingers artificially warm the wine, let it breathe catch the aroma—California yesterday, and pronounce it fit to drink. Friends are now into cheap wines, and I'm only too happy to drink with them, but for me fine wine is the way to go. Liliana looks at me, I'm not sure she gets what I'm getting at, she should, but only if she can read my mind, and I'm too old now to think of women as these emphatic beings, then I think how I would hurt Galina and I would never do that. Still I remember my mother thought she could tell what I was thinking before I even thunk it and recall deceiving her, telling her I was playing with friends when I actually snuck on the subway and traveled down to Harlem and saw my uncle, luckily he didn't see me or he would have told her and she would have known I lied, she never knew anything about me because I was a duplicitous child, lying so much I now don't even know what was true. I look back at Liliana's hazel eyes that have turned gray in the dark or maybe they were gray all along, at her turned-up nose, which is Roman—what a memory I have? Again she reaches out and touches my hand but I'm not sure what that gesture means: she feels sorry for me or she understands. But what is there to understand without her meeting me I would have become like them: my other friends, dull, boring, happy, or make-believe happiness, I have to remind myself I had to go through the breakup to become who I wanted to become and when I see my old friends, who I imagined were happy, I saw how unhappy they were even as they couldn't admit it to themselves they couldn't be alone. I should talk, I think. Are you happy? How can you answer that question? I know your type remember I lived with you and Jeffrey who were always going to start projects Jeffrey was going to start a novel that's what college graduates did in those days now it's film or tour with a rock band. In the sixties the word was holy now it has given way to MTV. A cultural chasm opened up when reading truly ended and concentration became limited to three-minute sound bites, even as songs went to long playing each record was still only three minutes long and now nobody reads unless in controlled situations like a subway, an airplane, the beach, and then only brainless claptrap, she says. I think of my uncle's opera recordings some even 78s and I actually bought a record player that played them because I didn't want to throw them out. Then ten years after his death a group of his friends invited me to a memorial in one of their houses, I'm surprised, they're friends, I'm family, these old codgers I was just a kid to them, but she too had a record player and asked that I bring some of his old records and we listened while reminiscing about him and what I realized is that he had a life outside me. Of course he did, but I never realized it—his American friends as he called them, in his new life, mostly younger than him, he loved helping out young people—giving back is what he called it, strangers helped him get started when he came here and he helped others in return, students, lost waifs, divorcing women, when it wasn't so easy for a divorcee to get started again, and we sat at a long table talking about him, each one stood up and mentioned a story about him and they all claimed to have met me at some time or another, but I only recalled one of them, it was like living with history—once I came into his apartment unannounced and saw a stranger there, I quickly looked around the room for a dead body, pulled myself straight up, I was young then I could take him until I saw he was built like a brick shit house and I would have been toast, but he introduced himself as a friend and that I must be his nephew. This little old man sitting in front of me, drooling, his false teeth in a glass jar, was this scary stranger. I found out all sorts of things about my uncle, what is spoken aloud in the family is not what is felt, it was to his buddies that the true sense of propriety which I didn't see then but now understand. He was gay. I walked out disappointed that he didn't tell me and that I had to find out from friends not from family, like it was some great big secret that he didn't trust me with, except even when I joined the Army he always wanted the best for me and wanted me to become cultured and he thought the life of the mind was a gentler life than a soldier.

I used to make fun of his life never realizing I would want to live it one day. His cosmopolitanism was an affront to my family, he cooked, a man cooking was just not done the excuse made for him was that he was a bachelor and had to eat, but we would invite him so that he had home-cooked meals. How he must have hated my mother's cooking? And one friend of his talked about how he came back after the war (he meant the second world war) and refused to go home to his parents' flat in Brooklyn and my uncle let him sleep on the couch encouraged him to go to law school and even lent him money to help with tuition. I remember my uncle offering to pay my tuition at a private school but I didn't want to be beholden to him, to take money from an uncle, my parents thought he was crazy (so did I) to pay good money for schooling when you can get it for free but he liked that one private school history teacher that he knew would take his charges to see off-Broadway plays, or to foreign films and education wasn't only confined to the classroom. Then I was too much my parents' son to be interested in intellectual thought, instead told him proudly that my class went to see the *Music Man* on Broadway, as if that would silence him. And nothing he could say would convince me of the joys of the life of the mind yet he did not abandon me and continued to visit even giving me a key so I could come anytime but I hardly ventured into the city, as we called Manhattan, mostly staying only in my neighborhood unless I had a specific reason i.e. school to leave. When I did go into the city I went with Jose and his bunch to hang out in Spanish Harlem and now that I could go on my own hardly left the neighborhood. These old men and one woman did and did not help bring him closer to me, they distanced themselves from him in being so old but they brought me closer to him because they were his friends and you're only friends with people like yourself, and my life seemed to be following his arc and these old men and women—not so old now as I look back on it, were a reflection of him. I don't want to go further with my thoughts but I was appreciative that they invited me to this reunion even if I was a relative. What I always loved about him was his difference from my parents, he was the only adult I knew who wasn't married, widowed, had children, grown or not, he lived alone without children, as a child that seemed weird to me, as a child I thought every grown-up was married and had children, the one couple who were married and didn't have a child was because she couldn't conceive and my mother said he was stuck with her. The concept of marriage without a child or not being married was not on their radar. I assumed my uncle lived in loneliness, not alone, but lonely that's the way I was taught, men who do not marry are lonely individuals, and only when I was able to change my orientation was I able to see it from his point of view. He didn't want to be like his older sister, he had made his choice when he started thinking and when I started thinking made my choice but accepted his choice not condemned it—all my parents did was give into their silences and I'm sure they didn't realize he was a homosexual, nobody was back in the day, he must have enjoyed furtive sex, I wonder did he pick up men in bathrooms the only place to meet them and did he feel terrible afterwards. He wagered his existence on not what was given, all he wanted was to embrace life, he didn't settle and life emerged between the spaces of dreams of happiness and happiness achieved—the difference is no perfect moment only failures that you try not to get too far out of control, that couldn't be expressed in prose only verse, only metaphorically, not concretely only moods had to be understood: I kept getting into fights, arguments, anger, all moods that I could not understand or my inability to comprehend because I couldn't accept then my uncle died and I just didn't want to understand how the world continued everything felt so different to me without him and I had to clean out his apartment and I saw all these opera records (he had given me the Bechstein piano long ago) and paintings on the wall and at first I tried to sell them but nobody was interested or wanted to pay peanuts, nobody really was interested in old opera recordings or avant-garde paintings of two generations ago that weren't famous i.e. couldn't be sold for gazillions of dollars; and in his abode I felt his presence more than anywhere else, in his recordings, the paintings he kept on his wall, his books, the complete works of William Shakespeare and decided not to put them up for sale but keep them because they are mementos of him alive in me. Whatever was left I gave to his friends. Even if I no longer listen to records keeping them keeps him alive within me—I would have stayed in the apartment if I could somehow get my name on the lease, and occasionally still put *Wozzeck* on scratches and all and be reminded of him by conducting the piece, that of course I imitate but the musicians don't come in where I tell them to. I cannot lead a life exactly like his nor can I take the solitude as well as him and many times I reach out in the middle of the night to touch Galina, especially when thinking about Liliana. But at times I am most with myself when I am alone in my thoughts, which I can only do with Galina sleeping in the next room, if she were to leave I would die. I want to go back to my isolation but know that is impossible and when sitting at some dinner party bored saying to myself this is terrible why can't I be home listening to one of my uncle's records with my colored lights on because stereos no longer have those green or yellow neon lights, and I have to light candles or turn on colored light bulbs. This may be the only place I am truly content especially after a bout with others, it's my reluctance to mix with others that constitutes my freedom or sadness that affects me more at certain moments more than others. I need solitude but it frightens me why my poems aren't more successful is that I don't have the guts to follow my calling all the way—the wager, that one (I) could change my life but compromised and have taken in more of the world than I should have. I need others, a companion, sex, but more important someone to hug and hold especially after my uncle died there was only one who would attempt to understand me but that didn't take away my isolation, my loneliness, especially when I started cooking for all my friends, helping to keep my uncle alive within me making all his favorite foods, except I knew I would use it in my poetry; finally doing what he did getting up at three to start the day alter my day's mood use the same motif as my uncle because what else could I do. It wasn't the stars or fate that governed my life but a privileged birth away from Hitler or Stalin—geography is destiny; I didn't have an enemy I could fight except myself and my laziness or fears. I didn't have the power or insight to stand up to it before but only struggle with it even if I couldn't defeat it I tried not to become defeated by it—the days went by slower the years faster, time is not constant, I was no longer imagining a moment of happiness like after our life ended together even as I knew we couldn't be together. You're dead aren't you? She shakes her head yes. Happiness cannot come by a wrongful act, illicit love, life became spectacle for me afterwards, she continues, answering my question, pure chance if I had left by another stairwell I could have walked all the way down, I knew enough not to take the elevator, it came upon me so suddenly I thought as I walked down won't I have an interesting story to tell even if I had nobody to tell it to, long ago at the office my mantra was don't ask me for anything and I won't ask you for anything and I had gone my own way, polite, friendly, but distant and when some colleagues started walking towards the roof, I wondered have they been watching too many movies where helicopters rescue people, it can't be done especially with all this smoke, still there wasn't that much that I couldn't see and I could still breathe. Immediately I think poetry is good for watching others' lives not for living. Art is good by itself, she says, how else can you give events meaning where there is no meaning. I'm not sure what she is saying any-more to be the subject of an event is not the same as the event itself but she was the singularity in the event and found her place in this world by not being in this world, and then I stop and watch as a woman walks down the steps to *Café Purgatorio* and slips on black ice and a man comes running to help only she can't get up and he comes inside to get aid because she's hurt and he doesn't know what to do and when we all go outside the barkeep calls the police who try and lift her but she says she feels dizzy and he becomes afraid to lift her lest he damages her head and he too feels helpless and waits for the ambulance and when they arrive the caretaker on the other side of the driver gets out of the vehicle carefully, I expected to see them running to an emergency, but no he gets out slowly, carefully, but still slips on the ice and now he too is injured and the driver has to choose between helping the woman or his colleague and goes over to his colleague then to the woman then back to his colleague back and forth, meanwhile calling for more ambulances—and all the time I'm watching from behind the glass door, there's not enough room on the stairs for the throngs of people who have gathered there, and more ambu-lances and police cars arrive to protect their own—it's almost like a drill with three ambulances and four police cars for a woman who needs help with getting on a stretcher and now an emergency worker who has hurt his ankle, knee, leg? and both are spirited away; I think god the city spends a lot of money on these drills, like the police racing up and down Ninth and Tenth Avenue in order to practice emergency training as if terrorists would use the same techniques all over again, and that this costs us a fortune in taxes and pretty soon I'll be taxed out of the city. While an officer is writing out a summons the barkeep is throwing salt all around and breaking up the black ice with a shovel. She comes back and says the woman broke her shoulder. What about the emergency worker? He had heavy boots on so they think it's only a sprained ankle because of his deep boots. I feel drained passion is no longer in me when Liliana was around it never left me, even thinking about her brings it back to me, reality is such a downer; once I was deeply involved in life and could taste it from a more refined distance, not of this world and not of another because there was only this world and I was only in this world not another, seeing myself as a cipher always playacting, a voyeur artist like the clown who wears funny clothes always wearing disguises, and this proved it again because I did not move from my spot off to the side by the window until all the ambulances and police cars had left each one blocking the other even as the two injured were put in the first ambulance, which couldn't leave until the last ambulance navigated backwards onto the main street because there was only one way out. Then I saw a little ten-year-old boy walking on the ice slipping and sliding but continuing as the barkeep yells at him why are you walking there, why are you walking there, and I answered for him because he ignored her, because I'm ten years old and that's what I do and this is fun and only when they all went on their way did I go back to my booth, and only then did I sit down at my table and review inside my head what went on (and also surprised that Liliana is still there) and realized it wasn't the barkeep running to the front of the bar that attracted my attention, I saw it but it meant nothing nor the man running to help her I saw him out of the corner of my eye but still didn't move to help, or the woman moaning that attracted my attention I heard it but paid it no mind, it was only when I recognized the man as looking like Jeff that I actually got up from my seat and followed where he was running to, then I realized I saw the barkeep going to the front door, I had seen the man running and heard her moaning because if I had seen the woman fall even in my solipsism I would have stood up to help. That made me feel better, I am not as isolated as I thought I still care about other human beings—save a human and you save the world. I still have compassion, my uncle would say that night turns to dawn only when you help somebody. What sets us apart from other animals is that we have compassion he would say and even if we now know that other animals also have compassion and it doesn't set us apart nor does language now that chimps know sign language, or even the thumb to be able to use tools because some animals use tools, ironically the only thing that separates us from other animals is either our religion or art. Liliana says that you still are a gentle human being and that she simply cannot imagine me as a killer. What else can we do for others, she says, except show compassion? we must be helpful and try to help others. So it was okay to feel sad at Jeff's funeral, I was wondering why my sadness isn't pure but tinged with excitement that I now recalled again, after all Jeff and I parted long ago, sure I'm sad recalling my first meeting him, or at least my first memory of meeting him, I must have met him before to even have this memory, being in a candy store with him and both of us accused of stealing two-cent banana candy, actually he was accused of that, I was stealing chocolate bonbons, and the owner was threatening to tell our mothers; but we had nothing in common for a long time, yet it upset me and I was surprised feeling the way I did and kept thinking about how Allisson found my name in his phone book (he must have changed phone books but never taken my name out?) and called me and said she was going to have a service in the city when I asked her about the funeral, I imagine I was going to drive up there, she said it was all done already, but we will have a memorial service in the city for all his city friends—he didn't have any friends in the city, I wanted to tell her, luckily I didn't because many people showed, most of whom I didn't know, and in a way I was glad that the funeral was already; he had started a another life, even if the other life was probably the same as the old one—all that I knew from the old life, his parents, his buddies, are gone or scattered that's why I was glad I had missed the funeral, his death didn't even make the *Times*, like yours did, I didn't know of your new life as a financial wizard and had no one to call and what could I say we were friends long ago, I certainly was surprised that you were working for a brokerage firm I never expected that—the cold sweat that overcame me the night before Jeff's memorial service was excitement not sadness—I switched back to vodka the wine wouldn't do to keep the illusion going, but I don't want her to fade away, and I drink so slowly it doesn't even warm me up. How can she be real? Except Liliana is more real than most of the people I know, I feel an intensity in my life I haven't felt in a long time. I know I must continue rather than go about the business of living everyday, which is all boring, thank goodness for boredom I usually say to myself but not today. In between the physical world and my waking world a reality exists that is a far greater reality than the one I inhabit with my lazy mind I don't have to figure out how it got this way only continue along the path I have traveled and follow it to the conclusion. Liliana drinks to that, she likens it to a first kiss now it's out of the way and you can go on to other things. However, now that I know it's different I doubt if the conversation can be the same. Maybe not with the same intensity, she says, but it will have similar meaning, she intones. She tips her glass into mine and says I am correct that whoever saves a life saves the world and she was sorry she didn't have a chance to say goodbye to me but when I left you the way I did I wasn't sure you still wanted to hear from me. Me who would dream about her naked, folds and all, her milky white skin and us making love, only to hold Galina afterwards as if feeling guilty that I had such impure thoughts, and never did I think of her when making love to Galina only when we don't make love in a while and say things like you know we should do it? Why don't we? And we'd have to make sure we went to bed at the same time, Galina unfortunately is a night person and misses the early morning—for me the best part of the day worshipping the rising sun. And now that our daughter is off to college the honeymoon has started once again, at least on weekends. I tried to keep you out of my mind by keeping busy computers, finance, buying real estate, going to the gym, raising children, all helped in not allowing me time to myself, which I used for a good purposes in making sure I didn't think about my past, losing myself in my life allowed me to live my life otherwise I should have worn black all the time, but the middle ages are over and I didn't want to wallow in the past, the past once completed is over even if I knew full well that was a lie. I would be at work early, even if nobody could see me, and come home late (I could afford the child care) and TiVo allowed me to organize my television watching, have a drink and relax and start over the next day—Sisyphean labor—my commute was such that I had to start like you with the rise of the sun and the commute is also better early before all the jam-ups. I enjoyed listening to the traffic reports safe in my office with my coffee and bagel. Unlike you I tried not to put anything into words that are lies anyway. I never read anything you wrote. All I write about is you. I didn't know. A lie, I say. I did send you one my first collection of poems, (*Por Qué/Porque*—Why/Because) I say. I took pleasure in burning that, she said. I wanted to keep you alive within me, I say. I took pleasure in watching each page burn, I'm surprised I didn't burn down the apartment and tore out each page and put it in a black cast-iron skillet and watch as the page crumbled under the gas heat and once one page burned put another one in and when they were all finished mixed up the ashes and put them into a dish and let the wind take them. I enjoyed that I have to admit. I did really try and read some but you have to be in the mood to read poetry and my life didn't allow for time to let poetry in. I remember being shocked that I did that, I shouldn't have been so careless with the written word: words are to be read not burned. In the beginning was the word. No in the beginning is imagination, I say. But the drawing of you on the back, she says, I kept in my wallet and I always said I would get rid of it when I changed wallets but never did, it must have burned up in the inferno and by then you weren't so important to me only as a reminder, a faint one at that, of who I once was. You were a lie to yourself, she says, I am the only one who you think about even when you think about others; it's me you followed or women who looked like me only younger versions of myself or whose personality drove you to them. What kind of person are you to lie to yourself, like that? You weren't like Jeffrey a different person when talking to different people, Jeffrey had the talent to mimic a person's accent, when talking to Gilly he would speak black, when talking to you Bronx, when talking to strangers within two or three sentences he could follow their incantations, their mannerisms and their accents you were always the same, you had a core identity there was always something there, conversation with you was always meaningful, you did not chit-chat, Jeffrey once wrote me a long letter explaining all this to me but he didn't include a return address so I knew he didn't want to be found. That's how I know you meant something to him. He actually called me after 9/11 wondering if you were alive, I say, but I didn't know so didn't respond. Besides you, I think, I knew nobody who worked down there, can you believe it? One acquaintance who I thought might work near there but I saw him on the subway a few days later so I knew he wasn't hurt and it turned out he only worked near there not in the twin towers. Jeffrey must have come down to the city to see what happened and if he could find news of me? He had a summer job, once, on Wall Street, before the Trade Center was built, but I doubt if he still knew anybody from a job in high school. I remember, thinking back to how happy he was the first day of school began and he didn't have to wear a tie. He was like that living existentially; he did that also when he ran away to Vermont. That must have been difficult, I say, when you didn't go with him, he didn't bring his sex with him, the movie theaters must not have shown avant-garde movies, no plays so to speak of, and certainly no *Filmore East*, he haunted places like that live musical concerts where you could get a contact high there was so much dope being smoked. We lived here all our lives and took it all for granted but you didn't you were the one who took us to all these places, showed us the city we lived in, we only knew our neighborhood, didn't really know the city, Chinatown, Little Italy, the Village, the off-Broadway shows, you even showed us the Italian section of the Bronx where we went for hero sandwiches we would never ever have traveled into other neighborhoods it just wasn't done—all I knew was Germantown and only because my uncle would take me to cafés around there, it's only strangers who get us out of our routine and show us new places in our old haunts. You took me to the Staten Island Ferry, the Empire State Building and the Statue of Liberty, she protests, made me feel like a tourist, she says. It was also the first time I had been to those places. And because of you, I say, even though I had been once before, we actually went to a serious Broadway play and hung out at Times Square one New Year's Eve. She laughs recalling that time when Jeffrey didn't want to go out and so she went with me but I made sure Jeff knew where we were, so it wasn't a date but that I was taking out his woman when he didn't want to go out. I was doing him a favor. It's true I learned the city through your eyes before that I would pass through it but never stop; thinking Village people were phony the only real people lived in our neighborhood. And you would show me celebrities that I would never have recognized, of course I was too cool to acknowledge their existence but you would always spot Mick Jagger stoned or Joe Namath drunk. I tell her that I did walk past *Studio 54* once when an actress got out of her limo and had the most bored look of all, yawned, and they immediately let her inside, but I never had enough guts to try it and I had no interest in night clubs. We went to the *Peppermint Lounge*, she reminds me, when the Twist was in fashion. My last night club it was so boring then we thought we could mingle with the rich and famous and be cool and we would be rich and famous because we were seen with them. Again we laugh. No longer do I even dream about being famous. All of a sudden the bar becomes silent, the juke box goes off, the murmur of conversation stops, the barkeep is quiet in the corner, I don't know why but all of a sudden it became quiet, rarely do you have moments like this and I would always marvel how it could become so quiet for one moment and then the noise would pick up again and life would continue again and I did enjoy the absence of noise and now believe if a tree falls in the forest and nobody is around to hear it there is no noise—noise has to be heard to be considered noise. It is in these moments that one begins to think, if experience has taught me anything, a doubtful proposition to say the least, it's that the only reason to continue is if you can be reincarnated but with our previous knowledge—what's the sense of perpetually coming back and starting all over from scratch I wouldn't do it any better the next time; does this show that a god has a sense of humor, our failures are always connected or we can only hear them in the sounds of silence and how we react in these moments, I tell Lilly the in-between is what counts. She says I never called her Lilly before next are you going to say how nice I look, the modern way of not talking to a woman by saying she is attractive—usually the noise is so loud I don't have to think these thoughts and we no longer have serious conversations only chitchat, it's all off the top of one's head like IM's not letters where you can actually think about what you are saying. Liliana does not apologize but we agree one changes the subject so as not to get to deep nor explore ideas, thoughts, moods, like me sitting here next to her and my penis telling me it doesn't like to take a vacation, but you can continue to chat using clichés like doesn't she look nice, or she has perfect manners, or my favorite she has such white teeth! It has taken me a long time to begin to answer that it's only appearance and when it's only appearance men wear suits and ties to void off seriousness, it's even better than language to hide thought. But it is only through the intellect can we finally realize the inadequacy of the intellect and want the body, but only after having sensual pleasures do we realize how limiting they are without the intellect. I've been so looking forward to seeing Liliana again to show her how much I've changed to impress her with myself, to show her I am not the same individual I was when she knew me—that I now would not bed her if she were my best friend's woman, to have been able to make holes in my character, not to have drifted along and as I think these thoughts I realize how tenuous my position is because as I moved away from my childhood friends I moved closer to her, never calling Jeff because we had little in common, we weren't interested in the same things, no longer would I discuss politics, civil rights, capitalism—we had all learned the mantra: the philosophers have only interpreted the world, in various ways; the point however is to change it. Never: In a country where the sole employer is the State, opposition means death by slow starvation. I became more interested in poetry than reform realized the world was ridiculous and the people who placed their hopes on revolution were doomed also boring, especially when all they did was quote Marx. Jeff had become a prisoner of his thought, always blaming the Man for his victimization and still to this day I have difficulty expressing myself directly and can only use indirect communication (poetry that has so much more intensity than prose) to figure out what I think, no longer having pat answers only questions. I wanted to live alone a solitary figure but I couldn't, even now must exist with others. You just can't know something you have to develop a taste; so when I no longer rolled up my tee shirt with a pack of cigarettes—to my credit I never did get a tattoo of my mother—Liliana shows me her tattoo of a little rose above the knee. I realized I had changed—I stopped smoking when I started jogging because I simply had no wind while the previous generation i.e. my uncle couldn't exercise because they smoked and had no wind. That was the beginning of a change but Liliana says that occurred when we lived together and we used to go jogging together. I don't recall. Yes, yes she says, and reminds me how she changed her name from Lilly Ann to Liliana at her guidance counselor's suggestion, when she came to New York, no longer would she be Lilly, which she thought was such a little girl's name but Liliana a more sophisticated name. I would take possession of my name she says, This is the human condition, which is a vague way of saying our finitude is part human and the rest is running on empty because we can only slightly alter our ideas, our thoughts, our moods and as we age we become more interested in our failures not our successes and complete failure is no longer an option anymore, nor is perfect happiness, and all we have are moments—your silences, that you just mentioned between the tree falling and the wonder if a sound emanates even if no one would ever hear it. Then she points to a little boy out playing in the snow (since when did it start snowing?) and his mother in a hurry pushing him along but he has no use for his mother's schedule until she has to come back and grab him by the hand—he lets out a howl, it pierces through me even though I cannot actually hear it because the bar door is closed and there is a constant background hum inside the bar—but even if he didn't scream I heard it. He has to exist on her schedule only when we become free can we exist on our own schedule. That's what true freedom is, Liliana says, being on your own time. It takes time to realize that and you are one of the fortunate ones who is able to do that, she says, because when we are finally physically and mentally able to do that the world usually knocks at our door and we say we cannot eat the dessert first, it's only after practice can we learn to do that. And when we learn that we can learn you can eat from the tree of knowledge. Enough of that stuff already I'm sick and tired of hearing about your struggles, get thee to a nunnery, the silence stares back at me, if I could stare at a blank wall for fifteen years then I would have a chance, I say, but I don't even have enough guts to run away like Jeff did, at least he got away from all this to an idyllic scene if even as I say it realize it must have been lonely for him up there, you can't easily start all over again, you're not leaving one place and totally transforming yourself, the same self comes along with you and he must have spent years being lonely before he fit in, if he ever did fit in, (I can see him lonely up there sitting in his bedroom watching television all the time) it isn't easy hooking up finding someone one you can be silent with, spend time with, who has the same sense of humor as you. I wonder did she? Or is it like our sense of smell the first to go when we became civilized, his sense of humor changed from being so isolated, and did his children (how many did he have?) know anything about his past life or by definition he was only their father not someone who had a life, who goes through the same things they go through, the same doubt, questioning, but the one who has the answers becomes the Law. You can't have the Law with humor only authority, Liliana says. He never contacted me forgot that I existed, she says. When we parted it was like we never existed as a couple. You left him! He continued with his life as if I had never been there and then runs away to Vermont. Did he go with a girlfriend? Did he have a job beforehand? Did he even check out the place? He simply left without a word packed up his bags in his old *Volkswagen Beetle* and drove off into the sunset, he always liked to do dramatic things like that; over there will be his new life not realizing the old life would follow him into his new life, I should know I thought I'd have a brand new life when I left Iowa, and I'm glad I left don't get me wrong, but it is the same life, nothing changes, but I would have gone crazy if I stayed home, so maybe leaving was also best for him—but to never see him again, that was hard for me. Seven years is not nothing we slept arm in arm when I first met him, you don't forget something like that, we slept together in his parents' home, he wanted me to sleep on the couch at first and sneak into his bed but I was a liberated woman and wouldn't put up with pretense and went directly to his bed to the shock of his parents. Unlike nowadays, I say, where my daughter makes sure her boyfriends stay on the couch out of respect for the parents. Finally we moved into our own apartment. We could do that then, now it's unaffordable. Not true, I say, students now move to other parts of the city Manhattan isn't the only game in town anymore and their movements bring vitality to other neighborhoods. The parties, the drinking, the sex, the people coming in all the time, the all-night conversations, you can only do that as a student once you have to get up early the next morning it's all over, she laughs. In Iowa they rolled up the sidewalks at eight at night. They did that in other parts of the city as well, I say, but not anymore, I say, a new vitality has hit the city, Manhattan is no longer called the city as young people have found Manhattan too expensive they have moved into the boroughs now even my old neighborhood now goes by the street name of SoBro (South Bronx), even if revolution isn't in the air people are living exciting lives I say. Exactly, she says, we were going to change the world now it's only to make more money, these guys know nothing of art and literature—there are no new theaters in these areas only bars and social clubs: remember the discussions we would have Stalin versus Trotsky, there is no more intellectual chatter, she says. I don't remember. However I do remember my uncle telling me there are only two important literary characters

Socrates and Faust, Socrates who professed to know nothing except about love and Faust who always tried to do good and ended up doing worse. How many people today are going to be changed by taking a poetry course? Or even take a Shakespeare course? Now it's all to get good grades to get a good job to make money and move out to the suburbs where they have their own house and are the dullest and most boring people you ever want to meet. And if you don't do this stuff when you're young when do you think you're going to do it, she asks. When you're forty I say and can't stand your life anymore, I answer, and move back to the boroughs it's not only young people moving into the city these days, it's also dissatisfied corporate climbers. Yes but they are only running away. When you don't read you have no idea what life is only what you feel becomes life, how many of my colleagues had to take vacations in the sun, i.e. get away, and only life is a beach, even if they hated the sun and the beach but that's all they know, no one even suggested they go to the theater, a concert, read a serious novel, or listen to poetry. They would only use art for relaxation not for thinking, she says. Do you realize how many times I suggested to my eldest that she not do what everyone does and find her own way but today schooling is not education! Schooling teaches you squat, teachers don't appreciate art or literature they only say they do and students pick up on their bullshit, never taking students to live theater, foreign films, art galleries, concerts, students don't even paint, draw use pastels past kindergarten. When the budget cuts came the first thing cut is art i.e. civilization. When I look at pastels these days, I say, I'm disappointed, most of them are done quickly with an eye on the market not on the beauty, mostly it's anti-art color without emotion unlike modern graffiti color with emotion I say, thinking back to the day when graffiti first started and how the authorities refused to harness it and let them paint subways instead kept trying to remove it. We would have had some beauty then, I say. It's the same intellectual dishonesty they use in teaching—do as I say not as I believe. It wouldn't have been as great art, Liliana counters if the Transit Authority would have allowed it, only in opposition did graffiti have a chance to develop. Look at all the writing programs now and no great novels, art only works in opposition to the dominant culture, you'd think people would learn that by now. All art is destroyed when it becomes acceptable it is only when it has something to fight against can art be/become serious, all great art is fighting against something only we've lost sight of what its counterpart was because the art is most successful when it destroys the old forms in its wake. I shut up, she has thought this through, I haven't she has a point. But why won't these images not leave me, they weren't disgusting like dead bodies but poorly thought out, the colors came right up to the border so you couldn't tell where the painting ends and the frame begins so I couldn't visualize the colors without visualizing the frame as well there was no space between them to let me know what in the watercolors melds into the wall, and it was all the same sunset, all blending together, and now I realize what I couldn't at the art gallery, yesterday, when I saw these watercolors of the sunset, the paintings had no meaning—they were pure color, pure form without substance unlike graffiti where there is distance between myself and the colors, it wasn't as if the artist wanted to share his vision with me, not even as the sunset might have appeared to him, it was not real in itself to give the appearance of being real, he didn't even look at the sunset from different times or angles, and it left such a bad taste inside my mouth that I had to cleanse my palate and ride the only subway left with graffiti (the number 6 line the train that went to the Bronx where it all began) to get rid of the bad aftertaste. When I first saw graffiti on the trains it had a bitter taste and only when after seeing them for a while (quite a while, the Transit Authority couldn't really eliminate them it was the power of the people, sometimes trains were so covered with graffiti you couldn't even see out the windows to know what stop you were on, and even if you could the stations too were covered in art) did a certain sweetness come to them, leaving a nice aftertaste. I would enjoy standing on subway platforms, sometimes even without my Beckett, and look at the art, you could always find new things in the drawings. I was drawn to graffiti after my first few dismissals of it as ghetto art being pissed that it blocked my view out of the window or onto the station until I learned initial impressions can be deceiving and only later upon reflection did I see I was wrong. You mean your wife told you they were beautiful and you should respect the native art, Liliana says. One of the joys of marriage is you no longer have to think what you like your wife can do it for you, I say. Just like your mother did, she says, men are little boys who never develop their own tastes, believe me I know I worked with enough of them in the banking world. If divorced they were useless. As usual we laugh together. Then she says all good living comes from the Roman elite, the house in the country, fine dining, free sex and a good education. Isn't capitalism wonderful, I say, it's now available to the masses not just the aristocracy. But then she says she likes how I can still talk art and recalls when we would do things together, walk into galleries when we didn't want to stay together but neither did we want to part and we needed something to do. I barely remember because we weren't living together but know I had difficulty sleeping and being with her was a way to calm my nerves down—I think I could have slept except for the dreams, now I hardly sleep but my dreams are fine—progress! My last dream about her, was it last night? was that we were walking down the street arm in arm, only she was this old black lady from my building whose husband recently died, and even as I dreamt it wondered why I was dreaming about an old black women whose husband just died and in the dream realized of course she symbolizes Liliana. She mentions that going around the city with me was her true education, the art galleries, the concerts at *Washington Irving* high school, the films, and especially the off-Broadway plays we used to go to. School is a place for mediocre minds and it was easy for me, but it didn't give me any pleasure it fact it offended me, she says, so much so I avoided graduation when they said I graduated with high honors because I didn't deserve it—what had I learned? You know we didn't even read Plato or Shakespeare; I just couldn't attend even if my parents were willing to come into the city for it. It's with you that I became interested in that stuff, school interfered with my education, I say. It was in one of these moments, she admits, that she started thinking of me as more than Jeffrey's friend. She orders another vodka.

I knew and didn't want to know simultaneously, contra Aristotle, who said you couldn't know and not know at the same time; Jeff knew what he didn't want to know like I knew even if I didn't want to know and had no idea that I didn't want to know and I too didn't want to admit that our relationship with Liliana had to end that we couldn't continue the way we were going: for me, it was this drifting for him this doubt, and I can truly say my life began, as Jeff probably could say for his, when I said I wanted to live my life the way I pictured it not the way it turned out, and even if he ran away and I did not, we both decided somehow we had to make a change—it would have been nice if the State had given us some advice, but now I know that is impossible that freedom is finding your own way, that we would each have to find a way to live by ourselves and that I couldn't stay with a woman who would not be committed to me nor Jeff with a woman who was not committed to him. At first I thought if I get contemporary furniture (i.e. new) I could be happy and it took a while for me to realize even if there is a fundamental beauty in mere appearance as I bought attractive china, which meant I had to learn to cook, you can't eat take-out, which was then coming into its own, on gold-rimmed dishes, I recall seeing a friend at a Chinese restaurant and I went in to say hello and thought I would eat with him but he said no he was only taking it out—to go! I never thought of that, and then fast-food places were opening up around the city, fast food, macaroni and cheese or frozen dinners didn't have an aesthetic appeal off *Hutsehenreuther* china; it all starting after my uncle insisted I have his *Bechstein* piano, (he wanted it to have a good home) now everything had to go together—so I took some of his fine china as well, and after he passed the rest of the set—I was the only one I knew who had a complete set not mix and match china. Boy was Galina impressed when we finally met, even as she was surprised that a "Jew" would buy a German product even if I never heard that before i.e. to hold all of the new generation responsible for the crimes of a previous one. And you know what happens after a good meal, especially in the pre-AIDS days and to our surprise we became one from the moment we slept together, or as she says, the next morning when she awoke and smelled the fresh coffee and was able to start her day playing the piano, albeit with the lid closed not because I wanted to be considerate of the neighbors but because it was a big empty space where I could keep my papers, and I began to realize even if mere appearance helps you had to make an inner change to be different but the masque of the outer helps change the inner. Liliana smiles, as if she recalls the first time I came to dinner with her, alone, and she made a chicken paprika braised with onions, garlic, caraway seeds, green peppers and cream with spaetzle and I had brought a sweet white wine—*Liebfraumilch*, what did I know? at least it wasn't *Manischewitz*, which we proceeded to drink out of paper cups because she didn't have wine glasses, and after that we went on a mission to find good wine glasses. Then I moved on to fine china and a complete set of silverware that Galina and I bought as our first purchase when we moved in together. Don't you recognize yourself, she says, in what you were doing, she asks, it was with me you were starting out on your new life, you don't want to use me as an excuse but it is *moi*, someone you bedded, your best friend's girlfriend even if I was the one who was courting you, and we were spending more time together than I was with Jeffrey, even if we were living together, I wasn't sharing you with anybody and I was proud of the way you were developing your taste and Jeffrey knew what we were doing, even as he refused to admit it, he knew we were together most of the day, that you would meet me after class, that we would wander the city together, that we went to see movies together, plays together, concerts together, what did he think it would only be Platonic. By then our relationship was like a marriage going through the motions, inertia, we would have continued indefinitely if I hadn't made a change, he was anti-war, fighting the man, the system, standing on street corners handing out pamphlets, feeling so proud when he got a portable megaphone—he could blare his words far and wide then, not be limited by the handout—he truly expected the masses to follow, and at home he became his father an old man with his tank-top tee shirt, lying on the couch, his pants unzipped, his hand on his crotch watching football on our new color television, playing with himself. I feel virtuous as she says that, they offered me their old black-and-white one and I refused not wanting to waste my time watching television. Liliana goes on he put the small one in the bedroom, and I realized our relationship was in trouble when we both watched the same show only in different rooms. You were the only one I knew who refused to own a TV set. When Jeff called once he said he waited until halftime but I replied I don't have a set, oh those were the days, I loved saying I don't own a television if anybody asked, but hardly anyone did, of course, because they all assumed everyone had a set—it was now more than just entertainment it was a crucial part of life. That and when women were

surprised that I had been a ball player in youth, you played ball? all
the time I was out on the street day and night playing street ball
never wanting to go home and do homework. When did you get
so smart Jeff once asked? Liliana says if you look into your eyes you
see none of your adolescence but I could never really get rid of
those memories: why did Jeff have to run away? he too had this
imageless moment, I think, where he realized his past would become his future unless he did something—he once told me that
he never looked in the mirror as a teenager because it wasn't him,
did he when he was older, balder, heaver? I who did preen in the
mirror as a kid always combing my hair trying to get the wave just
right, but not as an adult, now do look in the mirror once again to
make sure my beard is brushed just right, because who I see (even
aged) I think is me, in that I can control myself better, I now have
a greater link to my past than I ever had while living it. Liliana
laughs, you who wanted to add more layers of hell for your former
schoolteachers are complaining about your perception of yourself.
Yes until one of them said you can't treat us like that because of us
you can read Dante. Did any of my teachers actually know Dante,
of course, they heard of him, educated people know his name, but
did they actually read any serious works—that's why I assign them
to different levels of hell. No teacher reads! Didn't Dante assign
his former teacher to the fifth circle, with writers and other poetasters? Yes but for other reasons, which we wouldn't assign today,
(i.e. homosexuality or repressed homosexuals). When I lived for
my senses I couldn't wait to get my hands on you, I dreamt about
you, masturbated to your image even when you were beside me,
I was always thinking of things I wanted to tell you, couldn't wait
until we saw each other again to talk to you, I don't think I have
ever talked to anyone as much as I had talked to you—now that my
answering machine is broke I can go through a whole day without
having to talk besides to Galina, and have no conversation with

anybody; back then sometimes I wouldn't let you finish a thought before I would jump in with one of my own, to tell you what I had seen, heard, thought, but now being without others no longer frightens me so, I rather be alone even if afraid sometimes that I might slip into a deep funk that I can get out of—even if I still need others, i.e. Galina, the threshold is less now and I channel my energy into my solitude, and only occasionally will a perky young woman charm me—now it is difficult being with others. Yet I remember, even feel it in recall, how I always wanted to be with you and going with you and having someone to talk ideas with and see plays with. Now I only go by myself. Liliana nods because she stopped going, after you, she says, none of my loves liked off-Broadway plays, foreign films, music we had to listen to, so we went to mainstream theater or more likely stayed at home, men are good at doing that. When I became rich and could afford it never used the intellectual accouterments of the city, no longer inhabited the weird scene as one of my boyfriends called it; I never did shit and love in the same place that was my only intellectual activity, she says laughingly. That was a no-no, and besides men thought if they went to bed they owned me, that was my weakness, my desire, I still needed men to pleasure, and to pleasure me, how many boring movies did I go with them to, or Broadway musicals when they felt so proud of getting hard to get tickets, as if I would appreciate their persistence, or football games, one guy even flew me down to Miami for the game of the century *Jets* football game, spent a fortune on tickets, flight, hotel room, and for that expected me to be eternally grateful. Finally I stopped going out on one-night stands, or even with lovers, said I had to be home for my little girls, who really never wanted me home they liked our housekeeper much better, she had a room of her own in the house, truly you could say I was the guest and the three of them lived there. Also it was getting more difficult to navigate the streets of New York at night; crime was everywhere, while before I was never afraid to walk anywhere now I took taxis everywhere. And since I was now working all the time the only men I met were the divorced or never married businessmen, i.e. the never married were never trained, the divorced were helpless, and both had such lowbrow taste the kind god gives to important men who have big but empty brains so the culture of ideas was foreign to them. You'd think the law of large numbers should work in my favor and once in a while I would meet someone who was interested in ideas, but once men pass a certain age ideas hold no interest for them unless it's cost analysis, i.e. how much is this going to cost me, which is why I started fucking younger men—young blood, that was fun at first one even used to grab me in the hallway and I'd laugh to my- self calling him young blood, so this is what it's like when they can't hold it in, occasionally I would take them to a foreign film or an offbeat play but all they could do is talk, eat popcorn or snore they didn't know how to behave in public places—their mothers hadn't taught them manners. They had no clue that different behavior is required in art houses than mainstream movie palaces, where you could talk all the time, some even wanted to make out with me, as if we were sitting in a balcony i.e. that reminded me of Jeffrey all the time, not you. Where are you? I wonder. I asked them if you can't appreciate a work of art, to me that was the ultimate sadness of their lives, they couldn't question, wonder, discuss. Eventually it became easier not to date. By then I had a clear career path first in computers then in finance, and with money bought the house in Jersey and if I needed to go out went to a gym. After a while I didn't miss the absence of culture, there is so little of it, movies are blockbusters now, theater even off-off-Broadway doesn't deal with vital issues, only occasionally can I hear some good concert, books, nobody reads anymore, so I eventually didn't even miss it because there is nothing to miss and I thought money is the report card of life, I remember thinking that thought and all at once thought of you almost like you were this opposition to all I had become—and it was a moment of doubt, the kind you went through when you didn't like the direction your life was taking, only you did something about it, this unconscious that thinks where it wants to be not where it's at and you have become that image for me. Life was dull but pleasant, and I quickly forgot about culture, ideas, paintings, and I would say that was once but now I have other goals. Did the world become a better place because people wanted to change it, did it become better because people were interested in culture, no, she answers. And I say remember when we saw the double bill of *Wild Strawberries* and *L'Age d'or* and we knew then and there that Marxists had no imagination and only art could save us? No, now I can barely sit through one film and we would sit through two, I do remember that, she laughs, art can save us? Did we ever believe that? Yes and I recall because I remember seeing it in *Annie Hall*, that you would not go in the movie in the middle we had to wait until the first show was over, you said it was like opening a book to the middle, and I never heard of that before, and there it was in *Annie Hall*, and now because of Woody Allen now nobody walks into the middle of a film, but trust me when I was growing up that never stopped me. Liliana doesn't understand there is a gap in her knowledge about me even as I kept her informed of everything in my constant conversation with her, she still doesn't understand that I am not the same person that I was when we were together, and that good intentions as I eventually came to realize, are not enough, and that in renouncing what I thought and felt by thought itself allowed me to move beyond myself. You can't continue doing wrong even if she isn't a piece of property owned by someone else; she was certainly his girlfriend and even when it was pleasurable to be with her even if we could have forged a new freedom together, and sharing was almost permitted back in the day, (as my daughter now calls the past) and it truly was her choice to make, still there is a gap in my thoughts where I felt I could not continue—to continue would mean to agree and to my surprise I was able to control, or limit, or as she said, avoided her by taking an afternoon part-time job so that we would see each other less. Yet I simply couldn't give her up, she who could complete my thoughts for me; and the sex was too good and she was so pleasurable to be with—Jeff was similar but he had that ability because we came from the same neighborhood and grew up together, even if we hadn't grown up together by coming from the same neighborhood, (i.e. the same people—exactly the same, meant we viewed the world the same way) and with Liliana or Jeff or Jeff and Liliana we could all sit and be silent together and enjoy each other's company. And here's the kicker when I finally renounced her Jeff decided to run away and she decided to switch careers. I hoped that by keeping my desires under control I could make some progress, no longer was I searching for my other half, a twinning so to speak, but now searching for myself—who did I want to be?—a person who thinks, and started on my processes of late development. Unlike Jeffrey who peaked early, Liliana interludes, you drifted while Jeffrey had goals, we followed whims together, while Jeffrey kept his eyes on the prize—he was always involved in the world while we slowly had to figure out how we wanted to meet the world, you with your crazy stunt going off and joining the army to show the world you're a tough Jew, me in my civil rights days who thought the only thing needed to make America a better place was equal rights for Afro-Americans. You finally figured out you wanted to learn, to write your poetry, to get up at dawn and create—true poetry comes not from inspiration but from continued intellectual labor—imagine you get more pleasure from reading than hanging out. My uncle was proud of that, he always thought I had it within me he said he saw that look in my eye, but desire wasn't disclosed until my act of renunciation even as I couldn't believe I had done it and keep crawling back surreptitiously to see if I made any progress now from where I was then. But I can only examine the moment I live in not the ones I lived in with the woman sitting across this booth from me, and even here I keep the wine glass between us, and I can't believe I once believed that if I gave her up I would ever be able to find myself. What I thought was that I would never find another girl yet I, me, *moi*, found for the first time in my life, (excluding my time in whorehouses) plenty of women, which meant I had no women, until I finally found the one woman. At least give your analyst credit, I think, you had to tell him what you did, it made no sense keeping it a secret from him even if therapy is difficult because you try and keep these things hidden not only from the analyst but yourself as well, and even if you were embarrassed to tell someone because it means you are really telling yourself, even if your desire to explain means you were tying yourself up in speech you were getting to the essence of thought via language. Fraud's therapy, she repeats. The loneliness became more bearable in speech, but home alone with the idiot box always on, (when I left Liliana I had to get one) I wanted to go onto pills, or back to serious drinking but instead drank my red wine—becoming an oenophile turning the wine bottles every day a quarter of an inch so that the corks would stay moistened, continuing to teach myself to cook because it killed an afternoon to go shopping in different stores looking for ingredients and then listening to the simmering flounder, mushrooms and dill in my cast iron skillet at night having dinner with all my imaginary guests—which somehow always ended up as you, even as I invited Socrates and Faust you always came in unannounced and dominated the discussion. Now I can see why it has taken me so long to get over her which I still haven't done, as she sits across from me, it was with her I was having this never-ending conversation, and when the light is dim as it is now I can still see her chestnut hair not her salt-and-pepper hair, how she looked when we parted and when I thought my heart would break—and I would be waiting for her phone call (being one of the first to buy an answering machine when it came on the market so that if she called I would not have missed it) that never came. And my childhood came to an end, both my parents were now dead and my uncle would soon follow, Jeff had left, he who I could talk about anything was gone, and you were no longer by my side—I appeared to be not who I thought I was—I had a dream that Jeff visited me in my uncle's apartment and I told him he could take whatever he wanted, he picked a book with a chestnut cover and I got so angry that I slammed the book down, then he asked if I could drive his wife to Montreal she wanted to go to *Ben's* for a smoked meat sandwich but I said I am too busy and couldn't go right now and he yells at me she's used to men helping her and then his mother comes up to me and says you had something to do with this didn't you? That dream made my analyst very happy we spent days talking about it and my explanations never seemed to interest neither him or me, nor my silences either then I began to wonder what I am paying him for. Again Liliana puts her hand across the table and gently holds mine, first rubbing her hand through my beard, no longer could she rub her hand through my hair not enough there, and here I think she is going to forgive me, but she doesn't, catching me off guard not repeating what I had said or done nor the motives that I said but rather that she feels a certain anger towards me for leaving her because you should have acted differently and no matter how many times I repeat that leaving to live on my own meant I always come to the same conclusion that I acted upon what I assumed to be true even if now I can see her point of view and she was right to treat me in the way she does because she did not respect my reasons and she still feels anger at my behavior because in acting the way I did I did not conform to her ideas even if it happened over thirty years ago, she still feels the sting. She claims I didn't see the big picture and was only concerned with myself and I as only thinking of myself and that even if she were living with Jeffrey we did nothing wrong: she is disappointed in my actions, expecting me to be better than that; she thinks I should have shown her more consideration tells me you should have continued to converse with me and if you continued our conversation your actions would have been different and you didn't want to consult me in your actions because then your actions would have been different—intentions do count because your actions can then be different, and you had no reason to take such unilateral action that was binding on both of us without discussing it with me; that you were under some obligation to me because we were in love with one another to discuss this before you decided to leave so suddenly when you called and said you couldn't see me anymore and not allow me to tell you my side of the story and refused my calls in that I destroyed her right as a lover. You should have been willing to behave more like a lover even when your love interfered with your friendship. You certainly held back a lot over the years, I think of this unique person who I always carried around with me all these years, incorrectly as I now find out, she who entered my dreams, who understood everything about me, who understood why I did what I did is now thinking I now dissed her by not having a give and take with her hence ruining all our lives. Not true, I say. Even as I didn't expect that from her, I thought the two of them would continue once I was gone and I'd be passing fancy and only I would suffer, that was not the case, the world is not only facts it also has metaphysical and dogmatic beliefs connected to those facts and I was too cynical at the time, more cynical than I am now, and thought that was the only honorable way to behave. I knew what I was doing was wrong and solved it the only way I knew how even if I realize now it wasn't the best solution or was it? I expected her to drink after that outburst, I certainly sipped my wine and kept the glass in front of my face, but she was quite calm, but I hoped she was burning with anxiety inside, I certainly am but the wineglass in front of me offered no protection this time. How could I answer? She is right I should have spoken to her but I couldn't all I could do is run away—I was good at that—why do you think I joined the army. Now even as I can defend myself, then I probably was afraid and she would convince me to stay when what I wanted was to do no wrong. The noble sacrifice! I played hero in my mind acting with the noblest of intentions like when I joined the army to serve my country, not because I was scared or bored, and what I always needed to do is create adventure like hooligans mugging people or stealing from people just for the fun of it, i.e. the rush—to be able to have an adventure, even as Jeff was able to say he went to jail for a belief. Jeff must have known he didn't do it for beliefs but rather to impress Liliana. But to be a hero as I now realize is to support the existing order even if that's not what I had in mind when I performed my act of heroism or cowardice as Liliana sees it. Here all along I thought she understood my motives even if I never told her I was sure she knew that she was my true love and certain things you don't have to say to lovers, but I didn't ever give her a chance to explain that she isn't a trophy that Jeff gets as if he won it, and she wasn't allowed to be part of the decision because I only thought about me in the decision, even as I mentioned Jeff and her in my noble thoughts—and all these years must have been as painful to her as it was to me even as I thought that I did what had to be done cloaking it in such noble gestures as renunciation, for the good of our friendship, I was always assumed underneath she understood even if she didn't agree with my way of doing it. Instead I now see she sees me as running away. My last hurrah she must have called it. No that was Jeffrey running away to Vermont, she says. You had an implicit lover's obligation to discuss this with me; you could not decide what's best for all of us. Now what are you going to do about it? The past is over no act can change my actions all I can do is try and explain previous actions with reasons and maybe I can modify beliefs and this way the future can be changed, I say. But before I can begin to even do that I need more alcohol. For the first time I look at the smallness of the rim of my wineglass and realize from the shape of the bowl and the tapering of the rim that they are deadening the complexity of the cheap-ass wine—you need space to let the aroma waft. That didn't stop me from ordering another glass and realizing that in a place like this you can't expect a wineglass large enough to be able to swirl and stick my nose in nor a crystal glass with a long stem, and realized as Liliana suggests that I was condemned to live an ordinary life. I look across at her try and remind myself she's not real, but if she's not real then what is I wonder, even if she is not here in front of me she is within me, and what she does say does matter. My attitude towards her is changing and when she first spoke to me I couldn't have given a reason for my jealousy because I was afraid to admit it to myself as if I said it the world would crumble, or we wouldn't see each other again, or we would have to see each other on a more intense level not the person that she only did things with, which was the reason she was attracted to Jeff in the first place while in college, to have someone to do things with because it was difficult for her to go to events alone. With Jeff then me she was able to see the city. It was only after college that Jeff retreated into his own revolutionary world—only revolutionaries have implacable values, hung out with his comrades never at home and no longer did they do things together that I stepped in—and women, even feminists still insisted on attentions even if not gifts, i.e. baubles: rings, bracelets, ankle and arm, earrings, necklaces, no feminists insisted that women give up those superficial accessories, but attention and a man to do things with couldn't be changed or so easily given up. Even today one of my greatest pleasures is seeing a woman well dressed and love shopping for Galina; who admits I have excellent taste but complains we have nowhere to go with the exquisite stuff I get her, so we dress to the nines for our Friday night meal. Liliana wasn't ready for wifehood when I came along and wasn't afraid to go out with another man as many women were/are, thinking of it as betraying their main squeeze, but usually a woman can only be a friend of a man if a) the man is gay or b) she has a man of her own. What do I know about women/all I knew then was my mother, what I saw in movies, and the women I had met in brothels, I didn't have a sister to show me women were human beings? In fact I was shocked not even surprised when she insisted upon paying her own way; nowhere did I ever see that, a man took care of a woman. It continued because I was weak and it was fun, but she didn't sentence me to an ordinary life, I did not have to retreat into ordinariness if I did not want to, now finally forcing myself to admit to myself even with all the misrepresentations of language and even if she pounces on my thoughts, when I think language only says things poorly language is the only means I have to explain things to myself not as a structured whole or even to hide my real thoughts—what real thoughts? Who is the one I am afraid of saying how I really feel to? Is there only truth in retelling a story within a story, three times removed from the actual event: the actual event, telling it to my analyst and then telling it to myself before it is actually incorporated within me—is language is the limit of my world? Yes and no! I actually did hit upon a truth about myself when leaving her, I am a weak individual even as I found out I couldn't let go, even as Jeff ran away and the field was clear for me. We had something, Liliana says, and something is better than nothing, she says again, and even if it might not have lasted you had an obligation to continue until it couldn't last any longer not stop it in the middle. You didn't think that then and left without a reason. Wasn't it obvious? Obvious to whom? It was obvious to you not to me, she continues, I became an instrument in your life from which you forced yourself to change but what about the person you used. You used me in order to live an ordinary life, but what if I didn't want that type of life that you forced upon me. I have to admit I thought that would be the last thing I thought would occur, in my imagination that is not possible and never will be possible. Liliana had to become herself like I had to find myself even as I wanted her I realized I had to give up what I wanted if I was to find a self beneath all my masks. But life isn't kaput after a love affair unless you manage to kill yourself (god knows, I wanted to die) and I was lucky there was no new war for me to enlist in where I would have been sure to get killed—Vietnam was over and new ones hadn't started yet. I hadn't realized what I was doing in contemplating suicide, until I almost fell asleep at the wheel and knew I would be killed and said no I want to live: the imaginary thought is different than the real thing. I became scared, real scared, pulled off to the side of the road, felt my body shaking, couldn't stop my body from shaking, realized only Liliana would mourn me, I even had pleasure from that image of her all in black wearing a veil no less, and even as a momentary smile came upon my face, a cold chill ran down my body. I realized it was only play-acting, I wasn't real, otherwise what I wanted to come true could have come true, and now I had to be extra careful if I was to survive. As usual Liliana interrupts and says that I decided to leave only when she wanted to tell Jeffrey about our changed relationship because when telling him our relationship would have been officially put on a different level, even as we both assumed he had to know, otherwise why tell him? He knew we had long since been doing things together and he couldn't have expected me to remain faithful to him while he was in prison, and even if

he guessed we were doing things it's only in the telling that it becomes official and then he has to admit our relationship changed,
could change, would change, that was the issue why you left, she
says. I could not face that, could not admit that, did not want to
face it, did not want to admit it, I repeat. That was the reason you
did it at this juncture she repeats as well. What could I have said
to Jeff I slept with your woman now I am asking for your permission or for your forgiveness? What about asking me? only men can
think or behave this way, she says. It dawns on me I have not been
able to keep her silent because I am afraid in my silence she will
ask questions that matter and it's in my keeping her talking that I
don't have to confront my truth—my truth? the truth! What is my
truth? Is it this moment in time that I continually recreate or is it
living within the world that doesn't go back into time to stop at
this moment? Surely I am a product of this moment even as this
moment never occurred. But why this moment? Why not all the
moments back to my birth? After all my uncle once told me this
story of how as a toddler I screamed, yelled, cried when I wanted
to get out of my crib but my father lowered the crib so I couldn't
climb out, and he said he knew then I had the makings of an individual when I continued to try, freedom could not be hemmed in,
even as my mother said what if he falls and hurts his head. It's the
attempt, he said, that made him proud of me. But Liliana is now
saying we did not even get a chance to try. She was ready to give
it all up for me—not to be a mother to you, not to be trapped as a
parent for you, but to live a free existence with you but you didn't
accept my offer instead fled. Jeff ran away I stayed. You both ran
away she says. You fled as surely as Jeffrey ran away, he physically
departed you withdrew, he departed so that he could start over,
you withdrew so you could mentally leave. I had no one to go on
long walks with anymore, she says, to go to the theater with, she
says, to be with, she says, it's easy for men to go off but it is women

who have to call them back, and I had no say in your decision you made sure of that—I found myself with no man for the first time in my life, even in high school I always had boyfriends, I couldn't remember the last time I was without a boyfriend, maybe when I started junior high school, but even then I was one of the first girls to have my period and have an interest in boys. My father had always cautioned me, but he wasn't the kind of man that would oppose a woman and he supported me unlike my mother who said I was boy-crazy too early. And she was correct it's not good for a girl to get interested in boys too young, but I was too pretty for my own good and I engaged attention from boys even if I did have a head on my shoulders, which I knew I was going to use to escape small town life, and to all of a sudden be abandoned like that by the two people I cared most about in life, even if I realized the three of us couldn't live together that just couldn't work but I did at times fantasize and think that could be a solution to our dilemma, and it could have been cool to try it, but you guys couldn't even talk about it to each other let alone to me. You ruined my chance at happiness but your own chances as well—only in love can we find a true measure of ourselves. She looks me straight in the eye as she says this, no vodka glass between us, and my wineglass empty as the barkeep hadn't brought me a new cup of swill. She is right and she is wrong, I think, I couldn't speak to her I didn't have the understanding then, nor the guts then, and can only do so now because she has found me otherwise I would have buried these thoughts, pretty much like I have been doing all these years keeping them bottled up inside me—no wonder my poetry suffered I haven't been able to face the truth and if you can't face truth you can't write good poetry, your writing is going to be lies, unless, of course, you write academic tracts but then of course it's pure nonsense. Only time will tell if my poetry improves, does this mean I have leaped over an impasse? I never realized they were connected.

It's like watching a Tennessee Williams or Eugene O'Neill play now old-fashioned not about modern life but true nevertheless, all it needs to be made relevant is modern dialogue of the inner men and women laughing at their previous held beliefs. I have to have an inner dialogue where I laugh at my cherished beliefs and see them for what they are, cowardly, scared thoughts of a frightened man. But it just can't all end at one sophomoric moment—we age. Maybe it does, Liliana says, and all you do for the rest of your life is repeat that moment, only you disguise it better as you age circling around that moment in a ellipse, closer to it at some times further away at others but always taking up the same amount of space in equal time wondering what you did wrong and trying to figure out how to make it right. The question is which moment. The truth is in the living itself. Liliana refills her vodka glass and my red wine finally comes. Is this all I have been waiting for my entire life a confrontation with an old lover that would have changed our lives—why couldn't it have been different if we had lived together we probably would have divorced with children. But we could have tried, she says, to see if we could have made a life together and children born of loving parents have a much better chance in life than children born out of wedlock or the desire to procreate. Yes that is true I say able to see that now among my own and others, children born through love are less angry and depressed then those born for other reasons, even if they themselves don't know the reasons for their birth. Again, she says, truth is in the trying not in the not-trying. Again I am reduced to talking even if this time I remain silent because what can I say. I was afraid then, I am afraid now, I will always be afraid that's why I write: man lives his life in fear only disguises it in bravado, Jeff once told me that in an intimate confession that he acts so gargantuan because he is so afraid. I knew you were off limits and I trespassed those boundaries, which I should not have done. Hey she's in my fantasy not me in hers I should have some control, but once the Pandora's Box of memory is opened it can't be closed. Why didn't I call Jeff back? Yes I did receive his message on my answering machine, hey it's Jeff give me a call back and he leaves his number, my first thought being surprise that the machine worked, it must have had a heart attack, then who's Jeff, then I'll call a back later, tomorrow, when I have a block of time, I said to myself you know I should call but wouldn't, didn't, a week later another quick message on the machine, again I should really call back immediately otherwise I won't, a day or two goes by, then I get too embarrassed to call back, thinking I can say I didn't get his first one but eventually deciding what can we say to one another and do I really want to meet him again. What does he want to thank me for helping him get out of prison early? I have to play and replay it in order to understand the message; he didn't know my schedule to speak directly to me and I wouldn't call him back—my phone couldn't reach where he was going: I didn't realize he was calling to say goodbye. I wondered how we could meet again and now it looks like we won't. Now his former girlfriend is next to me and if he were here we might be rationally able to discuss the event and maybe even come to some sort of agreement, I laugh at that illusion, but still with Liliana sitting beside me, feel alive, blood flowing through my veins, not just my member, I can have a conversation again that might have some meaning, usually the only time I feel life has some meaning is at funerals. Or at least then I feel like an adult. Can I speak against the unknown? Shouldn't I know one thing by now, after all I'm a poet, and I'm over sixty-five years of age, I know multiple things but I don't know one thing that is true, or maybe it is it all diversity? With Liliana and Jeff I had answers now I can't even formulate questions. With Liliana and Jeff there was one true calling now only multiple questions—love, friendship, conversation, good food, they're all important. Forget about quality of life, Liliana says, living is what's important. But all I am doing is repeating again what I did before, I think. Liliana is waiting for an answer but I don't remember the question. I should never have opened up this can of worms. You were in my life for the longest time and I always knew that I couldn't live without you and if I had lived with you in my life my life would have been different but would it have been better? You'll never know? That's the difficulty we only go through life once and you can never know for sure but it would have been nice to try, she says, and once you left . . . Once, ha, I kept coming back to this moment. Once you left and didn't call or write or make any effort to go back . . . I kept you alive in my imagination, I had picked up the phone many a night to call, sat down and wrote you dozens of letters that I didn't mail, always spoke to you explaining to you the reasons I did things, it was to you I explained my life, you were always part of me, more than the outward events are part of me, I go through them with you I sit awhile and even as I struggle not to let you get to me it is to you that I expose myself and it is only you who knows my deepest thoughts. I love this difficulty of other minds, how do we know what others are thinking? I may not know what you are thinking but you know what I am thinking. In crying for you I kept you more alive than you actually were when we were together or when you were an individual person, always wondering what it would be like if we would meet again, would I have enough guts to ask you to stay. The gutless wonder that I/you are? Or would we stare at each other with nothing to say? Or would we be comfortable in our silences together? Would I have enough strength to ask you to stay so I could find out why I couldn't exorcize you from my mind? That would have been nice, Liliana, says, seeing me after all these years and then trying to get rid of me. Seeing you in the flesh would not have been better than the you I created. I am more alive now than ever. It is a fake aliveness not a real one. I am more alive with you than I was in my actual life where I was rather dull and uninspiring normal: you have created something of value inside me. I lived my life without you, I am sorry it's over, but I did figure out how to live a boring life and for that I am grateful, I was sick and tired of adventure. I say the same thing, it's when I have been able to shut the outside world off (not even reading the Wednesday *Times*, nota bene the Cooking section) like living in a monastery that I feel most alive, the arc of my day is solitude, slow time down by not doing useless tasks—even as I accuse Galina in the morning of sitting on the couch and thinking up chores for me to do. So you did get over me and marry. Marry yes, I lead a normal life on the outside but you stay inside me. You wanted an ordinary life, a real job, a place of your own, a woman who would be there for you, you wanted all that Jeffrey had, you made your money doing odd jobs still being supported by your parents, you were still living at home, your girlfriend was another man's girl, no job, no apartment, no woman—yes I thought if I could have a girlfriend all my other problems would dissolve, I could give my life some meaning. What I hated about this revelation is that it proves I'm just like everybody else, I'm jealous and that my attempts at the good life were really attempts to hide my jealousy (potter hates potter, beggar is jealous of beggar, poet of poet) like the time I would dream myself to sleep thinking that Liliana would kill her husband (even if I didn't know anything about her) and would run to me for support until I was in the kitchen one day chopping vegetables and Galina was in my way and I thought stab her, put the knife right in above her ribs, and immediately put the knife down scared that I had even thought that, I never had before nor since, and realized hey the dream was about me not her. You told me once that you wouldn't even think of buying anything permanent until you were settled i.e. married, as if you didn't have to live before marriage, you thought Jeffrey was the ultimate in coolness and he did enjoy his adult life while you were trapped in your childhood, he wasn't frightened of being an adult as so many men are. You taught me how to hold my arms so a woman can hold on, I think and say. But she continues since you couldn't get that yourself you did the next best thing destroyed Jeffrey's happiness by bringing him down to your level, and that's why you continued going with me I was a valuable commodity to you; you used me to get at Jeffrey, not because you needed someone to do things with but because you wanted to destroy his happiness because you yourself weren't happy and his happiness offended you and in destroying someone else's happiness I was only an instrument in your pleasure and when I succumbed to your advances you humiliated me even further by spurning my advances—that's what you wanted all along, and I fell into your trap because I was in a trap myself in that I liked my self-image as a liberated woman who lived with a man who I wasn't married to, and I didn't feel tied to him because I could go out with other men, and with both of you I could discuss ideas, like Simone de Beauvoir and Jean Paul Sartre. Only pretty soon I was washing his clothes, ironing his shirts, cooking dinner for him then for you, and he would come home and lie on the couch all night while I was doing my thesis and I had to holler at him to lower the television, can you imagine Simone de Beauvoir doing that. And after he graduated college he never opened up another book, and eventually we couldn't even do things on Saturday because he was getting up so late it was already Saturday afternoon, so it was more fun to go out with you Friday night, and Sunday ah Sunday, he would watch football all Sunday, so we saw shows on Sunday as well. If it wasn't for my going out with you my life was as if I was married without the benefit of the ceremony. The ceremony is important, I say, ritual is important, I say, when tradition changes the culture changes, you were not married to Jeff even if you acted like you were until you had the ceremony, I know, I lived with

Galina for a few years before we married when she became pregnant, and marriage is different we became closer with the marriage and we celebrate the ceremony not the living together. What difference is a ceremony I was trapped only I thought you were my salvation? We read books together, discussed my dissertation together, saw plays, movies, and did things only I didn't realize your hidden agenda. With you I got what I should have had with Jeffrey and you got to destroy his happiness. What I know now that I didn't know then is that a woman is ready to settle down when she meets the right man, but that's not true for boys. That's why he ran away he couldn't deal with it. Then you abandoned me and I was left alone. I want to stand up and run away from my own fantasy, please don't be so dramatic you refused to take responsibility for your own life is what I say instead. Me, I was a late bloomer coming into my own realizing what I was doing was wrong, life didn't come easy for me, I had to take the long way to find out who I am, I had to step off the old path; no longer was I satisfied to drift where my senses took me but stop for a second and reflect, and I thought solitude would be good for that, I thought maybe a year or two not realizing it is a lifelong quest to learn to balance my senses with my mind—even now when the urge strikes me I can barely control it—ergo we are here; to learn to breathe to see the shadows as well as the light takes a lifetime, not have one activity planned and then another, but to find out what I want and then try and accomplish it—not to succumb to temptation, it has taken me time to learn not to succumb and succumb means to avoid. I don't believe I wanted to destroy Jeff, I'm not that type of a person, I hurt him there's no doubting I have to live with that but saying that doesn't make me feel any better. If I had wanted to destroy Jeff I would have destroyed myself as well—he was glad that I was with you it helped me start my life after that stupid war—Jeff was glad that I was coming to my senses the war was wrong, this culture puts so many obstacles in the way of true learning. You wanted the life your best friend had. I interrupt, I wanted the good life but had to learn what that was. I knew I didn't want to continue trapped, drinking, screwing, a hedonistic life to blot the pain out, I knew that I wanted a life of the mind even if I couldn't figure out how to get it, even if I realized I couldn't sit six hours a day and revise my poetry, even if I only could work in short spurts (why poetry chose me). Jeff was more interested in being a revolutionary, fighting the system, I simply didn't want to be like everybody else, I wanted to find out how to live my life not change it for others, I had enough of that in the army—there's no freedom if somebody tells you what you must do, how you must live all you have is the illusion of freedom, i.e. follow orders or else and the or else means punishment or prison. I didn't want that kind of life, true I was jealous but also true I was trying to suppress my jealousy, but Jeff was surprised, even asked, how did you get so smart, when I started my serious reading, reading the books I should have read in college where if the professors had read serious literature, not textbooks, I would have started my quest earlier. Instead I read what my uncle said; you only have to read two books the *Symposium* and *Faust*, all the rest are footnotes. You were the one who told me college was crap if you want to read serious literature you will have to do it on your own; the important stuff is not in the curriculum. I was lucky I had a guide who could point me in the right direction; many of today's young don't even have that. You made my college career easy, you told me to buy a five-subject notebook so as not to have to carry around a lot of notebooks, don't ask questions just memorize what they want, as if I could learn like that. You were serious, she says, I knew that even as I got good grades, and remember this was before grade inflation, but girls were always better students than boys even as we were told girls were stupid and only men could deal with the complicated issues of the day, or that girls mature earlier, always an excuse to deny our brains, remember I am of the generation where girls were told to hide their intelligence, deny their brains from boys, boys don't like smart women—but that's what I initially liked about Jeffrey he wasn't ashamed to be seen with an intelligent woman, he liked it when I used my brain—you too, you just had a more difficult time expressing your emotions, but you were the one who encouraged me to go to graduate school because Jeffrey was too busy making the revolution—all for the revolution. It was cool being with two guys even if I should have known it couldn't last, that it would only be a moment in life not life itself but I didn't understand history then, that at certain intersections in history things change, but then they pass—Jeffrey and I had a waterbed but we didn't talk about the ebbs and flows of time. She laughs, a waterbed, you know how much energy it took to get that installed, first we had to get a landlord's approval because landlords were afraid that they were so heavy it would collapse into the apartment below, and, of course, he said no, then we got a structural engineer's report showing the building could handle it, he still said no, finally the threat of a court case forced the landlord to give in. All that and you didn't really sleep well on it the water would be like waves breaking and keep you awake all night. A minor technical detail as Jeffrey used to say. Why do I keep replaying this in my head? My whole life shouldn't revolve around Liliana, except my life is a secret to me. All that I think is really non-thought to keep away the one deep thought? What is real, what is make-believe? This seems more real even as I realize its only make-believe; my real life is only make-believe. Is there only one truth after all not a lot of little truths? Does this mean that all I have been doing is trying to cover up the one truth by little truths, like the Dog Star has no relationship to a dog? Who said that? I know it didn't originate with me: artists have no originality—poets lie, all they can do is mythologize, synthesize, copy, ideas. Ask my uncle who said artists only repeat old forms until they are worn out and new styles emerge similar to older forms but a shade different, and critics forget or don't know the older forms, so think artists created new forms but it has all been said before—if all poetry is a footnote to Homer, and he only copied down what was already a long tradition of oral presentation, codifying and changing it as he wrote it, or that copy cat Virgil who takes a minor character and makes him a major one in his work, making him the next big thing, until my uncle gave me Goethe and said here is something new, a new dimension in poetry, a man who reflects, then Büchner who actually adds a citizen, not making him ugly, cowardly and weak like Homer, Virgil or Shakespeare do with their common-man characters only aristocracy are important to them. Why you were able to comment on the paper I wrote on Virgil you knew *Faust*, I remember being very impressed by your thoughts, that's when I quickly realized you were smart. I recall seeing *Faust* on Broadway with Galina and they changed the ending I was livid wrote letters to all the newspapers, wrote the director a scathing letter, wanted to take out an ad in the Sunday Times, of course did none of that only stood up and booed the performers even if I was only angry at the director—my actor friends were pissed at me, but how else can you get your points across the devil doesn't flirt with Faust after he dies to get at him, the devil is too weak to claim Faust's soul, but the starkness of that was too much for a modern director. You were like Faust breaking off all your family relationships to change your life okay you didn't go as far as Faust and make a deal with the devil, but you realized you have to make a complete break if you are going to live the kind of life you want to live and you did it, with regrets, like Faust but you did it. When I left you it hurt you and are you saying I did that to Jeffrey. You knew what you were doing, I say, you went with me on your own free will, you stood by your action, you didn't flirt with Jeff as if you wanted him back when he left you, or more precisely when you left him because we were going together before he even ran away, before he was even in prison, it was your way of struggling out of Jeff; however it's only by flying backward at dusk that I can see that, we were caught in each other's web only with time does it become clear. Too bad we can't lead our lives backwards, she says, when I found myself for the first time without a boyfriend, this is difficult to explain, but I was truly alone for the first time, manless, when Jeffrey left and you weren't around anymore, I couldn't take it and went from man to man, and then in remorse, you and Jeffrey with your useless sacrifice, and me to a freedom I never truly wanted. We both gave up something we love in order to be pure, i.e. feel bad. We laugh at our foibles. I stealing my best friend's girl her being stolen by his best friend and we all gave up what was enjoyable. We were all capable of making decisions none of us wanted, all of us claiming the high moral ground, all of us trying to lead an independent life and each one of us saw that to lead an independent life we would have to make a useless sacrifice. Who said God is dead!? It means we had to give up each other, something none of us thought we could live without, I say, even if we had no idea where it would lead, I continue, all I knew was I had to get out of this place if I was to go on with my life, and even if we didn't know what we wanted, which was the case, I knew I wanted to be able to find out what I wanted. Did you find out? Yes and no. I'm not the same person I was then and looking back I would have done things differently but even as I say it know I would still blow it, still make bad decisions, still end up an obscure poet, still read the same works, still marrying Galina, only I would have studied more, tried to build up my stamina more to write for longer periods, have read more poetry earlier not come to it late in life. It is not too late, she says in a lament, like women of old who would sing the dirges while men went off to war and even if you can't be educated, she says, that doesn't mean you can't become smart—don't relive the far past which is impossible to alter. Brave words but even as she speaks them, I know I will go home tonight and become so afraid, not of dying, we don't die like we live, we die broken and pained, rather of living, fearful and scared, and all the practice in the world isn't going to help me live better or die easier—I want to finish this poem, you poetaster you! I still feel as if I am a fake. Yet you continue Liliana says, because for you it has value even if it isn't published, without reward—there's no justice in art, remember when you were on line at the photocopy store and you started reading what was in your hand because you were waiting and had nothing else to do and you stopped and said, hey, this is good then realized it was yours? But to be a poet you need more than your lover saying you are good.

Her lips aren't moving yet Liliana continues to speak that my prohibition against going out with my best friend's girl was mine not hers, and she wasn't bound by my rules, and in fact they were something she could be against since they were made without her consent—and that there was no trespass because she saw it differently, that I made things up as an excuse to feel terrible and this terribleness, that was made up in me, gave me a wonderful feeling. But what about your feeling of sexuality, of power, that you enjoyed over the both of us, I counter, it led you to a freer life because for the first time you understood your power came from within not from being the girlfriend of some man and this made you reel with pleasure which has never left you—this intoxication that has never left you and when you left Jeff and me you had a new-found freedom. Can I take credit for changing you from a mousy (which she never was) girl (but that is how she saw herself) who couldn't be without a man to a woman who could live on her own, who could take charge of her life and not be at the beck and call of some man, i.e. leaving her graduate program where she was only going through the motions into a job with career aspirations—I turned thirty it was time to get a real job. Nothing happened between me and Jeff that she had to tell him yet she felt this need to explain but does her act of explanation mean she no longer wanted to live with him only she was afraid to leave him even if she didn't come to that conclusion that was the result of her action. Why did she think it was cool to live with a man even as she agreed it was just like a marriage without the ceremony, if not for the freedom to separate? It was failure, it's always failure but which we can only see in the long view—hers and mine. This failure was a way for both of us to jump start our lives and not continue the way we began—why I can never think of any poem of mine as totally free of outside influences, now I see everything in relation to previous acts, and also I am not the same person with the same desires that I thought were free but only in holding back my impulses did I make a shift, a puncture, a breakthrough—not pissing on the fire, and afterwards folded the pieces of paper that was my life like a torn sheet of paper with jiggered edges and my fear became more palpable. Granted I didn't feel this until much later, then I felt I was absolutely right in what I was doing—it's a far far better thing I do then I've ever done before, but by then I started learning to think, was it Jeff? Was learning more profound then my fear of Jeff? was it the fear itself or what I would eventually think of the thought of what I had done or what I could do to myself, was that what kept me from repeating it over and over again in the eternal return of the repressed, at least when I finally shut up and let the silences grow. No! It was in the imagining that my freedom began, when I didn't want my freedom to only be my body—the distinction between mind and body, then there were the discussions with my analyst, always at the last moment so as to prolong the session—about the damage done by my parents, the war, you, the guilt and recriminations and I was always the first in the line of fire, until finally I reflected upon how I wanted to live the good life. I began to see things differently, especially as the Vietnam War started winding down i.e. with the end of the draft came the end of the protests that I could not continue only in opposition, I needed to find out how I should live. That was the moment Jeff decided to run away but I couldn't leave the city, I needed the vitality of the culture here to keep my brain focusing, and if I left would be trapped in the boonies with no alternative except solitude, or mainstream culture and would quickly succumb to stultifying life, especially as I didn't have a woman to bring with me; I certainly couldn't have asked you, you just escaped a place like that, and would like Jeff find one of them. He was married and with child in less than a year and the child of that first wife had just called and wanted me to give a eulogy. Yeah sure! I remember when she was born and he sent me an announcement, which I interpreted correctly as his way of saying let's get back together all I had to do was answer, but I didn't know if Allisson was a boy or girl's name and never responded, thinking I could wait and each day I waited meant I wouldn't respond until finally it was too late to respond. Now she wants to know what her father was really like as if they hadn't lived together all those years and he didn't say a word about New York once he left. Of course he spoke to his child but probably about nothing that was important, Liliana says. He could not have spoken about our relationship, you just don't say that to a child, about his time in prison, what can you say except it was horrible you can only paraphrase it not penetrate it, and about his best friend who abandoned him, what was he to do name his child after you. Just what the world needs another Simeon running around, here Sim or Simone as she might have been called. He did not speak for over thirty years about what was important, like the two of us, she says. Your parents never spoke, she continues, silence pervaded your house, you've told me that enough times, you gave them the sense of continuation otherwise they would have committed suicide, the only words spoken were spoken by you. Yes but they survived something unthinkable, our defeats were recoverable. Still we continue in the way of our elders. He could have confronted his, my parents had no choice there weren't even Holocaust support groups then. There are now? Yes and it gives nothing but nothing is better than hopelessness. Jeffrey didn't learn anything about himself in all these years, we at least tried. When his pain sprang forward he had no defense against it and hung himself. I came to see that you had no right to love me but you did and even if I can't totally recover from that—now I think I will dream that Jeff calls and whispers Liliana is dead but I blow him off, not being impolite, but gently tell him I will get back to him because I am busy at this moment, i.e. with something else: she is dead to me. I am not experiencing the craziness of man's inhumanity to man only my own *mishegoss* (madness) sometimes only a Yiddish word will do. In America at first when my father (my mother never could) would try to describe what he went through, others would look at him with sorrowful eyes and mourn oh my god what you had to go through, I feel sympathy with you but he saw they couldn't begin to imagine and really didn't want to hear the worst mankind can do to its people and they couldn't get over their American bravado that they wouldn't have put up with that—their individualistic ethic, they would have taken vengeance upon the guards, having no understanding of the culture of inhumanity where you too lose your humanity—my parents lived in a real nightmare from which they could not awaken—you, Jeff, I, could; we could attempt recovery but only when we were alone with ourselves did we realize the impossibility of living in the outer world. No Jeffrey never understood that, Liliana thinks, his depression was the illness itself and it finally drove him over the edge—we don't live twice so we can compare one life to another all we get is one shot, maybe it is better to have these prohibitions like you

Jews than have to confront reality. I'm still the Wandering Jew to you even if I haven't practiced Judaism in over a half a century, nor wandered out of New York. And I'm always the *shiksa* to you even if I didn't have blonde hair, blue eyes, or an upturned nose, we need these fantasies in order to see ourselves better, she says. Real life is not the life we live but the life we imagine, the fantasy life that we inhabit in our definition of ourselves, even if it has nothing to do with the life we live; the lunatic, the lover or the poet are the most important definitions of ourselves than our mere external roles. How philosophical you've become? Next you'll be talking that only humans are capable of happiness? You're so heavy you exhaust me? And we laugh. Yes we live in the best of all possible worlds, and I wonder can this go on forever? When I first left the armed forces I wanted to be a poet enrolled in the *Famous Poet's School* met with a fake poet, everybody told me it wasn't worth the money, but I wouldn't listen was convinced he could teach me how to write poetry paid the five hundred dollars and after the first lesson realized it was crap but never asked for my money back, too embarrassed, but realized you couldn't learn part-time and had to engage it, live it, write it, think it, and that I would have to only change my life if I wanted to be serious it wouldn't come just because I desired it I had to do it. To be an artiste you have to be like Cortez and burn your ships so that there is no way back. There are only long ways no short cuts. Poor Jeff he never had a chance to realize that and now his daughter wants to know about him. Liliana smiles and I see her teeth, still white not yellowed from too many cigarettes, when making love to her I wasn't with her usually somewhere else in some masochistic fantasy or working out some rhyme scheme of how I could describe this situation. The lunch crowd peters out and the barkeep/waitress comes up to us and removes our empty plates, I remind myself to give her a big tip we held up the booth for a long time and she could have made more in tips. We go sit at the bar. I think about what I just admitted to myself that I had gone to bed with Galina thinking about Liliana, fantasizing that I was making love to my old girlfriend, isn't that cheating in a way? Then who is my wife doing it with? Hopefully someone I can enjoy watching! But now that I am with Liliana she isn't as nice as my original conception of her, it is her mystery that made all the difference or the wonder why she let me leave. Did I really want to leave? Couldn't she have understood my true intent behind all the bravado, of course she did. The waitress comes up and asks how I liked the meal and says when she gets off work she will have oysters and a martini also, it's so New York. I think of Jeff would I have looked at his corpse, never. I want to remember him young and exuberant not how he spent his last thirty years a hayseed. Allisson walks in, I thought I would find you here, she says. That's why I asked the taxi driver to take me here all I had to do was look in a bar and I knew I would come across you. And I somehow knew you wouldn't go into these upscale places that dot the old neighborhood. Please tell me about my father, he never talked about the past, I know nothing of his life before he left for Vermont, and he never talked about his life in New York, she says, the mean streets as he called them, or the Bronx, which is what we would call the slummy part of Burlington. You have an exaggerated view of the city I say. It's not like it was in the fifties, we lived in a neighborhood and we became friends, best friends, but we couldn't wait to escape from our parents. In high school we shared a dream of getting our own place, only I got drafted and Jeff decided to go to college, he was the smart one, I had no chance to get into City College my grades were too low, besides then I wanted adventure, now I'm finally ready to go to college, I can be the crazy old man in a class—all good classes have to have one who can challenge the teacher, who talks and nobody listens to. Sit have a drink, I say. I don't drink she says and orders a wine cooler.

What's the younger generation coming to? They don't drink, don't smoke, all they are interested in is enjoyment without the dangers. Her father is dead she can now enjoy life. She can do anything she wants, instead she does nothing, Jeff and I at least had injunctions we could break on our way to freedom—her permissive father gave her nothing to rebel against. Remember I love you, and so she abided by the rules. How do you know? I know Jeff. Or at least I thought I knew him, after all, I am not the same person I was when he knew me so why should he be the same person when I knew him, yet Liliana had no trouble recognizing me and pushing my buttons, why do I think he didn't change only I changed? He might've thought out of sight out of mind, as he left New York, if only that were true. You can't change so easily by changing your physical address; it's the inner one that has to move. Once when Liliana and I were sleeping together she woke up in the middle of the night and couldn't get back to sleep, kept tossing, and actually got out of bed and walked around my room until I finally told her to come back to bed and sleep will occur, and to my surprised she listened. When Allisson leaves she tells me that she didn't fall back asleep and was astonished that I would tell her to go to bed, she only did so, she said, so as not to wake my parents. My memory is even less accurate than I realized. Allisson says she's glad to meet me, it's long past time we met, she then says, I may look like my mother but I think like my father and the proof is that I was able to find you. He never spoke about you but near the end his telling me to find you said enough, I knew you were close years ago and I just want to know about the life he had before I was born. He was always the Father to me, I never knew him as a human being and he wanted it that way, whenever I asked him about his life in New York he would say someday when you are older and now he's gone and there's only you to tell me about his past. I haven't a clue why he decided to kill himself and want to be memorialized here. Maybe he didn't want you to find the body and have to deal with all the funeral arrangements. Who do you think had to? His ex-wife, my mother, she wanted nothing to do with him. His new wife has enough trouble coping with my two step-sisters, besides she's a ditsy. Another *shiska*, Liliana would say after Allisson left. He also cleaned out his desk draw not to leave a clue behind of who he was before he moved here. Only his high school buddies are here, besides some of my friends who came to be with me, one ex-boyfriend came all the way back from Rome, none of his friends from Burlington had any interest in coming into the city, and my step-mother and his new family didn't think it that important to make the trek. The older you get the less people come to your funeral, I say. Did your mother come? No they stopped speaking a while ago and she felt it would be hypocritical to go to his funeral when she didn't see him anymore in life—for years they had nothing to say to each other, I only told her because I thought she should know. His new wife thought the children shouldn't be exposed to the city, my step-sisters who will now grow up father-less. The poor bastards, she says, my father was around for me he won't be for them. I'm not sure they understand yet but when they are older they will, their father committed suicide by hanging him-self and that will be a shame they can't live down. My step-mother wanted an open casket so the children would realize their father isn't coming back but I vetoed it they shouldn't have the last im-age of their father that way. Aren't you Christian? Yes but I am Jewish, I am my father's daughter and even though I am not of-ficially Jewish everyone considers me Jewish. My mother forced me to go to Sunday school; my father never insisted I go with him on the high holidays. And after my mother left my father and I and sometimes one of my girlfriends would always have a Passover dinner. Strange customs the Jews have, he would always kid them that we needed to drink Christian blood to make the Seder work, not realizing how many of them actually believed him. And some now are born-agains and Israel is the birthplace of Jesus so they no longer want me to convert but treat me with respect. Some have come down to New York so I wouldn't be alone but I really was looking forward to talking to you because this would be the only chance I get, I gather you never leave the city. There's nowhere to go. You're always welcome in my place and she hands me her business card, I am well versed in business card etiquette and examine it, and put it in my wallet, even if I don't have a card to give her, I don't have to pick up girls. On a paper napkin I give her my phone number, who even knows if my answering machine still works I receive so few phone calls. I have to get back to the memorial service my friends are waiting for me. We are now going to a restaurant to celebrate my dad's life. Please let me know why my dad took his own life. I don't know, I've been asking myself the same question, maybe he had an illness? No I spoke to his doctor and he said he was healthy for his age. Maybe he feared old age? He wasn't depressed, or at least no more than usual, all of a sudden he goes down to the basement the only note is all the information, insurance for his burial. I had no idea he would do this. You knew him long ago I figure you must have some idea why, he wouldn't do it for no reason out of the clear blue sky. Maybe he didn't want to be with two babies all over again, one crying all night the other clamoring to get into bed with him. She makes a face. I apologize. She says that her step-mother Valerie wouldn't marry him unless he agreed to have children and he was surprised that they came so quickly but I don't think that made him do it. Did you see how ugly she looks chewing gum? Liliana asks, after she leaves, why didn't you tell her? I'm back to drinking straight vodka again. What could I tell her that her father is ordinary who simply ran away when his relationship became too difficult; that he is not the hero she makes him out to be? Now at least there is a moment of mystery of him in her memory, she thinks he made this great renunciation in giving up New York even if she is not sure why, maybe if I were a better storyteller I could embellish it, but he left, ran away when the pain became too great, he didn't want to accept reality, what kind of story is that to tell her, so that she should lose her image of him? We thought we were special but in the end we were ordinary, she says. You could have told her he made a sacrifice didn't want to get in our way, like you thought you made this noble sacrifice he didn't want to interfere and probably felt good knowing he made the correct choice in leaving, because if your best friend had stolen your girl it meant she wanted to be with him and who were you to get in the way. Jeffrey hated his father, I knew that, and when he ran away I called and said you're acting like your father. What did he say? He screamed. I think I know the truth about him because I think I know the truth about myself, I think to myself. When you asked Jeffrey if it was okay to sleep with me he told you and I realized when he didn't put a prohibition on me he didn't care for me; forget his bullshit of freedom or that it was my choice, he should have told you no and not told me. That was the moment I realized I couldn't always be with him. I had totally forgotten that incident, I say. At that moment I knew I would not live with either of you, but I had no one to talk about this with, the only ones I could talk about this with were the two of you. I had no close girl friends, only men friends, only two close male men friends who didn't care who I slept with. I could not explain my dilemma to anyone, no one was close to me who I would be able to explain it to compare to you two and you could play martyr for, each giving me up for some alleged nobler cause. I like hero better! Cute! Hero is not acting so others can see you but an inner sense of right. You were both using me to do what you wanted but didn't have enough guts to do so on your own, you to go into your Fraudian analysis and change the way you were living, Jeffrey to leave New York and start a new life without me. You were tired of living from moment to moment with no plan saying you want to be a poet but doing nothing to become a poet; Jeffrey the memories of the failed revolution, the wasted years in prison too big a burden for him to stand. And you want me tell Allisson this? Isn't it better she sees a moment of mystery in her father's behavior rather than the end of a love affair? She should know the truth? He was an ordinary human not a hero. The difficulty he had, I say, is in his believing the ordinary isn't heroic. He killed himself on the anniversary of the day we met, Liliana says. How could you know that, how did you know you would become a couple? We don't know the day we met? We knew right away we were for each other only we were too embarrassed to tell people, we met at a teach in for civil rights, when Marymount actually let in heretical ideas, and when he stood up and defended freedom and that you could not deny anyone the opportunity to be free, it is not the speed that we should be worried about but rather where we are going. I was taken by him and it was on the real Lincoln's birthday, so the date became enshrined in our consciousness. Like I was taken in by you when you threw your medals away in an anti-war protest. Do you want me to tell his daughter that he was a coward that didn't want to confront life, she would only hate me not love her father more; maybe if I loved Jeff more I could do that so that she doesn't follow in her father's footsteps: if I tell her Jeff convinced himself that he died a heroic death when all it was was a lonely death it could let her get on with her own life? I didn't really think quick enough that she shouldn't hold her father up as some kind of hero because of his silences, the silences were not the limit of the world, of what could not be said, but of what he was afraid to confront, afraid to relive the situation, like my parents who couldn't talk about the horrors, legitimate horrors, grand horrors to be sure, but the silences made the terror worse and only in exploring them would they have been able to what? Come to grips with them, no, understand them, no, maybe let them sleep a little at night? It was too late for them, it is too late for Jeff (i.e. me) but a limited understanding of the ununderstandable is all we can hope for. There is always a gap between man and God. Religious thinkers can always say it is God's way because God is inscrutable the rest of us are damned to trying to understand what either cannot be spoken or we won't speak. How do you know if you can't think and think to me means converse about it? If you put all the pieces together God does not exist; that's why we have to believe more than ever. We are so utter failures that there is no chance of achieving our goals and only belief makes us human—giving reasons beyond reasons, i.e. the absurd because as far as I can see there is no reason to actually believe, but if we make up Law the laws can be almost universal i.e. no killing, and now only States do killing i.e. violating the Law, and now too easily because of modern technology, we don't have to see the horror of the killing like when I see homeless men on the subways, no matter how our mayors try to hide them, they are still there and I cannot look at them one, because they are ugly, and two, they remind me of my failures yet I am too embarrassed to even feel their pain only their repulsion—I give at the office. Sometimes though I will look, never give money but offer him my solace, especially to those who get down on their knees and tell me their horror stories. Unfortunately sometimes my eyes insist upon looking even when I can't stand to see even as I am surprised that my eyes want to see this and sometimes even ask did you enjoy this? I began to realize my body has a will of its own brought home to me while driving on long car trips and getting stuck in traffic, i.e. counting the cars on the New Jersey turnpike, and I couldn't hold it in and wet my pants, it was warm, and now carry an old water bottle for just such emergencies. Is it better than deserting your lover and going into analysis to justify it? Liliana asks.

I didn't grasp it at first, I respond, the connection of my mother's silences and my need to justify myself, I reply, that ugliness was repulsive and that I wanted to find beauty, I say, which had to be a different path than drifting, that was the wager I had to make with myself that I could change my life—okay not change my life that is too histrionic even if then I was into dramatic gestures, but modify it somewhat, let thinking be a guide not a hindrance. I was forced to learn in school hence never learned a thing, only afterwards when I wanted to learn could I begin to learn. It wasn't the end of the world. It was to me. I started piano, it was as if I turned my eyeball inside out like a God looking down on the universe from the outside—which of course is impossible, and observed all my actions—my eyeball focusing in on me not the world—my erotic actions no longer a justification and the act of observation changed my behavior into becoming the being I wanted to become but in no sense was destined to become. Only in giving up me, you say, did your life take on meaning? It was in my leaving that your life took on more meaning to me, you became an imaginary goddess actually you are quite ordinary but in my imagination your charm, your desires, your fantasies stayed with me. If we had stayed to-gether I would have had no reason to change, I would not have attempted it was in the act itself that I changed. She now wants to leave but I gently put my hand on her sleeve we shouldn't part like this who knows if we'll ever see each other again. Are you afraid it will leave bad karma? After we parted I never saw your friends again, I say, the people who knew you and Jeff stayed loyal to you and I didn't even invite them to my wedding because I was afraid they wouldn't approve of me as I am now. Because you found your better half? My other half! Surprisingly she stays. I thought she would get up and walk away like when I bumped into her on the street she was always in such a rush that she had no time for me now she has all the time in the world, even when I wrote my paeans to her she was always on the go, surprising what a death can do? My life is entangled in your thoughts, I say, and know no way out but to continue. Liliana continues to drink but I refuse her offer to pour me another glass because my head will explode, beside the reason I don't drink anymore is how long it takes me to get back on schedule after a night of boozing. After drinking I can go through the motions of a day but not feel the arc of the day, and it is in feeling the day that I can get through the day, I do my exercises to loosen the muscles up, this is the critical decade I tell myself, how I get through this decade will determine how I will live out the last years of my life, and so now exercise more readily, and even if I am no longer shocked when these physical ailments happen to me—I too thought I was special, am surprised as my body deserts me. I practice cross-training, drinking with either hand. I haven't been to a bar in years, now the only time I go is when old high school buddies come to town since I won't visit in the suburbs—how can they waste their lives like that? they have to come in to visit with me and we still do it even if all we can talk about is the past, they don't know culture, hardly see a play (unless it's a Broadway extravaganza), never read a line of poetry, but are willing to talk about their children, health or money, and boy can they drink, unlike me. I turn and twist gently looking at Liliana hoping the pain in my back disappears, realize I have been sitting for hours and have to do my exercises or the ache will worsen— which always embarrassed my daughter when I would have to stop while driving and stretch, or after sitting in her classroom listening to her teacher—I was ordered on the pain of ostracization not to say a word about their poor quality of teaching—daddy they will just give me a lower grade. My one joy in life is being able to do things for her and if she gets lucky one day will be able to do things for her children. I had been trying to get her interested in *Oxford University* (it's only three years), *Charles University* in Prague or even *McGill University* in Montreal, but American high school did a number on her and she has little or no interest in intellectual ideas. If we begin talking about something before I even get into it she already says that's enough if I ask you the time you try and tell me how clocks work. Too bad you can't pass on anything, Liliana says. My daughter once asked me about the Constitution and I began talking about the jealousy between the different branches of government, the difficulty with the idea of political equality and laws supporting economic inequality, but all she wanted was the failures of the Articles of Confederation, and went to the Internet for answers rather than having a discussion—even her classrooms all had smart classrooms i.e. computers but no interest in any type of discussion. My parenting skill was I shined by my absence in both my daughters upbringing, she says. I look at my uncle's pocket watch, Liliana says that's over a hundred years old, not yet, well save it you can sell it, it is valuable, I'm happy to be able to carry it again after all those cheap watches I had to buy in the eighties because of the fear of muggings i.e. my friend's brother died in a bar robbery when he asked the hooligan to let him keep his father's watch and the guy simply stood back and shot him. Enough of your shilly-shallying, she says you had your life let others have there's. Mine's not over yet until my body totally leaves me, I say, but, really don't want to think about, since I can make the distinction between body and soul. My poems aren't great but they give me pleasure. Too bad art can't be passed on seeking can, learning can, trying can, but art itself has to be desired. Arts aren't cumulative like the sciences, Liliana says, you have nothing to complain about you're not alone, and you've had a privileged birth even if it didn't look that way at the start—you overcame your beginnings, what more do you want? An interesting question—action, glory, power don't particularly interest me and I know I'm leading a privileged life bitching. She asks that I stop stretching, even if there is only the barkeep in the place, my back feels a little better so I stop but remind myself to continue tonight but exercise is so boring, people now do it as another avoidance tactic so they don't have to talk have social conversation even with themselves either they have an iPod in their ear or a television blasting, no solitary thought going on inside their head. I happen to like exercise bikes because I can read. Few exercise the brain—the mind is a muscle, use it or lose it. Seeing her again reminds me that she didn't ruin my life, or me hers, renunciation forced me to confront my life and I began to live not exist because of her, and it wasn't me who caused her to live a miserable life, I swear to that. Liliana continues not even allowing me to finish my defense because she couldn't get over me and we had no right to abruptly leave like that as if there is any other way of leaving. We could have had a nice life together, not wonderful but nice, with someone I cared about with deep intensity who left because of some misguided notion of heroism that I belonged to another when I am a free individual who belonged to no one, especially when I was young. Jeffrey didn't own me and neither did you. I understand women who don't want to be home-wreckers especially when older and you realize how fragile the bonds but not from the one I enjoyed being with from the moment you wanted to see *MacBird* and *Hair*, do you remember you wanted to see two plays in one day. I interrupt but she pays it no mind that we didn't see what I wanted instead saw *Six Characters in Search of an Author*—you introduced me to theater of the imagination, intellectual imagination, I say. She continues those pleasant times we had at off-off-Broadway plays and then to stop like that without telling me you couldn't continue to see me and now having the nerve to say it was against your will. Whose will was it then? Running away and not telling Jeffrey or me where you were, I couldn't take it that the two men abandoned me like that. I see tears in her eyes as she recalls that moment. I want to say grow up it's over only it's part of my life as well and I understand her feelings—her eyes turn away from me but before they turn all the way I say that I left for myself and I may have done a poor job but we couldn't have had a life together because of how we started, that I couldn't build a life without an ethical center but because of you I was able to change my life and search for an ethical center, with no more hustle, and if my life has meaning (an absurd thing to say about the universe—but not about an individual life—we can try to create meaning i.e. beauty) even if the meaning would only be valid for me and not fall for the gruff pleasantries of the flatterers who said live for the now, take advantage of each situation rather than begin climbing the ladder searching for beauty, truth, goodness. It is too easy in this culture to fall for them (i.e. money counts bullshit walks) I wanted no part of that world and mere knowing what I didn't want led me to try and explain myself to myself, somehow I always thought you'd understand. She gets up and walks out on me. I continue, still wondering if I have come any closer in my search because each time I come closer I see the truth receding and this time I thought I could grab on to it and hold it a little tighter like when younger I thought I needed friends around me all the time or I was lonely. I cried myself to sleep after I left wondering if I would ever meet another woman like her. Now I say to myself I shouldn't be so isolated it'll only lead to major depression and I won't be able to get out of it, but in leaving Liliana I was able to search for myself, thinking all the time I will never meet another woman and I soon found a better woman. Only Jeff wasn't around to confirm that statement because he left me as well as her. Did he meet a better woman? The difficulty is you can never verify, and even if I could verify it in a hundred cases can I assume he did the same, the hundred and first case. Was Liliana's name on his lips as he died? He must have been depressed stuck in the backwoods of Vermont, I would, and then it becomes too difficult to do anything else—he never came into the city again that I know of, his parents died in Florida. What is there to say, I was not, I was, I am not, I care not. It was said long ago. We should have met halfway, I've gotten over my fear never to leave New York again, in Montreal or even Albany—a fate worse than death. Better Montreal we could have met over a meal that had some taste unlike most American cooking which uses lots of spices and still is flavorless. We could have had a good conversation over food and wine—there I go again thinking only of me how do I know Jeff would even like this? What were his intellectual transformations like? After all he's still not getting stoned at the *Fillmore East*. It could have been fun to see how much he changed as well. Would we have grown in different directions, like I seem to think? Would he have become like his hated father?—the ultimate irony. The picture his daughter showed me looked just like his father; Jeff became roly-poly too bad his father wasn't around to see his morph. I have to get out of here and be alone with my thoughts, but it's going to feel strange not having them around with me, not having people I can explain myself to and who immediately understand me. I should have been disappointed we all went our separate ways and you can't go home again, but who says we can't be like a turtle and carry our home with us. When I finally moved out of my parents' place into my own with roommates and then into my own and then in with Galina did I really have to break with Liliana and Jeff. The sun blinds me as I leave the bar I can't even see my shadow on the steps, but I know I must leave the world needs me? After I'm gone I assume I'll be like Jeff the only one who will mourn me is my daughter then she will get on with her life. And so it goes! Where to? Why don't I think of these things when I'm in the bar? Allisson gave me an address of where she's staying but do I want to go there? Enough drinking for one day, I won't go back inside. I feel wobbly walking toward the bus wondering do

I need friends, no I don't need them the way I once did. Walking feels good, a nice buzz now that I'm out in the cold air, I forgo the bus and walk even as I think I should write all this down in my journal so I can mould it later into a love poem, but my natural laziness takes over and I continue to walk instead. It is easier to walk than to write. My uncle once asked who requires us to read Goethe, and answered poets' wake us up you have to answer them, debate them—why is there not nothing. Only Plato goes further he asks that we don't dabble in life but learn and learning takes time to absorb the ideas and not simply quote them—poets only make sense when you learn to live, oh boy, it is only when sensory experiences don't dominate that you can you climb the ladder towards knowledge. How did Allisson find this hotel? She told me she gets *New York* magazine and knows all about what's going on in the city and I should read it. I meet her in her room, she dresses for dinner with her back to me. He knew about you and Liliana. No small talk with her. Daddy told me all about it and I was waiting to see if you would tell me. I once asked why he left the city, I couldn't imagine anyone wanting to leave the city for a small town, I had told him I was saving up for the day I could move out of here don't save money for a wedding give it to me as a way to escape from this backwater. And he told me he was living with this woman once but she was having an affair with his best friend and it hurt him to the quick, he knew it all along and decided to leave so that they could be together, they probably were too embarrassed to tell me and this way they could be together and I wouldn't stand in their way. And she said that no matter how much it pained him he thought he had done the right thing, because he would now allow the two people he cared about the most to have a happy life, a life they could not have had if he had stayed put. I thought he had made peace with it and was surprised that he wanted to be buried in the city. Maybe he wasn't so pure and noble, I didn't say, why would he make this great sacrifice and then many years later take his life when he has children who love him, ex-wives forget you, mistresses forget you but not your children. I look at her, yes I am pregnant she says, and not married, she concludes, when I see no ring on her finger, I am too old for an abortion and I want this child. The father? He doesn't know one day I will tell him. My father didn't have to end his life this way; I had it planned that the three of us could live together when he separated from his new spouse, I knew that wouldn't last. He wasn't ashamed that I was single even told me he would help take care of the baby. It surprised me he wasn't what you would call a hands-on father, he hardly spent any time with me growing up, I'd play in my room on weekends when I came over and he was around physically but not as a presence. Now he wanted to make up for that, that's what he said but did the exact opposite. For his friends he makes this great sacrifice but for his family he does the exact opposite. His death was a precise death showing full well that he never meant what he said and he always lied to me because if he didn't mean it he wouldn't have done it, and he didn't have to say it I was not counting on him, I never counted on him—my mother, his first wife insisted that I learn a skill so that I wouldn't be dependent upon any man like she was when they divorced, she had to struggle to become a nurse. I'm stymied keep my mouth shut—her father told her the noble (parental) lie she sees him as this hero not this confused man that we all are, and she thinks he's the one who didn't give her the opportunity to be free. Now she can live her own life, I assume Jeff thought, without having to worry about what her father thinks—the king is dead long live the king, a child can only be truly free when their parents are dead. I would bet the house he left her enough money so that she won't use all her savings up in childcare. Who knows? I walk over and shut her television off only I can't find the off button and Allisson does it by remote, I can't think with it on and she always has it on—a trick I always learned from my father he always had it on and made it louder or lower depending upon who visited. The television was always on growing up, she says, and I don't even realize it now.

You Jews are still sacrificing to your crazy unknown God, sacrificing other peoples happiness for your craziness, I can still hear Liliana's words ringing inside my head even as I've long since gotten past the stage where I fear listening to my own thoughts or believing my thoughts can becomes reality. When I wished my parents' dead they didn't die and my mother replied is that what you learned in the army. No. The army only teaches sacrifice for tradition, it was in reading that I learned to break from that tradition that I didn't have to follow along the old path but could transform myself or at least try to learn to think. After shutting Allisson's television off, I had to go into her bathroom and shut the radio off, she couldn't be alone for one yoctosecond. Now we could continue talking but the talk at first produced silence as if she were listening to her iPod and I had to face my self and not roll my eyes because she would think (correctly) that I didn't respect her like my mother would roll her eyes at me when I told her I couldn't stand how she led her life, even now as I realize that she saw, heard, felt hell and I should be more sympathetic, I still couldn't (can't) be sympathetic to her whose only concern was did the teacher's compliment me on the way I looked. It was only clothes there are more important things in school, i.e. teaching me to read good literature which she was never concerned about. It has taken me a lifetime to figure this out—where I would have to train myself to awaken early, read, write, play the violin, learn how to ignore the chatter of civilization—once in a bar Jeff asked if I wanted to go bowling later that night and I responded no I want to stay home and read *Faust*—where did I get such guts to say something like that. I have to tell Allisson something but I don't know what to say. Jeff would have wanted her to meet me; I assume that's why she is meeting with me now even if she feels uncomfortable with a friend of her father's. When my father wanted me to meet one of his friends' I wondered if he had friends. Luckily Allisson can't stand the silences that interfere with her noise, she tells me that her father and her always spoke over the sound of the television or radio on, and she now keeps something always on to remind her of her father. She explains that she always watched football games with him, I didn't know he liked soccer we didn't even have it when we were growing up, until I realized she really meant football. His sudden gestures have to be explained, she asks, leaving New York, killing himself, were they sacrifices to a hidden god, she wants to know, I don't know that much about Judaism, she says, all I know are some rituals but not the meanings behind them. Manipulative acts, I think, how could we have ever done things like that, sacrificing for ourselves and claiming to do it for others? She's about to rise and put something else on, I gently tug her sleeve and try to break the silence and say her father's act was a misbegotten act a sacrifice of himself not realizing when he left we could not have stayed together or maybe making doubly sure we would not get together. How could he have stayed she wants to know when his best friend and his lover betray him like that. A good question and like all good questions there is no easy answer, because we didn't betray him we were free people who were thrown together a lot and we both enjoyed doing the same things, and since we were friends at first there wasn't the current of sex between us, or so I thought, because we were both off limits to each other, but it was the temptation that brought us together and when there was no more temptation we parted, and your father's gesture didn't mean that much because by then we had succumbed to temptation and the fruits are never as good as the fruits imagined. He gave up his life for you and you treat it as if were useless. He changed his life for himself we were his excuses, he used us. Blame the victim like my mother blamed me for the divorce saying I was a rotten child. That must have shattered her life is this what I'm doing breaking up her life into smaller pieces yet her father's act was important in my life in forcing me to change, to begin analysis, to reflect upon myself—not to go on as before, and this changed state allowed me to transform my life upon the backs of others, but now I realize in behaving no longer wanting to live with my unquenchable desire I had to learn to listen to the silences—get over my fear of living alone, of always being busy, fill my head with thoughts that I could live with instead of sensory ones that I could masturbate to, which helped me get through the day while drink helped keep the night. Can this help Allisson? Life is a series of eddies and byways leading to who knows where, not simply two paths and you have to chose one and you can change course, it's difficult to change course. How can you tell the thinker from the dabbler? Anyone can do it if you pay them. It's only when you give it up and how many times does the artiste wish he has never been touched by the muse and simply gives it up, stops it, ends it, yet always is drawn back to it; it's when you continue to accept your solitude, your humiliations, that come with not being able to articulate the perfect phrase, picture, rhyme, whatever your particular skill is as the world shits on you—there is no consolation in art! Her father didn't do that he fled and in flight ruined it for the child as well, does Allisson have a chance or has her father's actions ruined it for her as well? Now she is beautiful and I can tell she has all the self confidence of a modern woman i.e. she feels she's flawed even if she received straight A's in a name-brand college and never reads a line of modern poetry. What she has to find out is what she likes then pursue it. Enough preaching, I'm sounding like a tired old man, what do you read I ask? Read? Poetry, novels? Read? I read magazines and the In- ternet. Read more give yourself a chance. Enough preaching did

I ever listen to my uncle? Why should she listen to me? At least I
had my uncle as a model. Who did she have to introduce her to the
theater, concerts, poetry a coffee house? My uncle gave me money
for the grand tour, he was worldly enough to see the importance
of travel, my father saw no use for travel, he thought I should work
never understood the life of the mind. Was Jeff the same, college
fine, but what you learned there was to get a degree, Allisson seems
smart and wants me to know it i.e. she's comfortable in her skin,
working in an Aquarium she had taught elementary school for a
few years before getting burned out and went for her Masters because she lacks imagination and didn't know what she wanted to
do with her life and now teaches children about fishes. She asks me
what I do, and I told her I am a poet and she's almost impressed,
longevity has its rewards when I said that younger strangers would
look at me and wonder if I was a school teacher. She tells me she
has a sweetheart who wants to marry her but she's concerned he
still lives at home with his parents, and she's afraid she will simply
replace his mother. What can I tell her about her father that will
help her? I want to know why he left New York like he did, why
he killed himself, she asks. I wish I knew but the other is a stranger
to me, as I am a stranger to myself, I say. My mother never really
loved him because she didn't like sex only did it because she was
suppose to but never really had a passion for it or him not realizing
that love is part of the equation of being in love. He never found
a woman who would have him. How do you know this? They divorced quickly, she tells me, daddy told me, he didn't even send
an invitation to his wedding just an announcement when his new
children were born, which she tore up. She didn't even come to
his funeral. He told nobody about his suicide plans. He called me,
I say. I didn't know that. How could you? What did he say? You
bastard you ruined my life, as if somebody could ruin another's
life. It's easy to blame difficult to continue—there is some kind of

existential pleasure in looking far back and enjoying your hatreds. Tell me more? He left a message I didn't call back. You can't let his event be the true event of your life otherwise you only relive his life not your own, I say, that was his life now it's your turn to fuck it up—bad enough we have the shit of our past, which isn't even in the past but always in front of us. It's in our nature to mess it up and I can almost see her yelling back at me that is not what I was taught, but you have to grow-up someday. Allisson has enormous technical skills and I don't doubt that she will make a good living but will she be able to reflect upon herself, that I wonder. The old triumvirate of truth, beauty, goodness seems lost upon her and she has no idea what I am talking about and doesn't have a clue how to live. Years ago I might have been attracted to someone pretty like her but now I only love women who have some mystery to them who understand (i.e. Liliana) the desires of life and the failures that go along with those desires, I'm surprised she doesn't even get me hard. There is no key that will unlock her door, and I don't even know if she is flirting with me, all I think is what can I tell her that would help her get out of bed in the morning. As I am thinking this she tells me that when her father left her mother, her mother would refuse to get out of bed in the morning (and I recall my mother napping in the fetal position daily) and she had to awaken her, feed her, I used to come home from school and she'd say she was napping but was still in her PJs, so I knew she hadn't even gotten out of bed yet, it helped me learn to cook, one of the reasons I couldn't wait to go to college because I wouldn't have to be my mother's mother. I was surprised that I was so frightened being away when I thought I would just love it, and I was only a few miles away living in the dorm. I accepted four years of intense boredom leading to a boring job and dad says he couldn't wait until I settle down, settle down to what more of the same boredom. Here my mother came in handy made sure I had a skill so I wouldn't be dependent upon any man and thus not be poor. She always says she was raised to be a wife and mother and when my dad divorced her she knew of nothing else she could do. I smile she too was a child of the sixties but it didn't seem to take hold, as Liliana had said the sixties only influenced one percent of the population even if it was everybody we knew. Now is the time to begin living your life, to transform your life don't wait for a lover to do it for you, change and you will find a lover who will help you. I'm too old, washed up, she intimates and what is she thirty-five. How quickly your life can end if you let it. I am not one to give advice and here I am giving advice, school's out she has to live her life not relive her father's life—how long did it take me to realize I was a child of a holocaust survivor not a survivor and how many of my poems are living in the past—will my child finally end my past? Let go. I can't. He ended it so quickly we didn't have enough time to settle things between us, a slow death might have been easier for all concerned because besides saying goodbye we could have discussed things but he wasn't up to doing that, he just upped and left, she says, like his other times he didn't want to deal with issues, you guys in New York, my mother, and now me, and now I'll have no chance in asking him why I was raised the way I was, why he abandoned my mother never took me in only allowed me to visit on weekends. And even there I was always worried about my mother would she get out of bed on the weekends, did she have enough to eat, you know I was the one who told my grandmother when I visited her in Florida they were separating: she nana was putting me to bed telling me that soon she would come up for a visit and I asked at which house she was going to sleep at, and she wondered what I meant and I told her at my mommy's or dad's, because dad now had another girl sleeping in his bed and mommy never gets out of bed, and then she goes and asks my father why she didn't tell him they're separated and he tells her he doesn't want to talk about it so for two weeks the only information my nana has is me, I was also the one who delivered messages between my mother and father. As she says that she can't stand the pauses in her conversation, and walks over and puts the radio on because the silences frighten her so. But not enough to deafen conversation it's only background music. Her silences frighten me as well, I'm no better only have a little more experience and I can see how little that's worth, I can't even help her lead a nicer life, all I can tell her is that she has to find her own way and life is difficult. Liliana always said I was a good listener. Or should I leave her with her illusions about her father, if Jeff had wanted to say something he could have, do I have the right to interfere? Ah the prime directives an excuse not to change old customs, traditions, not to give people a chance to live. What is real? They didn't have a chance to clear up the mystery between them, I can bring peace to her—he ran away once, he killed himself another time so as not to have to confront these issues, like walking across the street in the middle of a problem and saying car hit me that will solve it. Isn't it great how we mature? Jeff probably didn't even know why he ran away in the first place nor why he had to commit suicide—self-reflection wasn't big with him. He lived in darkness never truly understanding his reason for being—not that I am much better, but it's easier for me to see his pattern than it is to see the pattern of my own life. My father didn't want to forget because he didn't want to forgive. It's the empty space between thought and action that determines who we are, where you can see how mysterious we are. At Auschwitz the only ones who acted in truth were the Muslims, the Muselemann, the ones who gave up living who had lost their will to survive his body lived but it had nothing to do with him living, he no longer cared what happened to him so much that even the other prisoners shunned him, he had no will to live, not even to survive and assumed this would be his last day and it would have been, only the Germans fled as the

Soviets approached. The Soviets saved my father's life otherwise he would have been dead he had accepted his fate, hence called a Muslim fatalist or Muselemann by inmates, he was resigned to death but the Soviets brought him back to life, he is only alive because the Soviets came. Jeff could only be who he was because he ran away. Now Allisson wants to know why he ran away because she thinks by knowing his thoughts she will understand his actions ergo she would know about herself. Ha. But none of us understand our desires and we give different reasons for them but after all the tortures of the body I am slowly beginning to understand mine. I wasn't going to be a coward like my father I was going to show them (who's them?) I was tough, could kill not be killed, hence a ghost. Who expected those lives to haunt me? But still shouldn't Jeff remain a mystery to his daughter like I am to myself. Allisson offers me a drink but I have had enough today, I need to get back on schedule and look around but see no clock in this room and I can't tell time by the stars, besides you can't see stars in the city, if you are lucky a star or two, I couldn't even see Halley's comet back in '86 that I was so looking forward too because my father told me he saw it in 1910, didn't even know which way was southwest, that's how bad my stellar orientation is. Allisson claims she could see the globe of the heavens when she was younger but now Burlington is getting so built up its like New York. The world is not like the Garden of Eden of our youth. She's waiting for an answer. I believe she has a right to know so she can break free of her illusions, why should she be a prisoner of her father's ghost, but at the same time since he told her nothing, he only communicated by his silences, like my father, why compare the two they are not comparable, that's why I compare the two, I can only see the familial not the cosmic. Now at least I know the difference between horror and discomfit. But her survival depends upon her learning if she can talk about the past—what happened after what happened. Yet something keeps holding me back, I don't speak as freely to Allisson as I do to Liliana. It's always like that never could I write the truth from 'Nam, everything was always excellent— why worry my parents, even to Jeff I never expressed my doubts, but Jeff also didn't write of his new-found love, or his fundamental radicalism, which he only told me about after I came back to the world. It has taken me a long time to develop this sense of awareness where I could learn to speak the truth to myself and here it is failing me again, younger I went along with my friends for fear of being unpopular, unfortunately I am easily influenced by who sees me last—a smile crosses my face of how a prosecutor once didn't want me on a jury because he thought I would influence the jury not realizing the exact opposite would have been the case. I'm easy. When I go I should go so easy not linger around and have Galina exhausted and need sleeping pills or anti-anxiety medication to get her through the night, and my daughter have to fly in, just do it I say to myself; but my words are not spoken from on high, I laugh, recalling when I was younger and my parents older saying I will kill myself rather than become like them, and now cling to life. Yet all I can think is how luckily I had my uncle who showed me another direction, there is something more than following the leader—oh what a platitude, even if it looked weird growing up eventually it sunk in; imagine he had more books in his house than simply an encyclopedia bought because a salesman knew enough to get the addresses of parents whose children went to working-class schools and sell them to parents as a way of educating the *kinder*. Only my uncle asked me what I want out of life. He also would ask what books I was reading. To that I would laugh. Now I am in a situation similar to that with Allisson, Jeff's daughter, and am behaving like my parents not my uncle. Maybe freedom isn't all it's cracked up to be? Maybe now our whole cultural dialogue against anti-reflection is correct. No I can't/won't believe that—you have to find a space for solitary thinking or you succumb to temptation—ask Liliana. I did. She told me how she had over fifty men real love affairs not just one night stands and do you know how exhausting that can be, I wasted so much time. I refuse to give in and want to push forward and somehow find the energy to do it, like a child running uphill to increase his speed, I wanted to run away from my birth, even as I got tired and my mother had to carry me until I could get my second sailing even as my soul wandered all over the place. It's always uphill, against gravity, even if outwardly I am no different than my neighbors i.e. a job, a spouse, a child, it's not the same a transformation came over me—my Faustian soul. An inner voice says he only meets freedom and existence who wins them everyday anew. Allisson can't remain silent for long and lights up a cigarette, I can't remember when I met someone who smokes, I look at her white teeth and realize they will soon yellow with tar as the air instantly becomes smoky, and you can't even open windows in these modern hotels. Our ersatz conversation has nothing to show for itself, her life is not about her father but how she will live in the world and what we can hide from ourselves—the person we know least is ourselves, I say, and I don't think I can be of much help to you, I sprinkle out between coughs from the smoke. My uncle who loved me could only do so much I had to struggle myself before his attempts fell on deaf ears. I leave walk out into the moonlight discombobulated, almost lost, but in the city, like in the Bronx I can never get truly lost and start to walk towards home, a woman passes by looks just like Liliana until I realize I will not see her or Jeff again, never, never, never; as usual only in death throes do I feel like an adult, and speaking to his daughter makes me truly realize they are realize he is no more. Both were crucial to me and my memory is clearer of them than it is of me. I hesitate, wanting to go back inside, but you can't step into the same stream twice, and I had my chance and blew it, my words, as usual are pointless, weak, but I'm not thinking about Allisson nor Liliana, nor Jeff, my chance encounters are not signs, and they ended up the same way as if they hadn't existed—nothing changes, it was an accident I was born and I've done nothing to alter that situation; you can't live half awake and half asleep and even if I think I tried to awaken myself you are either awake or asleep, and as the door closed to Allisson's hotel room, she not even walking me to the lobby, I realized I blew my time here and it couldn't return: the paucity of words, I had nothing to say to her even if the nothing is not all I have to say nothing more would come out. If younger, now that I am on the street I would have jogged like I did once when spying Liliana on the street one afternoon and I went home put on my jogging clothes and ran a half-marathon. I expected just to run once around Central Park but I jogged more than I ever did before, one loop around the park, one loop around half the park and topped it off with a burst around the reservoir for a mini-marathon. Where did I get such stamina? I did it to show her my life had meaning? Show myself I should say. Now I bundle myself up, walk around puddles, and decide to walk home to try and get them out of my system, besides walking is better for my knees than jogging, once a foot doctor suggested I need orthotics for my shin splints, and when he told me how much orthotics were and that my insurance wouldn't pay, I knew I could live with the pain. The sound of a car horn beeping reminds me where I am, how could Liliana go to sleep without the sound of car horns, I like this better than the cackling of cuckoo's, the squawking of the larks upon the dew laden grass—I remember once being taken on a trip to a new housing development in Jersey, to visit one of Galina's Russian friends, and asked her where are we, seconds ago we were on a highway to nowhere and all of a sudden this huge complex in the middle of nowhere springs up, and she says Florida, and she tells one of her old Russian superstitions that a cuckoo's wail tells you how many years you have left to live. I must not have heard any because my inner ear failed to hear this one, it wasn't a car horn but a car wanting to turn and the driver yells at me, luckily some stranger on the other side of the street yelled louder and caught my attention otherwise I would be no more. I thank her for her random act of kindness, and tell myself to be more careful, as I walk over towards the water. The beauty of New York again is that the city is safe and you can walk in the parks at night. And we must thank New Jersey for embarrassing New York by decided to fix up their waterfront so the city felt compelled to do so as well. I'm walking along the same stream but not stepping into it twice wondering why I write poetry that can take you to places you're afraid to go but is useless in times like this—words fail in the face of death even as poetasters want to make hymns to feelings, you can't practice dying. When I get home I will burn everything—Liliana had the right idea when she burned my first book of poems. I may have started out wanting to write but I can't continue for that reason any longer. The winter wind feels good coming off the river, luckily I started wearing a cap when I lived close to the river, and now with my hat on backwards look like an aging hipster, and realize how foolish I am, think maybe I was right as a little boy to ridicule my uncle's teachings because he seemed so different than everybody else we knew, and he was the only one who seemed interested in my education. All I believed in were cowboys and sports until he insisted I go to an opera with him, which I promptly fell asleep at, he tried to talk to me about the ideas but I was more interested in the spectacle of scenes, the dress, the audience except for my uncle in his tux (now mine), I smile recalling Büchner describing people trapped in circumstances beyond their control, his endings like his beginnings with no pat solutions—the characters couldn't think their way out of it, couldn't refuse and had nowhere to go. It was in my first attempts to stop letting my body do all the thinking that

I started to become who I wanted to become, my first instinctual denial when I no longer wanted to kill, to be with the boys, it was dramatic meeting those shoeshine boys in 'Nam who had been orphaned that made me realize that I could no longer kill, from then on my sniper days were over, missing all my intended targets, firing over their heads, thank goodness I was never in a firefight who knows how I would have behaved then, but certainly not like our brave soldier boys now killing at a distance, I had to see what I didn't want to hit, my first act of not doing what was expected of me helped to define some being inside of me who wasn't going to continue along the same path as what was expected of me even if I never could go in the total opposite direction, I never had the strength for that, at least I veered off the path, and since I give in to the mob started avoiding the mob, my instinctual no instead of yes led to a break in my life where I could learn to think, and I became a man who was waiting for his jig to be up and no longer a killer. No outright resistance, I was too afraid for that, the Armed Forces would come down hard on those who resisted so I created a space of passive resistance—in the infantry the solders fragged (shot at) their officers while they led platoons into the jungle. Even if now I am not able to change the past at least now I can see it as a moment of doubt even if I couldn't understand it then and thought again I was following my body and didn't realize this new way of thinking was not an ending but a beginning, my first conscious effort even if the person I would become still did not exist it was the beginning of the person who I wanted to become—my first anti-instinctual act, of course it wasn't totally mind-thought, there must have been other reasons but I have no memory of those, I cherry pick my past but it slowly comes back to me, I couldn't stop crying on my bunk, I just want to die, I just want to die, I moaned over and over, I'm so messed up, I don't know, I want to go home, even if I joined to get away from home, but the memory I pick was the one that set me off on a new course of being a different person than I thought I was—join the army, visit foreign lands meet exotic people and kill them. Seeing myself made me look at my image and I saw it differently than how I looked in the mirror and as my uncle once said become like a god create works of art, artists get to the essence of things, I didn't think of it that way in my initial refusal, then I had no idea I would find a fundamental shift of life, even as I was amazed when I came back into the world how quickly the new becomes like the old unless you fight it, luckily I had Jeff then Liliana, someone who did things with me, and in choosing my act of freedom was limiting myself to who I wanted to be not become what others expected of me. A touch of the poet? How can you make a living writing poetry, others thought I wanted to become an English teacher, as if I had enough strength to go into an American high school, especially knowing what I did to substitute teachers? Only my uncle understood writing is a full time occupation even if you don't spend all day at your desk, but we live in a culture where you can't make enough money to survive by only working a few hours in the morning and writing in the afternoon—I don't have much it flutters but I try and maintain it in the flux without being stubborn so that my initial refusal is not a grand but empty gesture. But I always did good when my back was against the wall, fighting the good fight, not giving into the bastards, the belief that I was fighting for freedom, justice, the American way, Jews always believed in something called Cosmic Justice, Liliana said, but not in living. Now I say to nobody in particular or anybody who would listen, and now you can talk to yourself on the street because everyone thinks you're talking on a cell-phone, remembering as I left therapy thinking that both Abraham and Jacob are like Antigone and Creon, two pathologies. There are no ultimate tests except in living, except my parents were the dead living in that they didn't die during the Holocaust but they couldn't live afterwards either, me with my privileged birth have been able to avoid that, or as my uncle would say you have to forgive your parents—and I am almost ready to do that now, they had seen too much horror to believe in man or God, but you can look for truth in life, beauty in life, goodness in life, he said, even if I didn't understand what he was talking about then I do now. All I knew is I didn't want to be like them, I enlisted to get as far away from them as possible, besides looking for adventure or to prove to them that Jews aren't cowards, am I becoming like them even if I wear tank tops he wore t-shirts, he smoked, I don't. I wear jeans he wore trousers (the only time I remember him standing up for me was when I no longer wanted to wear dungarees and wear slacks instead and my mother didn't want to spend the extra money on trousers that I would simply tear to shreds, and my father said he is not a little boy anymore he wants to wear trousers). I am becoming like him and if I saw myself in the mirror right now my father would be the one looking back at me. Then that thought scared me and I had to do something but he was right and it is something I never got a chance to say to him, when he told me go to listen to your uncle he is an educated man and educated men live better lives even as he despised my uncle because he didn't have a family and always talked book knowledge. I started listening to my uncle, met Liliana evolved moved away from my roots, condemned like Liliana, because she too wanted to get away, to live alone not with family, except I have Galina and my child but no large extended family, Liliana died alone, the noise must have been awful going down the staircase from the 105th floor, she was on her cell phone trying to reach Jeff because she had no one else to call leaving a message telling him she was safe and leaving the building when all of a sudden she hears screams and screams herself and the last thing Jeff hears from her was her screaming as the building collapsed on her, and Jeff left another one of his messages on my answering machine telling me this, which I never responded to. Still it's taken me a long time to get over her as I fall back push forward, two steps backwards one baby step forward, and I didn't want to go backwards again, if I learned anything it's that I can only by myself, make-believe alone (I have a family), I am a surprise to myself I thought I could call back and go with Jeff to her memorial service if she had one, be next to her daughters who I assumed would come out of the woodwork to bury their mom, yet I couldn't do it, wouldn't do it, didn't want to be a knight on a white horse again, it was more pleasant to mourn by myself. Thinking has become my refuge even if I think only banal thoughts yet thoughts helped me refine thoughts and helped me become the driver over my body until the body will again assert its role—I needed more than clever phrases—poetry in motion, I needed a philosophy behind it, not clever images but substance, even as editors said they weren't sure they got my meanings and rejected much of my work, yet my poems are no better than me. Poetry fueled my passion even as I live by my senses—I want to be present at my death to be able to describe it to myself before there will be no more self to describe it—ah something to look forward to, of course now I can laugh when it comes I won't be able to laugh nor will poetry be of much good then either. Don't you think I should have learned something by now? I look at all those youngsters with full heads of hair, who piss into the urinal with such power, who are shaped so powerfully, and see them aging soon they will be fifty and won't have as much hair, nor will it come out so energetically, nor walk as fast—even if fifty isn't as old as it used to be, I have a letter my uncle wrote my father where he said I'm turning fifty the end years, still something happens the body goes kaput, the healing takes a little longer and all of a sudden you start thinking seriously wondering if you should prepay for your funeral—all of a sudden you believe in the old stuff, when I heard about Liliana dying I remember sitting on the floor—

never before did I like the floor, but I was sitting *shivah*, mourning for the loss of a loved one and wanted to feel uncomfortable, I didn't do that for my parents or my uncle, didn't believe in the old ways when they died but all of a sudden I found myself sitting uncomfortably following ancient mourning traditions wanting to hold onto something even as I fought myself and said don't give into the old superstitions. And all of a sudden you start thinking about what is behind you not what is in front of you, the old forgotten past not the non-existent future—when does this happen? is there an exact date like if you got ill on a certain date you could say up until so and so I was in perfect health then I became a sick man, by fifty-five you realize you're closer to sixty than fifty—still healthy but soon you will get sick, now is the time to learn something else I remember telling myself, you always wanted to learn to paint, do it, but I didn't, someday, but the day soon will be no longer—what good are you you can't learn anything else and nobody is interested in what you know. You think, sit in a pub with the other old geezers but those men lead conventional lives nice but boring. Besides by then you have no interest in others. It took me a while to realize I could no longer be with others, even lunch with women where we would drink a bottle of wine, and wine is important because it means you eat slowly not gobble down your food, no longer held out the promise of a nice afternoon. What was enjoyable after the lunch and wine was the solid deep nap. I had to give up my passion to climb higher, after all it takes strength to go with women when all you need is a woman, what I had previously thought was false, I wasn't connected to the world at night but at dawn where we can see the shadows on the wall—there may be no truth, only confusion masquerading as truth like when Renaissance painters put angels into pictures—imaginary realism creating what's not there—Joan of Arc painted with angels in a tree but it was there truth, maybe we can't leave the cave nor go back inside the cave because we are the shadows on the wall made by ourselves, and then only poetry can help us understand a language that has been pervaded by newspeak (words meaning nothing) or sports clichés and now only poetry can get behind nonsense concepts, this becomes clear to me as I walk home. I stop pull out an index card from my jacket pocket make a few notes so I won't forget—fight my laziness and capture a thought on paper (my joy is of being able to capture a fleeting thought into a well-formed image) from whence I can transfer it into a poem, moving, the line always moving not in a rhyming way which is an ornament but in blank verse looking for substance, even if there can be no such thing as ultimate meaning there is the value of poetic thought, of putting words to images. All of a sudden my inner radar spots some young men hanging in the park but times have changed and I am not afraid, still I walk on the other side of the street. Still I haven't the slightest clue who I am—funerals are tough they make you think about yourself. What could I have done better? Should I have become a contender earlier? Impossible! Always nice to put the moment way in the past so you don't have to do anything. Here I stand I can do no other! Now I think and hope when I get home I'm not too tired because I have to put some of this down on paper—I can now imagine myself at my wooden desk surrounded by my uncle's Plato and Goethe, writing notes to myself, reminding myself instead of painting I am studying old Greek and German to read them in the original, *Wozzeck* playing on my record player and red wine in a glass helping to keep senility away.

Galina greets me at the door, how was your day?

Drawing by Nicholas Vagenas

Frederick Mark Kramer is a novelist, playwright and amateur musician living on the Upper West Side of New York City.

Printed in the USA
CPSIA information can be obtained
at www.ICGtesting.com
JSHW021144300723
45567JS00002B/106